Madison's Angels

Madison's Angels

By

Elaine LaForge

Strategic Book Publishing and Rights Co.

Strategic Book Publishing and Rights Co.
12620 FM 1960, Suite A4-507
Houston TX 77065
www.sbpra.com

ISBN: 978-1-62516-748-4

To my family who supported and encouraged me
To my friends who shared the excitement along the way

Chapter 1

It was a dark cold December evening in New Mexico. The temperature was dipping below freezing, which was about average for that time of year. The dark clouds in the sky hid the small sliver of a crescent moon, and threatened to drop snowflakes on the ground below. A young Mexican woman ran down the sidewalk, constantly looking over her shoulder. She was shivering from the cold. She was wearing only a long sleeved flannel shirt and jeans. She wore sandals on her feet that slowed her pace. The young woman knew her life depended on getting away from her captor. She had been lucky to escape from his car at the gas station while the large box truck had blocked his line of sight to her while he was inside paying for the gas he had pumped.

The young woman turned into a dark alley and tried to run faster as she knew she only had a few minutes of lead-time. Just when she thought it might be safe to stop and catch her breath, a car pulled across the end of the alley blocking her exit and the man she feared greatly emerged from the driver's door.

She tried to turn and run back into the alley, but he quickly overtook her and grabbed her arm. He began to shake her.

"Where is she?" he demanded as he shook her.

The young woman tried to yell for help, but there was no one on the street. She would not answer him.

"I asked you a question. Where is she?" the tall bearded man demanded as he shook her again.

When the young woman again refused to answer, he slapped her hard across the face. She was exhausted from her failed escape and the slap knocked her unconscious. The man opened the back door of the car and shoved her still body inside.

"Damn", he muttered. "I guess it doesn't really matter, neither one of you will survive this cold night."

He tied her hands with her own scarf, which was in the backseat of the car and returned to the driver's seat. He had to quickly change his plan. He was deep in thought as he started the car and drove out of town.

A few blocks away, in an outdoor nativity display at a neighborhood church, a baby stretched as she awoke. First a fuzzy bootie on a tiny foot appeared out of the straw bedding and then the second foot appeared, this one with little pink toes wiggling in the darkness.

Chapter 2

Twenty-seven years, five months later

Madison Rose Cavanaugh parked her car and hurried into the Biltmore Square Mall. It was the Friday before Mother's Day and she was picking up the special present for her mother. She was on her lunch break from the Hendersonville General Hospital in Hendersonville, North Carolina where she worked as an Emergency Room Nurse. She was dressed in white slacks and a brightly colored floral scrubs top. Madison preferred to wear colorful scrubs as opposed to the drab solid dark colored ones. She felt the patients needed all the brightness they could get in their day. Madison knew that if she ran late, her friend and fellow nurse, Heather Cooper would cover for her. She was working a double shift in order to have the upcoming weekend off.

Madison had ordered a lovely sterling silver necklace for her mother. An outer circle was engraved with the words "Mother," "Daughter," and "Friends." Inside the circle were entwined hearts, one smaller than the other. On the inner point of each heart, a small gemstone would be mounted. She special-ordered it with their birthstones inside the hearts and their names engraved on the reverse side of the circle. Her red ruby for July and her mother's blue sapphire for September would certainly put a sparkle in her mother's eye.

Madison and her mother had a very close relationship. Being a single mother, Rosemary had worked multiple jobs at a time and foregone many things in order to provide for her daughter. Madison was very grateful to her mother and wanted to mark this Mother's Day as extra special with the necklace. Madison had been an RN for almost four years. She had worked in her current job for the last three years. She truly enjoyed her work.

At twenty-seven, Madison was a stunning young woman with shoulder length shiny brown hair. She had large round brown eyes that seemed to always twinkle with life and happiness. She had a slender build, was five foot seven inches tall and had a lovely olive skin tone.

Madison had just recently moved into her own apartment in Hendersonville. Her mother had encouraged the move. Rosemary thought it was a good idea for her daughter to be on her own to be able to establish her own routine and relationships. Madison sometimes felt like the baby bird the mother pushes out of the nest to teach it to fly. She knew it was the right move, but sometimes it felt strange to be alone in the evening. She and her mother had spent many hours sharing the details of their days over leisurely dinners.

Madison was preparing a nice Sunday brunch for her mother in her new apartment. They usually went out to lunch or dinner, but this year, they were invited for an afternoon party and buffet dinner with the Davis family. The Davis family, though not related by blood, was the only family Madison had ever known. They, and her mother, were all Madison had ever needed. She had been raised to respectively refer to them as Uncle, Aunts and Grandparents.

Once inside the mall Madison walked briskly to the entrance of the jewelry store. She walked up to the counter.

The clerk behind the counter asked, "May I help you?"

Madison replied, "Yes, I am picking up a necklace. My name is Madison Cavanaugh."

The clerk went into the storeroom and soon returned with a velvet box. He opened the top to allow Madison to view and make her approval. The necklace was breathtaking. The entwined hearts were beautifully set with their respective birthstones, which were shimmering. Madison was sure that her mother would be surprised and pleased with this gift.

Madison paid with cash while the gift was being wrapped. Soon she was on her way back to work, and if the traffic on Interstate 26 wasn't too heavy, she would have plenty of time to return before her break was over.

Chapter 3

Rosemary Cavanaugh had an hour left in her workday. It was a perfect day in May. The sun was shining, there was a slight breeze and the temperature was hovering in the mid seventies. Mothers' Day was among the busiest holidays at the elder care facility where she worked. You could count on at least one visitor for almost every female resident. When Madison was younger, Rosemary would bring her daughter to visit those few residents who had no family.

Rosemary had never known her father and had lost her mother while she was still a child. She had lived in many foster homes during her pre-teen and teenage years. Rosemary envied her elderly patients with large loving families. She hoped one day that Madison would marry and have children, her grandchildren. Rosemary would turn fifty this coming September. She hoped to live to a ripe old age surrounded with grandchildren and maybe even great grandchildren.

Rosemary had light brown hair and blue eyes. Her skin was slightly lighter than her daughter's and she was two inches shorter.

Rosemary started at the Blue Ridge Senior Care Facility more than twenty years ago, soon after coming to the Asheville, North Carolina area. She started as an aide to the faculty and sometimes even the nurses. Rosemary had no formal secondary education, but quickly learned what needed to be done and impressed her supervisors. She worked hard and after several promotions, was currently supervisor of resident activities and handled the staffing schedules. That meant Rosemary was in charge of everything from the annual Fourth of July resident and family picnic to juggling the staff's requests for vacation days. She had managed to arrange her own schedule for the coming weekend so that she was not working. The next two days were going to be busy for her.

As Rosemary was going through the papers on her desk, one of her co-workers, Phyllis Baker, stopped in her doorway. Phyllis had a petite frame, auburn hair and green eyes. She was a few years older than Rosemary.

"So I understand you have big plans for this weekend."

Rosemary smiled as she responded, "I sure do. On Saturday I will be helping my friend Debbie Davis as she prepares for a large party that her family is giving on Sunday. Not only is it Mother's Day, but Debbie's mother, Charlotte, turns eighty early the next week. The family decided to combine the two events into one large party. Ever since I moved to Asheville, Charlotte has been like a mother to me."

Phyllis said, "That sounds nice, but probably means a lot of work as well."

"It sure does. But on Sunday I'm going to Madison's apartment in Hendersonville for brunch before the party. I am so looking forward to the time with her. It's only been five months since Madison moved to her own apartment, but to me it seems much longer. I really miss her."

Phyllis nodded. She had been divorced since her two daughters were quite young. She and Rosemary had found much in common over the years as single mothers.

"I remember when my youngest moved out, the feeling was bittersweet. As mothers we know our children must venture out into the world on their own, but we still want to nurture them."

The two women laughed and Phyllis moved on leaving Rosemary to finish her paperwork, and think about her daughter.

Mother's Day always caused Rosemary to do much self-reflecting. Sometimes she wondered if she had made the right decisions all those years ago. How different their lives could have been. She worried about the time when she would have to tell Madison the truth of where they had come from. Each year she decided it was not yet the right time. They were happy. Madison had had a wonderful childhood, had excelled in school and college, and had grown into a respected young woman. Rosemary could not risk bringing something into their relationship that might drive them apart. She also could not imagine how she would live if the Davis family were to become ashamed of her. They had welcomed her into their family with no questions asked. She had been lucky to meet Ray Davis at that diner in New Mexico when Madison was just a few months old.

Rosemary put those thoughts out of her mind and got back to work. She had many tasks yet to finish if she wanted to leave work on time today.

Chapter 4

Ray Davis was cleaning up from a busy day at work. The Davis family owned and operated a gas and diesel station just off Interstate 40 near Asheville, North Carolina. The business had been in the family for three generations. Ray's grandfather, Floyd Davis, had started the original service station in the late 1940's, soon after the war ended. His son, Ray's father, George Davis, started working at the station as soon as he was out of high school. The small service station quickly became a booming business and expansions were made over the years. Today the station had twenty gas pumps and ten diesel pumps in a large area behind the station for large trucks. They managed a truck repair and 24 hour towing service as well.

Ray was approaching sixty-two, but was not likely to retire anytime soon. He liked keeping his hands busy and his mind filled with new business ideas. He was just over six feet tall with a slightly stocky build. His salt and pepper hair had started to recede. He knew he was starting to look more like his father as each year passed.

Ray was the manager of the station now with his father, George, helping out a few hours a day. Ray's son, Matt, was the first Davis family member to graduate college. With his degree in business and accounting Matt soon took over the supply and money management of both businesses.

In the early 1960's the family built a small diner next to the station. The Hungry Driver's Diner served its customers at a long counter with round blue leather stools and in ten red and white leather booths. It soon became a favorite stop for many travelers, tractor-trailer drivers and locals alike. In the mid 1970's the small diner was expanded to add a large room that accommodated a dozen more booths and several square tables. The menu had always consisted of home-style meals like Tuesday's meatloaf and Thursday's chicken and biscuit specials.

In those days, Ray's mother, Charlotte, had managed the diner. She was an amazing woman. Ray was thirteen when Charlotte became pregnant for his sister. She never stopped taking care of the business. She brought that little girl to the diner with her while she organized the cooks and made sure the waitresses were tending on the customers according to her standards.

Today, Ray's wife, Susan, and his sister, Debbie, managed the diner together. His mother still attempts to supervise the ladies on how much of this, or how a pinch of that would make the soup of the day taste just a little bit better.

Debbie is a single mother of a daughter, Megan, who Ray was more of a father to than an uncle. He remembered when Debbie first told him she was pregnant. She had come to her big brother first. She hoped that he would help her break the news to their parents. Ray immediately wanted to know who the father was so he could have a little heart to heart with the man. Debbie was steadfast in not naming the father. She knew that Ray would have brow beat him into making an honest woman of her. In the end the entire family supported Debbie and her child in any way they could.

George could not stay an idle, retired man, even at eighty-two years of age. Ray knew it did his dad good to stay active and be around people. George enjoyed walking and talking to the truck drivers as they took a break and stretched their legs around the parking lot. He convinced many a driver that the diner next door was the best place in North Carolina to get a meal.

Ray heard his father's voice echoing through the large building.

"I'm back here," Ray shouted.

George Davis walked across the shop floor. He carried his six-foot frame well for his age and with snow-white hair and blue eyes that still sparkled, George was still a handsome man.

"I just wanted to see if you or the girls need anything from me before Sunday." George frequently referred to Debbie and Susan, as 'his girls'.

Ray continued to wipe the grease from his hands. "I think they have everything under control. Tomorrow Susan, Debbie and Rosemary are tackling the food items that can be prepared a day ahead. I think Megan and Madison are doing the decorating. I think you and I will be called in for any heavy lifting. Probably have to move some tables and chairs around."

George pretended to flex his muscles. "I can still do that".

"I sure hope Mom sees how much we all appreciate her. And it's not just Debbie and me. Rosemary often says she feels like Mom's other daughter and I know Madison sees you and Mom as the only grandparents she's ever had."

Ray and George were both remembering when Rosemary and Madison had come into their lives. Ray had been driving trucks at that time in his career. He met Rosemary in a small diner in New Mexico. Rosemary was alone with her baby and what few belongings she had stuffed into a tote bag. She reminded him of his sister. Debbie was about to become a mother herself. He could not imagine letting his sister and her baby travel alone across the country. He offered Rosemary a ride and she hesitantly accepted. He could understand the hesitation. He tried to convince her that he was an honorable family man.

Ray seldom traveled that far into the southwest, but on that trip there was a delivery to Abilene, Texas and one to San Bernardino, California. He was cutting south across New Mexico and Arizona. Rosemary had no particular destination in mind, though she implied California might suit her. She told him that she needed to get away from a harmful situation. He assumed she was trying to escape from an abusive boyfriend. He had been brought up to never raise a hand to a woman, so he was happy to help her.

By the time Ray and Rosemary arrived in California, he had convinced her to return with him to North Carolina to make a fresh start for herself. It was December and he didn't want to wonder where she and her baby would be spending the holidays. Ray knew that not every family would understand if their son returned from a road trip with a young lady and her baby. He suspected that not many families would also then welcome those strangers into their home. But he knew his family would and that was exactly what happened.

Ray told his father, "We invited some other special friends, workers and customers to stop by as well." Ray knew it was cliché, but one never knew what might happen next in life. He believed in celebrating every milestone as it came.

George was reflecting as well. "I'm sure she realizes how loved she is."

They were hosting the event at the diner, so it would be closed to outside clientele. They had posted signs of the closing for almost a month, but if a weary traveler appeared at the door, his family would welcome them to join the festivities. The Davis family was always open and welcoming to strangers, just as they had been to Rosemary and baby Madison.

Chapter 5

Debbie Davis was busy in the kitchen at the Hungry Driver's Diner. Fridays were typically busy, and today was no exception. She hoped to be able to start preparing a few dishes she planned to serve at Sunday's party. Her best friend Rosemary was planning to spend the entire next day with her helping to prepare the feast she planned. They would certainly be busy. She planned to serve the food buffet style. They would have a roast of beef and ham with their famous southern fried chicken for the meats. She planned several hot side dishes in addition to four cold salads.

Debbie was making and decorating the cake herself. Years ago, she had tried her hand at cake preparation and decorating. To everyone's amazement, she was excellent at it. For the past ten years, she had sold more birthday, anniversary and wedding cakes than she could count. With the diner's baking and refrigeration capacity, she created a rewarding side business that aided her financially. Being a single mother, she found the extra money a great help to her and her daughter Megan.

Debbie was forty-seven and had blonde hair that was just starting to have some gray streaks. Her eyes were blue, as were her daughter's. She had never married, but was currently dating Steve Edwards. Steve was slightly older than she. He lost his wife to cancer four years earlier. Steve was a respected surgeon at the Hendersonville General Hospital, the same hospital that Madison worked at.

Debbie met Steve at a cancer awareness fundraiser sponsored by the hospital. It was Madison who suggested to the fundraiser committee that Debbie would be perfect to prepare the sweets for the event. When contacted, Debbie gladly offered to prepare the desserts at cost, donating her time for the cause. Steve attended the event and commented on how delicious Debbie's preparations were. He asked to meet the baker and Steve and Debbie were soon having coffee and getting to know each other. Steve had two grown children, a daughter Amy and a son Jason. Before long Debbie and Steve grew quite fond of each other and she wondered whether he might be the right man to spend the rest of her life with.

Debbie and Rosemary had been best friends since their early twenties when Ray brought Rosemary into their family. She thought it strange at first that Rosemary remained in North Carolina and never wanted to return to the southwest. Rosemary told Debbie there was no family for her to return to and no close friends.

Rosemary immediately started working as a waitress in the diner while Debbie, being eight months pregnant, watched baby Madison. After Debbie gave birth to Megan in January, the women took turns watching both babies while the other one worked. After a few weeks, Rosemary was able to get a small apartment for herself and Madison. By then she and Debbie were best friends and the babies were destined to grow up inseparable, being only six months apart in age.

As a single mom, Debbie had her reasons for not wanting her family to know who Megan's father was and she assumed Rosemary had her own reasons for not discussing Madison's father. For that reason, she never pushed Rosemary about her past.

Debbie was a waitress at the diner since her teenage years. After graduating from high school, she began working full time. She never planned to go to college. She knew that one day she and her brother and sister-in-law would be running the family businesses. She was right and quite content on how her life turned out.

Chapter 6

In Deming, New Mexico, Father Francis Gomez was packing the personal items from his office in Saint Gabriel's Catholic Church. He was retiring from his position as Priest at the church. The Father was a tall man with a thin frame. He was an extremely fit seventy-eight year old gentleman with gray hair. His dark eyes were vivid above his short, full beard and mustache, which now grew with as much white as gray. The Father had mixed emotions about the upcoming Sunday's mass, which would be his last in the church he had called home for over forty years.

Father Gomez was moving to a retirement community about fifty miles east in Las Cruces that was highly populated with other retired clergymen. In three days, Monday, a moving van would appear to take all his meager possessions to what would probably be his last worldly home. Father Gomez was not planning on having an idle retirement. He had volunteered to provide services and communion for residents of the several elder care homes in Las Cruces. He knew he would deeply miss his faithful parishioners that he had come to know over his many years at Saint Gabriel's.

As he was sorting the files in his bottom desk drawer, he came upon the faded, sealed manila envelope that he had been holding in his possession for over twenty-five years. The young woman who gave it to him left explicit instructions that he was not to open the envelope. She instructed him that he was to give the package to any person who might come to him in search of her. The young woman had labeled the envelope simply "For M".

Father Gomez liked the young woman, and had known she was searching for some kind of purpose to her life. He counseled her for five years. She was a lost soul when they met, but she quickly put her energy into helping others. She helped organize many events the church held. The young woman set up a small day care facility in the basement of the church to assist the young working mothers in the congregation. She asked for volunteers to help staff the project, which allowed the church to only charge a nominal fee. She was certainly quite a resourceful young woman.

The Father often wondered what had become of her, and how her life had turned out. She disappeared into the night that December so long ago. She left only a short personal note to him with the instructions to keep the fading envelope he now held in his hands until someone approached him asking of her by name. Sadly, however, except for those inquiries from within the church, he never heard her name again. He wondered what he should now do with the envelope. Should he transfer its safe holding to Saint Gabriel's new Priest?

Father Patrick Finney was in his late thirties; about the same age Father Gomez had been when he accepted the position at Saint Gabriel's. The elder priest looked around the room that had been his office for all these years. He saw the heavy dark draperies that hung in front of the tall windows. He suddenly felt that the darkness of the cherry paneling and bookcases reflected the age of the room as well as his own. Father Gomez knew with certainty that Father Finney would be remodeling the room to his own liking. He hoped that bringing a younger priest with more modern ideas would not only brighten up the office, but also bring new families into the congregation. Thinking of the congregation brought Father Gomez back to his current dilemma. What should he do with the envelope in his hands?

As if sensing he was being thought of, Father Patrick Finney appeared in the doorway and lightly tapped on the open door.

"Good Morning Father Francis. Is there anything I can help you with?"

As he was deep in thought, it took the elder Father a moment to realize he had been spoken to. He turned and saw the younger priest, who was a few inches shorter than his predecessor with blondish hair and green eyes, standing in the doorway.

Father Gomez addressed the younger priest by his given name, the manner in which had been requested of him. "Good Morning Father Patrick. I was just reflecting on the many years I have spent in this office. I realized that I have not done much updating to the décor over the years. I am sure that looking at this room with fresh eyes, you must be anxious to make it feel like your own."

Father Patrick Finney smiled. "I am sure this office has fit you well over the years. But I must admit I am looking forward to taking down the heavy drapes and seeing if I can lighten the room up a bit. I don't want to spend much of the church's hard earned money, but I am sure I can make a few modest changes."

Father Gomez added quickly. "I know the first thing you will do is hook up a modern computer. I admit I have not kept up with technology over the years. There have been many changes in the world, as well as within the church, over the past decades. You are now able to use the latest technology and the Internet to broaden your knowledge and stay connected to world events. Just remember this one thing. An electronic message can never replace a face-to-face visit, a firm handshake or a warm hug. Everything has its place. Always remember to stay connected in person to your congregation."

Father Finney replied with sincerity. "I believe in touching individuals within the church in many ways. Some people need an in-home visit; some need a welcome handshake after mass and some, those who feel their lives are just too busy, need an email from time to time to let them know the church has not forgotten them."

Father Gomez could not agree more. As Father Finney turned and walked out of the office, the retiring priest felt more confident that his parishioners would be in good hands with their new priest. However, Father Finney never knew the woman who left in the dark of night so many years ago. Father Gomez now felt even more strongly that he must not violate her wishes. He carefully added the envelope to his box of personal items that would be moved with him to Las Cruces. He made his decision. He would continue to hold the faded envelope.

Chapter 7

Early Saturday morning Susan Davis prepared to leave her home to help her sister-in-law Debbie and their close friend Rosemary prepare for Sunday's celebration. There were many food dishes to prepare and they needed to arrange the larger dining room to seat the guests.

Susan and Ray had been married thirty-eight years. Susan had been hired as a waitress at his family's diner and she had seen Ray from a distance on several occasions before they officially met. Ray had been driving eighteen-wheelers at the time. One hot August evening, Ray, who was just returning from a long haul, came into the diner for a late hot dinner and a cold drink. Susan waited on him and they started talking about everything from the weather to politics. There were only a few other customers and Ray's mother, Charlotte, tended to them. Charlotte spotted a connection immediately between the two young people. She wanted her only son to settle down and raise a family, and she liked Susan as soon as she had hired her. Charlotte thought Susan was smart, hard working, witty and quite attractive.

As they say, the rest is history. Susan and Ray dated for less than a year before he asked her to marry him. They had a small wedding and enjoyed a short honeymoon trip to Myrtle Beach. When they returned they found a cute house to buy outside Asheville. Before long they started a family and soon had three children. After a few years, Ray gave up driving truck and began to work with his father at the station. By that time, both of Ray's grandparents, Floyd and Phoebe Davis, had passed away. Susan was happy with his change in careers. He was home more and able to be more a part of their children's lives.

It seemed impossible that their children were adults now. Matt, now thirty-five, worked in the family business and had recently married Alison. Their only daughter, Claire, was thirty-three, married to Ben Webster, and was about to deliver their first grandchild. Their youngest, Ryan, was twenty-nine and an engineer for a large corporation in Hickory. Ryan was still single, but Susan was hopeful that he would find someone special soon.

Susan was fifty-seven years old and her brown hair was lightening with age. She had green eyes and a smile that still lit up Ray's day. Susan dressed in a pair of khaki crops and a red and white striped tee shirt. It would be a long, hot day in the diner's kitchen. She left their home at nine o'clock.

Chapter 8

Megan Davis had long blonde hair, bright blue eyes and a pleasant personality. She was twenty-seven years old and a second grade teacher at a small elementary school in Hendersonville, North Carolina. She enjoyed her job and took great pride in your students' accomplishments. She loved children and hoped that one day she would have a few of her own, although she was not currently dating anyone seriously.

Megan moved into a small upstairs apartment in her grandparents' home after college. George and Charlotte Davis created the small apartment when Megan's mother was pregnant with her. The elder Davis's felt their house was getting too large for them to care for, so they moved completely into the downstairs rooms and made the second floor into a pleasant apartment with its own outside entrance. When Megan was four, her mother bought a house and moved them into a cute little cape cod just a few miles from her grandparents.

George and Charlotte never rented the apartment to strangers, but used it over the years for family members in need of short-term housing. When Megan graduated college and secured her teaching position, her grandparents approached her with a proposition. They started to think about what special care needs might arise in their golden years. They suggested that Megan could live into their upstairs apartment in exchange for helping her grandmother with a few household chores and watching over them in case of an emergency. Megan jumped at the idea. She loved her grandparents dearly and would have done anything for them. The apartment was just the right size for her.

Today, her best friend Madison Cavanaugh was coming over to help get the decorations and gifts ready for her grandmother's birthday party. Charlotte firmly stated that she did not want gifts, but the family knew she wanted to visit Nashville one more time. As a group gift they purchased two tickets for a three day bus excursion designated for senior citizens to Nashville in late June. They knew Charlotte would be thrilled.

Madison arrived at ten o'clock and they got busy making centerpieces for the tables. They decorated a large white wicker basket with bows for people to put their cards to Charlotte in.

As they were working, Megan asked Madison, "Have you ever wondered how your life would have been different had you had a father at home?"

Madison thought for a moment before she replied. "I used to wonder about that, but to be honest, I can't think of my life being any other way. My mother has given me all the love and guidance I ever needed, and I never went without any necessity."

Megan reflected. "Remember when I was ten or so and I was determined to know who my father was?"

"Yes. And I remember how adamant your mother was that you didn't need to know."

"My mother always told me that when she informed my father of her pregnancy, he denied that the baby could have been his. He accused her of trying to destroy his life and wanted no part of us."

Madison tried to comfort her friend. "I think we were both better off without fathers who didn't care for us. I remember the one time I did ask about my father. My mother stated she didn't know who my father was."

Megan felt that was a curious response. "Did you believe her?"

Madison nodded. "She swore it was the truth. Something in the way she told me, made me believe her."

Megan was puzzled. "Makes you wonder what the circumstances were."

Madison had long ago settled on a theory. "I sense my mother was attacked by a stranger. That is the only conclusion I could think of knowing the kind of person my mother is. I decided to never ask questions that might cause her to reflect on what must have been a horrible memory."

Madison also knew her mother to be a devote Catholic. She knew that even if Rosemary had been raped and a child had been conceived from the violent act, her mother would never have considered an abortion.

Megan changed to a happier tone. "You know that my Mom is dating Steve Edwards. She seems really happy when they're together. Steve seems like a great man and his kids adore him. Now that I'm out on my own I do wish that Mom could find true love and share the rest of her life with someone. Maybe it's not too late even for me to have a father figure. I would like my children to have a great set of grandparents like I grew up with."

Madison only knew Dr. Steve Edwards slightly on a personal scale, but she knew much about his reputation at the hospital. Dr. Edwards was a highly skilled surgeon. She heard of near miraculous surgeries that he performed on accident victims that she had seen in the emergency room. She thought that if she were ever in an accident, she would certainly want him to be her surgeon. She was anxious to get to know him better outside of work and hoped he and Debbie would be happy together.

Megan and Madison moved on to conversations about their work and respective new apartments. The time flew and by four o'clock they had everything loaded into their cars. They would meet at the diner the next day ahead of the party to set up the decorations.

With their work done, they decided to go out for pizza. Madison and Megan had worked up an appetite and both wanted to sit back, relax and be waited on.

Chapter 9

At Hungry Driver's Diner, Debbie, Susan and Rosemary were hard at work preparing the food for the next day's party. They prepared three cold salads, a layered jell-o dish and a large bowl of mixed fruit. They put together a pot of baked beans, a special hot potato casserole and Susan's famous macaroni and cheese. They would put those in the oven a couple hours or so before the party. They would start a large turkey and spiral ham earlier Sunday morning as well.

Debbie had baked a large sheet cake and was about to start decorating with a frosting version of Charlotte's favorite flowers, yellow roses. She had also made a smaller carrot cake with cream cheese frosting decorated with bright orange frosting carrots.

The ladies' conversations took many directions during the course of the day.

At one point, Rosemary asked Debbie, "So, how are things going with Steve? Will he be here tomorrow?"

Debbie blushed when she replied. "Things are going great. I'm trying not to take things to fast, but Steve might be *the one*. His children have made me feel welcome and he treats Megan like he's known her all her life. He and Amy will be here tomorrow. Jason still wasn't sure if he could get home for the weekend. He works in Greenville, South Carolina. I think Mother's Day is still hard on Amy and Jason, but Amy said she wanted to meet the rest of my family. She and Megan get along quite well."

Susan added her comments. "Ray and I think Steve is just wonderful. We really hope it works out. You've worked hard and deserve all the happiness you can find. I'm looking forward to meeting Amy tomorrow and maybe Jason will surprise you."

Chapter 10

While everyone was preparing for Charlotte's party in North Carolina, Nina Theresa Garrido Perez was in Las Cruces, New Mexico, on her way to pick up her young charge from ballet lessons. At forty-six, Nina was a petite woman of Mexican heritage. She had long dark wavy hair and dark eyes. She had a long face that bore scars on her left cheekbone of a long ago accident.

Nina worked as the nanny for the Baxter children. Sarah was six and Colby three. Sarah had been taking ballet lessons since she was three. She was quite a limber little dancer.

As Nina waited in the dance studio lobby with the other mothers and nannies, she reflected on her own life. Nina had been the nanny to Sarah and Colby's mother Melissa from the time Melissa was a young child. Nina and her husband, Hector Perez, came to the United States over twenty years ago. They secured positions working for the Jackson family. Carter and Jillian Jackson were career professionals. Carter was a banker and Jillian was an attorney. Nina was hired to be the nanny for their children. At the time, Melissa was eight and Todd was four. Hector was hired to be the gardener and handy man for their large home. The Jackson family was great to work for. Though they had busy careers, they made great efforts to spend plenty of time with their children.

Being a lawyer, Jillian assisted Hector and Nina with applying for and getting their green cards. They were most grateful to her. As Melissa and Todd grew older, Nina's role drifted to be more of a housekeeper and meal planner.

After Melissa married Bryce Baxter and had her first child, she asked Nina to become the nanny for her young children. Melissa had a great job in Human Resources at New Mexico State University and Bryce was an engineer with a local company. Melissa adored Nina and knew her children would be well taken care of.

Suddenly a familiar squeal of delight brought Nina's attention back to the present. Little Sarah was still dancing as she crossed the lobby carrying her small bag that held her ballet clothes and shoes and waving a pink sheet of paper.

"Miss Nina, we're having a recital. Can you and Mr. Hector come watch me dance?"

Nina took the sheet of paper and read the announcement of the upcoming recital.

"We would love to come, Sarah. You know how much Mr. Hector and I love to watch you dance."

Nina and Hector never had children of their own. When she was younger, Nina had felt quite sad and ashamed that she could not give Hector children. Hector always consoled her by saying that he loved her and if they were not meant to have children, he would just have to love her more. Nina never told Hector the whole truth of why she felt ashamed. Hector knew that Nina had been in an accident a few years before they met. He believed Nina's explanation that the accident may have caused her to be unable to bear children. Nina never explained the full truth about the incident to anyone.

In reality, the Bad Man nearly beat Nina to death. He left her for dead in a desolate field just over the border of her home country of Mexico. Nina was sure that in addition to the outward scars she still wore on her face, the inward scars were what caused her barrenness. She could never explain what she did in her teenage years that led up to that beating. She only hoped that her last heroic act saved that precious baby's life.

Having prayed earnestly for all these years, she still searched the faces on the streets and in crowds. She continued to hope that one day she would see that baby girl's face in that of a young woman. That would be proof to Nina that indeed that baby girl had survived. Though she hoped never to see the Bad Man again, she searched the faces for his as well. Nina knew that if he should ever spot her first, he would kill her.

"Enough of these unpleasant thoughts", Nina told herself and reached for little Sarah's hand.

"Do you remember what we have to pick up now, Sarah?"

Sarah's eyes continued to sparkle. "Yes, I do. We have to get Mommy's present, the secret one from me and Colby and Daddy."

"That's right. I'm glad you remembered it was a secret. Your Daddy really wants to surprise your Mom tomorrow."

Sarah and Colby's father, Bryce, had made an appointment to have a portrait of the children done and selected a heart shaped frame. Nina had taken the children for the sitting and was to pick up the finished portrait today. She was almost as excited as Sarah to see it.

Chapter 11

Mother's Day dawned with brilliant sunshine and just the right amount of breeze. Charlotte Davis was awake early with anticipation of her party. She fussed over her children going to such work to celebrate her birthday, but secretly she thought she was blessed to have such a wonderful, caring family. She also felt blessed to have had such a good life for eighty years. She was looking forward to seeing her family all together with many of their close friends.

As Charlotte reflected over her family memories, she remembered the year Ray introduced Rosemary and baby Madison. She admitted to having some doubts at first. A mother's instincts are to always be cautious when inviting strangers into your family's home. But she almost immediately saw that Rosemary had no ulterior motives. Rosemary was a good woman who desperately longed for an extended family in which to raise her daughter among.

Charlotte remembered how it seemed that Rosemary and her baby were not truly bonded until they were among the Davis family. Charlotte saw a slight awkwardness when Rosemary tended to baby Madison. Charlotte was happy to gently guide Rosemary on infant care and soon she was a natural. Mother and daughter had been closely bonded ever since.

She thought she should start getting ready for the day and headed to the kitchen to start the coffee. George would be back with the paper in a few minutes and they would enjoy their first cup together quietly before their busy day started.

Chapter 12

Rosemary was up early on Mother's Day as well. She attended the early mass at her church and drove to Madison's apartment for brunch. She was looking forward to the day ahead.

Madison saw her mother park her car and hurried to open the door and greet her with a big hug.

"Happy Mother's Day, Mom," she proclaimed as she released Rosemary from her arms.

"Thank you dear. This is such a nice idea for us to enjoy brunch alone before the busy afternoon. Something sure smells delicious."

"That would be the egg and sausage casserole. Let me pull it out of the oven and let it set while I fix us a cup of tea."

Their friends often teased the mother and daughter of being the Tea Toting Twosome. Neither of them had ever become fond of coffee.

Madison placed the casserole on the counter and poured the boiling water into a white ceramic teapot to brew. As she reached for the cups, she told her mother to sit down and relax. She used a tray to carry the tea to the sitting section in her apartment's open design. Madison and her mother chose to sit in the two light green padded chairs that complimented her floral designed love seat. As they relaxed and sipped their favorite brew, Madison reached for the velvet box with the big white bow.

"Mom, this is for you," Madison said as she handed the box to Rosemary.

"You didn't have to buy me anything. Having you as a daughter is all I've ever wanted or needed."

"Please, Mom, open the box."

Rosemary slowly removed the bow and lifted the cover on the oblong box. When she saw the sterling silver necklace and the gemstones within the two entwined hearts tears began to form in her eyes. When she read the words engraved on the outer circle, 'Mother, Daughter, Friends', her own heart swelled with pride.

"This is so beautiful. I truly don't know what to say. Thank you so much. I love you Madison. I have loved you since the first moment I held you in my arms. You are the most wonderful daughter any mother could ask for."

Madison was a bit teary eyed as well. "Mom, I'm so happy we have such a great relationship. The necklace symbolizes how strongly we are bonded together."

Madison stood up. "Let me help you put it on you. I want to make sure the chain is long enough."

Rosemary held the necklace in front of her and let Madison take the ends. She took a moment to wipe the tears from her face. The chain length was perfect. Rosemary clutched the circle of hearts in her hand and pressed it to her chest. She thought to herself how proud she was of the young woman Madison had become.

It was moments like this one that Rosemary knew she made the right decision all those years ago. She reassured herself that she had raised Madison with love and kept her safe from the dangers of the world.

Still clutching the circle of hearts in the palm of her hand, she said to Madison, "I will wear this always. I can't tell you how much this means to me. Thank you again."

"Our birthstones look nice side by side as well, don't you think?"

"Yes Dear. I guess we were lucky right from the beginning."

The mother and daughter ate the lovely brunch Madison had prepared. In addition to the tasty casserole, Madison had prepared home fried potatoes, sliced melon, English muffins and fresh squeezed orange juice. The meal would surely hold them until their late afternoon luncheon for Charlotte.

As they ate, they discussed Claire's upcoming baby's due date. They also made plans to attend the annual Black Mountain Arts and Crafts Show on the first Saturday in June. Madison made a mental note to put her request in for time off on the hospital nurses schedule.

Chapter 13

At shortly before one o'clock, Madison and Rosemary arrived at the Hungry Drivers' Diner. They were happy to help with the finishing setup tasks. Madison and Megan set the fresh lily centerpieces on each table. Rosemary set up a side table for the basket that would collect any cards for Charlotte. Ray and Matt hung a Happy Birthday banner high over the counter.

Family and friends started arriving and soon the diner was packed with close to one hundred well-wishers. Charlotte beamed with joy and pride as she greeted the guests. She was wearing a pale blue linen pantsuit with a floral silk blouse. With her shimmering white hair and rosy complexion she looked elegant.

The afternoon held all the closeness and happiness that Charlotte's family could have hoped for. Charlotte's sister Bernice was able to attend. Her daughter, and Charlotte's niece, Shirley, had driven her from Atlanta, Georgia for the occasion. Shirley announced they would be staying a few days to allow the sisters to visit more. Charlotte was only twelve months younger than Bernice so they had grown up very close. Charlotte was looking forward to having time to catch up with her sister.

George's brother and wife were also in attendance from Hickory. George and Stanley found a corner in which to talk, away from all the commotion.

Ray and Susan's three children joined the crowd. Matt and Allison had arrived early to help with the preparations. Claire and Ben arrived a little later. Claire was looking every bit like a pregnant woman in her ninth month. She couldn't wait to deliver her little one. Ryan had driven from Hickory and brought a date. Susan was pleased to meet Jenny and hoped she would see her often in the future.

As promised, Doctor Steve (as Debbie's family called him) was at Debbie's side most of the afternoon, looking quite happy and natural. His daughter, Amy, helped Madison and Megan set up the food.

"I really like your Mom. I haven't seen my Dad this happy in a long time. I was beginning to think he would never recover after my Mom's death", Amy said to Megan. "It was hard on all of us, but Mom made us all promise to remember that what she wanted most for us was to be happy. I miss her every day, but I know she wouldn't want me to dwell on the sadness. Jason is having a little tougher time, but I think he's getting better."

Megan smiled. "Your Dad is really cool too. I've never seen my Mom like this. She seems to glow with happiness. Let's hope things work out for all of us."

Chapter 14

At three o'clock Ray stood between the two dining areas of the diner to make an announcement. "I want to thank each and every one of you for joining us here today to celebrate my mother's eightieth birthday. About half of you in the room are family and have known Charlotte most, or all, of your lives. The other half of you have been such good friends to my mother that I'm sure she considers you family as well. One thing we all agree on is that Charlotte Davis is a terrific lady. She worked hard raising her family and helping to build the family business. My sister and I wanted to take today as an opportunity to show Mother how much we appreciate and love her."

Ray took an envelope his pocket and motioned for Charlotte to stand beside him. "Mom, you always say there is nothing you need besides our love, but we couldn't let this milestone birthday go without a special gift. We have arranged for you and Dad to take a little trip to Nashville. We hope you enjoy yourselves. But, as you always cautioned Debbie and me, please behave yourself and don't get into any trouble."

Laughter filled the room and someone started the applause that soon took over the crowd. Almost no one noticed when Jason Edwards slipped in the door and stood alone in the back of the room. Almost that is, except for Steve and Debbie. A tear slid down Debbie's cheek and Steve squeezed her hand. As if one, their minds silently told them that everything was going to be just fine in their relationship.

Susan quieted the applause and announced that the buffet table was ready. She asked that Charlotte and George start the procession.

The remainder of the afternoon was filled with laughter and much reminiscing. The elders in the room told many tales to the younger generation.

Chapter 15

On May 25th Claire gave birth to a beautiful baby girl. They named her Erica Michelle Webster. Claire and Ben were the proudest parents and Susan and Ray beamed as first time grandparents.

After Claire and Erica were home, Rosemary and Madison visited, armed with bright pink gift bags that were overflowing. Susan, Ray and Debbie were also at Claire and Ben's home that day. Susan was a glowing grandmother and Rosemary had a hard time not envying her. Rosemary could not wait until her daughter was happily married. She knew that Madison would make a great mother and she wanted to be a doting grandmother for many years.

Rosemary never knew her grandparents. Her mother, Ellie, grew up in a small town in California and left in her late teens. Rosemary's mother told her that her parents, Rosemary's grandparents, died before Rosemary was born. Rosemary often wished for grandparents to love her. Ellie become addicted to drugs and died of an overdose when Rosemary was only six. At that time, Rosemary wished she had grandparents to live with, rather than the foster home system she was put into.

Everyone was taking a turn holding little Erica. She was a beautiful child with a perfect complexion and dainty facial features. Susan could see Claire in Erica's face. Susan was so proud and happy for her daughter.

The conversation turned to the subject of labor and delivery.

Claire was the first to say, "I had a period of very hard labor pains, but as soon as I could start pushing, the pain seemed to ease. When I heard my baby's first cry, I knew it was all worth it.

Now I can't remember much about the pain. I'd always heard that, but never thought it would be true. How about you, Mom, did you forget all the pain us three kids put you through?"

Susan laughed as she answered. "Yes, I forgot the labor pains, but there were certainly a few headaches over the years that are hard to forget. You kids could be quite a handful on some days when your dad was on the road and I was home alone with you."

Ray had to lend his comments. "That's why I gave up trucking all those years ago. I needed to stay closer to home to help your mother deal with all you wild kids." Everyone laughed.

Madison looked at her mother and asked, "What about you, Mom? Was I an easy delivery, or do you have memories of me causing you pain?"

Rosemary seemed to pause in reflection before she replied. As she had for many years, she chose her words carefully. "I don't dwell on your delivery either. I just remember how I felt the first time I held you in my arms. I knew, at that instant, we were meant to be a family forever."

Chapter 16

On June 1st, in San Angelo, Texas, Catherine Wallace walked slowly toward the grave of her only daughter in the Lawnhaven Memorial Gardens Cemetery. Today would have been her daughter's fifty-fifth birthday. The name on the large tombstone read Lydia Jayne Wallace Meriweather. The date of death read almost twenty-eight years ago.

Catherine Wallace was a very agile seventy-seven year old woman with beautiful white hair. She kept her hair styled and her makeup applied perfectly. Catherine's height had slipped over the years to five feet, five inches but she had maintained her slender frame.

Catherine used to believe the saying that time passes quickly and heals wounds. But to her, the last twenty-eight years had dragged on forever and her wounded heart still ached on days like this. She hoped on several occasions to awake and learn that it had all been a terrible nightmare.

"Happy Birthday my dearest Lydia," she whispered as she knelt in front of the tombstone.

Lydia was taken from this world in her prime. Struck by a hit and run driver, someone who was never brought to justice for his or her crime. Catherine thought often over the years that if she had someone to blame, someone to divert all her anger toward, that she might have been able to move on more than she had been able to.

Catherine had tears running down her cheeks as she talked softly to the cold stone. "I still miss you so much. I feel like I have nothing left to remember you by. I wish I could reach out and touch your lovely face and hear you sing that favorite lullaby to your daughter."

If only there were some part of Lydia left for Catherine to love. But even Lydia's dear baby girl had been taken from them. The mystery surrounding Olivia's disappearance still haunted Catherine's dreams.

"Your Dad was in his study when I left looking at some photo albums from when you were young. He misses you just as much as I do. He just holds it inside himself."

A few years ago, Catherine's husband, Nathan, stated he had to put his sadness and anger aside and try to live a fuller, happier life in his remaining years. He no longer visited Lydia's grave with Catherine. Nathan felt he honored Lydia's memories better by looking at the smiling photos of his daughter that he kept in his study, than at the sight of her tombstone.

Catherine respected Nathan's decision. She often wished that she too could set aside her sorrow and enjoy remembering all the wonderful times with her daughter. Then she worried that she would feel guilty, as if she were forgetting her daughter's tragedy.

Catherine smiled proudly as she talked. "Your niece and nephew both had great years in college. They are home now for the summer break. They are quite smart and will go on to have good careers."

Nathan and Catherine had one son, Lydia's younger brother, Luke. He was married and had given them two precious grandchildren, Holly and Nicholas. Catherine spent quite a lot of time with her grandchildren over the years. Though she adored them, she was always haunted by the thought of her first granddaughter. She supposed one always wondered what would have become of their loved ones who were taken at such a young age.

Nathan often tried to get Catherine to join a support group for parents who had lost children. She always thought that no one else could know her pain; never thought it would be helpful to listen to others' painful stories. She wondered today if she might have been wrong. At seventy-seven, was it too late to let go of her grief?

Chapter 17

Catherine Wallace had three yearly traditions she remained firm about regarding Lydia. Today, Lydia's birthday, she always visited her daughter's grave. She could not imagine not spending time with her daughter on the day she had given birth to her.

Catherine's second tradition occurred on July 14th of each year when she placed a phone call to the Abilene police department. She spoke to the now Chief of Detectives Brian McGregor on the date of her first granddaughter's birthday. Chief McGregor had been the lead detective on Olivia's kidnapping case. Catherine called to remind him that Olivia was another year older and still missing. She never referred to her as dead. That would have meant giving up hope; hope that sometime in her life, she would be reunited with the grandchild who was stolen from her so long ago.

Both the Wallace and the Meriweather families had agreed on one thing. There would not be a marker bearing Olivia's name placed over an empty grave as long as there was any hope left that she might still be alive. Chief McGregor still headed the missing persons division in Abilene. Though he never had an update on the case, Brian McGregor always offered his sympathy to Catherine for her loss.

In October, on the anniversary of the day Lydia was hit and killed, Catherine's third annual tradition occurred. Catherine would place another call, this one to the homicide detective in Abilene, who had been in charge of Lydia's case. Catherine knew that Detective Luis Fuentes would not have any updates to this case either, but she made the yearly call so that Lydia's case would have to be looked at once a year, and her name would not be forgotten. Detective Fuentes was always courteous to Catherine, and seemed truly saddened that her case had never been solved.

Over the years, Catherine tried to keep track of Lydia's husband, Graham Meriweather. Although the two families had not spoken in many years, she wanted to keep track of the Meriweather family in case any new developments came to light. Graham's family made a fortune in real estate, banking and Texas oilfields. Catherine wondered whether the Meriweather money might have been the root cause behind Lydia's death. She assumed it was surely the cause in Olivia's kidnapping and disappearance. Catherine knew that Graham still lived in Abilene; in the same house he shared with Lydia during their short marriage.

Lydia had been hired to be Graham's father's private nurse. Oliver Meriweather had a terminal kidney disease. Catherine heard that Graham inherited his father's kidney disease and required a transplant a few years ago. She hoped that he was doing well. Catherine made a mental note to herself to send a short note to Graham as she ran her hand across the lettering on the tombstone.

Catherine placed the bouquet of white roses along the base of Lydia's grave and wiped the tears from her eyes.

"Remember that I love you. I promise to visit you again next year."

As she walked back to her car, she wondered how many more years she would be able to make this annual visit. Catherine also wondered if anyone would visit Lydia's grave after she was gone.

Chapter 18

Milton Donovan was also visiting Lawnhaven Memorial Gardens Cemetery on June 1st. He watched Catherine Wallace from behind a tree. He too was there to remember Lydia. Milton knew today would have been Lydia's birthday. He often visited her grave on this date. Over the years, he learned to wait for Catherine to leave before he approached the grave to leave the small floral bouquet he purchased at a nearby supermarket next to the white roses Catherine left for her daughter.

Milton was a tall man who was slightly overweight. He was fifty-nine years old, with salt and pepper hair and a matching thick mustache. He walked with a limp from an accident that had left him disabled many years before. Besides the physical damage, Milton was also left with mental scars. He was often delusional and paranoid. Since his disability, he had lived a meager life. He was forced to move back into his mother's home. Between her social security and his disability checks, they were able to just make ends meet. On this day, he was dressed in blue jeans, a light blue tee shirt and wore his favorite baseball hat. Milton was a devoted fan of the Houston Astros.

"My Dear Lydia", he whispered, as he knelt in front of the headstone. "You were supposed to belong to me forever. Remember when you said you would always be there for me?"

Milton's voice started to become louder and more agitated. "You did tell me that. And I believed you. Then you left me. You married that rich man."

Milton could feel his anger rising. "If you had stayed with me, you would still be alive. We could have been happy. You were

43

supposed to be with me. If I couldn't have you, I didn't want anyone else to."

"That's why I followed you that day. The day you died."

Milton wiped a tear from his eye and patted the tombstone. "Now no one has you. I'll see you next year, Lydia."

Milton Donovan walked back to his car. He needed to get home in order to prepare dinner for his eighty-five year old mother.

Chapter 19

The first weekend of June arrived, and as they planned on Mother's Day, Rosemary and Madison were preparing to attend the Black Mountain Arts and Crafts Show. Madison was working that Saturday morning, but firmly stated that she had to leave at noon, as soon as her short shift was over. She was to meet her mother at one o'clock.

As the morning rushed by, Madison got caught up in the many activities and cases arriving in the emergency room. It was almost noon and she had not taken a break. As she ducked into the break room and was preparing herself a cup of tea, she heard the dispatcher's announcement.

"Attention ER. There is a multiple motor vehicle accident on Interstate 40. The critically injured are being routed directly to Asheville Trauma Center, but we are getting multiple victims. ETA of the first ambulance is fifteen minutes."

Madison thought, "I can't leave now. I have to stay and help. Mom will understand. We can go later this afternoon, or tomorrow." She pulled her cell phone out of her pocket and pressed the speed dial code for her mother. Her call went directly to voice mail. She quickly left a message apologizing and asking her mother to call her back as soon as she picked up the message.

Madison put on a scrub gown and grabbed a pair of gloves. Many of the ER staff headed toward the door to meet the ambulances as they arrived. They were a -trained team that worked well together under pressure.

The first three victims had various broken bones and were sent directly to x-ray. The fourth victim was covered with blood. The paramedics shouted the statistics as they rolled the gurney through the doors.

"Female. Age approximately fifty. She has multiple broken bones and probable massive internal injuries. We started fluids intravenously. Pulse is weak and her breathing is labored."

Madison took one look at the woman on the gurney and asked the paramedic, "Why did you bring her here? She should have been routed to the trauma center. This woman has life threatening injuries."

The paramedic replied. "She demanded we bring her here. She was having a difficult time talking, but I think she was trying to tell us that she knew someone here."

Madison was opening the woman's shirt to listen to her lungs when she spotted the sterling silver hearts covered with the woman's blood. Madison's breath was taken away and she suddenly felt faint.

"This can't be", she shouted in her mind.

She tried to get a hold of herself. She lifted the oxygen pump from the woman's face and looked into her mother's pleading eyes.

"Oh my God, Mom, it's me, Madison. I'm going to take good care of you. You'll be just fine."

Madison waved her arm in the air to catch her co-worker Heather's attention and shouted, "Call Dr. Steve Edwards to the ER, NOW."

Rosemary was quickly wheeled into a room and gently moved from the gurney to an examining table. Madison tried to clean the blood from Rosemary's face and body, but it had started to dry. She hooked her mother up to oxygen and a blood pressure monitor. Rosemary's pressure was low, probably due to internal bleeding.

Dr. Steve Edwards appeared at Madison's side in record time. He took one look and realized the patient was Rosemary. His heart sank and he touched Madison's hand as he moved closer to his patient.

"Let me examine her. I can take her into surgery as soon as I assess her condition. I want you to sit down and take some deep breaths. We're in for a long day here."

Before he started the exam, Dr. Edwards stepped outside the room and motioned to Nurse Heather Cooper.

"Heather, I need you to call Debbie for me. She should be at the family diner. Tell her what has happened to Rosemary and ask her to get here as soon as possible. Madison is going to need a shoulder to lean on while I operate on her mother."

Heather understood Dr. Edwards' concern and hurried to the break room to make the call in private. She wanted to do all she could for her friend.

When he reentered the room Dr. Edwards told the technician to order a portable ultrasound machine to be brought to Rosemary's exam room. He needed to see where the bleeding was before he operated.

Chapter 20

Debbie Davis was in the middle of the lunch hour rush at Hungry Drivers' Diner when she heard the business phone ring. Megan was working her usual Saturday shift and ran behind the counter to pick up the phone.

Heather Cooper's voice was shaky and rushed. "May I please speak to Debbie Davis?"

Megan glanced toward the kitchen as her mother came through the door carrying several plates of food. "She's quite busy at the moment. This is her daughter, Megan. May I take a message?"

Heather was relieved to hear she was speaking with Megan.

"Hi Megan, this is Heather Cooper. I work with Madison at the hospital. You and I have met a few times. There is an emergency here at the hospital and Dr. Edwards asked me to call your mother."

"Is Madison all right? Is Doctor Steve okay? What's wrong?"

Heather hated to give Megan the bad news before she spoke with Debbie, but she sensed she was not going to be able to avoid it.

"Megan, they are both fine. It's Madison's mother. Rosemary has been in a bad car accident and she was just brought into the emergency room. Dr. Edwards is with her now and will be operating on her soon. He would like your mother to come sit with Madison. Needless to say, Madison is quite shaken up. Do you think Debbie can get here as soon as possible?"

Megan practically slammed the phone down as she was replying. "We will both be right there. Tell Madison we're on our way."

Megan had felt the blood drain from her face and she had tears rolling down her pale cheeks as she approached her mother in the aisle.

"Mom, I have something to tell you. It's bad news. Please, can we go into the kitchen?"

Debbie could tell that Megan was truly upset. Her hands began to shake as she grabbed her daughter's arm and led her through the kitchen door. As soon as they were through the door, Megan lost her composure.

Megan was sobbing as she tried to get the words out. "Mom, Heather Cooper just called from the hospital. Rosemary has been in a car accident. Doctor Steve asked Heather to call for you to come to the hospital to be with Madison. He has to operate on Rosemary soon. Heather said it's bad. We have to hurry."

As soon as Debbie heard the word "accident" she was ripping her apron off. Susan Davis and Scott, their short order chef, had been watching and knew something was wrong.

Debbie looked at Susan and said, "There's been a car accident. Rosemary is hurt. Megan and I are headed to the hospital to be with Madison while Steve operates on Rosemary. That's all I know. We'll call you as soon as we know more."

Susan, shocked at what she heard, said, "Go. I'll take care of this. I'll call over to the garage. I saw Matt and Allison's car there. Allison can help me. I know Ray and Matt will want to know. Give Madison our love. I'll be saying a prayer for Rosemary."

Debbie and Megan raced out the back door to Debbie's car. Debbie started the engine and both women buckled their seat belts as they sped out of the parking lot.

Chapter 21

At the hospital, Rosemary became semi-conscious. Dr. Edwards was checking her vital signs. He had called upstairs for the next available operating room. Rosemary's condition required surgery as soon as possible.

Rosemary's eyes opened slightly and she was able to whisper to Dr. Edwards. "Where is Madison?"

Dr. Steve Edwards replied. "She's just outside the door. She'll be right back. You hang in there, Rosemary. We will operate soon. You're in good hands."

Rosemary started to get agitated. "But you don't understand, Steve. I have to speak with Madison. I never told her the truth. She doesn't know where she came from."

Steve blamed Rosemary's apparent confusion and agitation on the trauma, shock and meds she had been given. He wanted to calm his patient, so he walked to the doorway to locate Madison. He saw her just as she was rounding the corner.

Steve motioned to Madison that it was okay to come into the room.

"Your mother is asking for you. Please try to keep her calm. Reassure her. She needs to conserve all the strength she possibly can."

Madison quickly stepped around Dr. Edwards and made her way to her mother's bedside. She took her hand and said, "Mom, I'm here now. Don't try to speak. You need your strength. We can talk later, after surgery."

Rosemary did not want to wait. She struggled to speak. "I'm so sorry I never told you the whole truth. I always meant to.

You've been the best daughter. You and I are a family. You are my whole life. I love you so much. I've done my best to always keep you safe. You need to know some things in case I don't make it."

Madison tried to quiet her mother. "Mom, stop talking. Whatever it is we can discuss it in a few days. Even if it seems important right now, I'm sure it can wait. You need to stay calm and keep your oxygen levels up. You know I love you too."

Rosemary was determined to get her message out. "Madison. You must go back to where you and I began. Find Father Francis Gomez. He's at Saint Gabriel's Church in Deming, New Mexico. He has something you will need. Tell him I sent you."

After the tremendous effort it had taken her to talk, Rosemary fell unconscious again.

Though her mother seemed quite coherent when she spoke, Madison was very confused by her mother's last statements. She too blamed the meds and the trauma. But Madison could not forget her mother's instructions. She planned to ask Rosemary what they meant in a few days after her mother had time to recover from the surgery.

Chapter 22

Debbie and Megan Davis arrived at the hospital in record time. Debbie quickly parked the car and the two women raced across the parking lot into the emergency room entrance.

Megan spotted Dr. Steve Edwards first and grabbed her mother's elbow as she said, "Mom, this way."

Steve put out his arms and gave Debbie and Megan a group hug.

Debbie was crying as she asked, "What happened? How is she? Please tell me the truth. Where's Madison?"

Steve tried to settle Debbie. "Calm down. Let's take one question at a time. There was a multiple vehicle accident on I-40. Rosemary was conscious enough to demand the ambulance drivers bring her to this hospital. She has considerable trauma, internal bleeding and a punctured lung. The truth is that she's in critical condition. Rosemary needs surgery now. An operating room and a trauma team are standing by. I was just going back into her room to escort her upstairs. Madison is with her now. You can come with me."

Steve showed Debbie and Megan to the room Rosemary was in. They found Madison sitting at her mother's bedside, holding her mother's hand and weeping. Rosemary was still unconscious. Madison was so deep in thought that she was startled when she felt Debbie's hands on her shoulders.

Madison stood up and collapsed into Debbie's arms. Madison was shaking and she sobbed into Debbie's shoulder.

"Why did this happen? We were planning to go to the craft show this afternoon. She was probably on her way to meet me.

If we hadn't made these plans, she wouldn't have been on the interstate. She wouldn't have been in the accident."

Debbie tried to console her. "Madison. None of this is anyone's fault. Your mother loved going places and doing things with you. She's happiest when you're together. Don't blame yourself for this. Accidents just happen, even bad ones."

Madison got a grip on herself. "You're right. I have to focus on helping her get through this. At least she was able to speak for a few minutes. She wanted me to know she loves me and is sorry for something I couldn't understand. Then she said some very odd things about a priest from New Mexico. I think all the medications have her confused. But at least I got to tell her how much she means to me while she was awake. I think she understood that."

Debbie could see that was important to Madison.

"Honey, she has always known how much you love her. She'll be able to feel that whether she's awake or not."

Madison let go of Debbie and went to hug Megan, who was silently observing her friend and Rosemary's monitors.

Debbie then got her first opportunity to look down at her best friend as she lay in the hospital bed. She could see that her injuries were major. Debbie gently took one of Rosemary's hands and squeezed it.

"Rosemary. It's Debbie. We are all here for you. I'll be with Madison until you wake up. Be strong and we'll see you after surgery."

Dr. Edwards noticed the nurses and technicians standing at the door. He knew it was time to move Rosemary to the operating room.

"Debbie, Madison, Megan, we have to go upstairs now. You three ladies can wait in the surgical waiting area. I'll send someone out with updates as often as I can. You know I'll do my best to fix everything wrong. I'll see you soon."

Dr. Edwards and the team wheeled Rosemary out of the room and toward the elevators.

As they walked by, one of the nurses handed Madison her mother's pendant necklace. The blood had dried on the hearts. Madison closed her fingers around the necklace and wept.

Chapter 23

Rosemary Cavanaugh was not the only person fighting for their life that first Saturday in June. In Abilene, Texas, Graham Meriweather lay on a hospital supplied Gerry bed within his spacious bedroom suite in his estate waiting for his private nurse to return. Graham had once been a very active man. Standing just over six foot, two inches, with dirty blonde hair and green eyes, he was still a very attractive fifty-five year old man.

Ten years ago Graham was diagnosed with the same kidney disease that his father had died from. He received a kidney transplant seven years ago, and all had gone very well. Quite well, that is, until recently. Over the past few weeks, for no apparent reason, Graham's body started to reject the donated kidney. He was put on stronger anti-rejection medications and was receiving dialysis treatments in his home.

Graham was the only child of Oliver and Victoria Meriweather. His mother died from cancer when he was only nine. Graham's grandfather, Malcolm Meriweather, had been a very successful businessman and had created a family fortune. Malcolm's two sons, Oliver and Owen, Graham's father and uncle, were the second generation to run the family business. Graham and his cousin Harrison were currently the heads of the corporation. The Meriweather family had real estate and banking institutions throughout the southwest and was heavily invested in the oil fields along the Gulf Coast of Texas.

Graham knew that the latest of his in-home nurses, Julie Collins, would arrive soon to start his treatment. Patricia Meriweather had hired Julie about three weeks ago. Patricia married his widowed father when Graham was in college. Though she was legally his stepmother, Patricia Meriweather had never been a warm figure in his life. Graham thought Patricia was somewhat of a fortune hunter. Patricia had a son from a previous marriage, Preston Hamilton, who was a few years older than Graham. Graham's father paid for Preston to attend the finest universities and, upon graduation, had given him a position in the Albuquerque, New Mexico branch of the Meriweather Savings and Loan bank. Preston worked hard and was currently the branch manager. Oliver and Preston had never been what anyone would call brotherly. They tolerated each other on holidays and at business events.

Right on schedule, Nurse Julie Collins spoke as she entered his room.

"I'm ready to check your vitals before we get started. How have you been feeling?"

Julie Collins was barely into her twenties. She was a slender five feet three inch blonde with short hair styled with layered curls. Her eyes were bright blue.

"I'm feeling about the same Julie. I thought I would be feeling stronger after being on the dialysis."

Julie knew she should not allow her patient to feel discouraged. "Mr. Meriweather, sometimes these things take time. I'm sure we'll see some improvement very soon. Do you need anything before we start today's treatment?"

Graham heard sincere kindness in Julie's voice that reminded him of his late wife. He shook his head and said, "No, I'm ready. Let's get this started."

After Graham's treatment began he started to share some of his memories with the young nurse.

"Julie, did you know that my wife was a nurse?"

Julie looked up from making notes on his chart. "No, I didn't Mr. Meriweather."

"Please, Julie, call me Graham. It looks like we might be spending a lot of time together."

Julie nodded and motioned for Graham to continue.

"My father was stricken with this same kidney disease when I was just out of college. Lydia Wallace was hired to be his in-home caretaker. She was a beautiful young woman about my same age. I was taken with her looks and the kindness that she bestowed on my father. The short version of the story is that we fell in love and were married within two years. She continued to care for my father until his death."

"That's a wonderful story. Did you and your wife share many happy years together?"

Graham's eyes watered a bit. "No, unfortunately we did not. Lydia died in an accident just a few years after we were married."

Julie could see how troubled Graham was. "If you would like to talk about it, I'm a good listener and neither one of us can go anywhere right now."

Graham looked at the tubes running in and out of his veins and nodded.

"Yes. I would very much like to tell you about Lydia. As I said, she was beautiful. She had the shiniest brown hair that had reddish highlights. Lydia had the most beautiful brown eyes I have ever seen. We were very happy. Within a few months of our marriage, Lydia became pregnant. We were ecstatic and my father was thrilled to have a grandchild on the way. Unfortunately my father's illness took his life just a few weeks before our daughter was born."

"That's so sad", Julie commented.

"We were quite upset at the time, but then when our little girl was born Lydia's and my world was filled with happiness again. She had her mother's big brown eyes. We named her Olivia Catherine. Olivia in honor of my father and Catherine was Lydia's mother's name. That little baby brought us so much joy. I gave my wife a beautiful ruby and diamond necklace to commemorate her birth."

Julie couldn't help but smile with Graham. However, she soon noticed that Graham's face had gone solemn. His voice was filled with sadness when he began to speak again.

"Tragically it seemed as if Lydia and I were not meant to live happily ever after. When Olivia was only a few months old, Lydia went for an afternoon walk. She has struck by a car just a few blocks from our home. It was a hit and run accident. The police never found who was responsible. My beautiful wife died at the scene."

Julie didn't know what to say. She reached out and touched Graham's shoulder as he hung his head and tried to compose himself.

Thinking how close she was to her own mother, Julie said, "It must have been difficult for your daughter to grow up without her mother."

Graham's eyes filled with yet more tears. "I lost my wife that day and Olivia lost her mother. But just a few weeks later I lost my daughter as well."

Julie looked at her ill patient and felt as if no man had ever suffered as much loss as the one before her. She offered Graham her sympathy. "I'm so sorry to hear that. Do you mind telling me what happened?"

Graham took a deep breath, "Just a few weeks after Lydia's accident, my daughter was kidnapped. I received a note asking for a large sum of money. I sent the money exactly as I was told, but I never saw my daughter again. The police think our former nanny may have taken our daughter in retribution for being fired. They believe Olivia was killed. But I have never given up hope that my daughter is out in the world somewhere alive and well. My greatest wish is that I see her once again before I die."

Graham started to sob harder. "I just can't die without knowing what happened to her."

Julie tried again to comfort her patient and then changed the subject. "Looks like it's time to unhook you and get you resettled in your bed."

While his nurse was doing her duties, Graham's head filled with thoughts of his family. He remembered Lydia. He remembered the necklace he had given Lydia upon Olivia's birth.

He hoped that piece of jewelry would become a family heirloom that could have passed to Olivia. It saddened him to think of that necklace having been stolen by someone he and Lydia trusted; trusted enough to invite into their home, and entrusted their baby's care to. That young girl from Mexico who Lydia hired as their nanny turned out to be a thief and quite probably something much worse.

He also thought of the four multi-million dollar trust funds that had been set up upon his father's death. Graham, Lydia, their unborn child, and Patricia were given equal trust funds. Their main home, this estate in Abilene, was left to Graham with stipulations that Patricia was allowed life use. Upon Lydia's death, her trust fund reverted to Olivia, as her only child. Olivia's trust fund had stipulated a release date of her twenty-fifth birthday. Since Olivia was still listed as missing with no proof of death, when that date arrived, Graham had the stipulation changed to a release date of Olivia's thirtieth birthday. It was also established that if Olivia were not present by that date, her trust fund assets would revert back into the primary fund. The last surviving recipient inherited control of the entire balance. Knowing his own health was failing, Graham cringed at the thought of his stepmother, Patricia, inheriting the Meriweather family fortune.

Julie's voice broke into his thoughts. "You're all set now. Would you like to relax before lunch?"

Graham was always tired after a treatment and his illness and the medicines he was taking caused him to require much rest.

"Yes, Julie, I would like to take a short nap. Could you please close the drapes to darken the room?"

Even as Julie was closing the drapes, Graham was slipping off to sleep with visions of his lovely wife and beautiful daughter bringing a smile to his face.

After Julie left the room and Graham was fully asleep, a figure moved into and across his room, staying in the shadows. Gloved hands reached for Graham's medicine containers. Carefully the intruder opened a pill container and poured the pills into a plastic sandwich bag. The intruder then opened a second baggie and dropped identical looking pills into the pill bottle. Graham and his nurse were unaware that his medications were being replaced with placebos.

The intruder whispered to a sleeping Graham. "It won't be long now before you join your dear Lydia and baby Olivia. I hope you all rest in peace."

Chapter 24

In operating room number five at Hendersonville General Hospital, Dr. Steve Edwards made a large incision the length of Rosemary Cavanaugh's torso. He was assessing the multiple procedures that needed to be done. He requested two additional physicians to assist him. One was an orthopedic surgeon, Dr. Ethan Stone, and the other an internal medicine specialist, Dr. Sanjay Patel.

As suspected, Rosemary had multiple broken bones. Her left arm would need to be set. One rib had punctured her left lung. Repairing her lung would be critical to restore Rosemary to stable breathing. Her spleen was damaged and would have to be removed. While the surgical nurse was suctioning, Dr. Edwards noted that her pelvic bone was also fractured. He noticed something else that made him pause for a moment.

"That's strange," he thought to himself. "I don't have time to examine this now. It has nothing to do with her injuries."

Dr. Edwards noted that there was a great deal of blood in her abdomen cavity. He needed to locate the source of the bleeding immediately.

While Dr. Edwards was examining Rosemary's kidneys, Dr. Patel assessed her liver. He spoke calmly. "Steve, I think her liver has been damaged. That could be where the bleeding is coming from."

The doctors quickly focused their attention to Rosemary's liver. As they prepared to repair the tear in her liver, Dr. Edwards noticed that one of the main arteries to her right kidney had a small puncture in it. Dr. Edwards quickly gave the order to obtain more blood. Rosemary was going to need several units while the team of doctors worked on her injuries.

About ninety minutes into the surgery things were going about as good as anyone could hope for. Dr. Edwards was beginning to have hope. Suddenly blood was spurting from Rosemary's open abdomen.

The three doctors, almost in unison, called to the surgical nurse, "Suction, here, please. Quick."

Rosemary was losing blood faster than it could be put back into her veins. The anesthesiologist reported that her blood pressure was dropping. The team of doctors tried in vain to clamp off the bleeder.

Rosemary's vital signs were dropping, and the bleeding continued.

One of the nurses yelled. "Doctors, we are losing her."

Chapter 25

In the small surgical waiting room, Debbie Davis was trying to keep the conversation light between herself, Madison and Megan. She had gotten sodas and candy bars from the vending machine. None of them wanted to wander far from the operating room doors.

"It's been over two hours," Madison said in a low voice. "Dr. Steve said he'd send someone out with updates."

Debbie tried to console her best friend's daughter. "Madison, I'm sure everyone is just very busy in there. Someone will be out soon with good news for us. I'm sure of it."

Their hopes were soon shattered when Dr. Steve Edwards walked into the waiting area. Debbie could tell immediately from Steve's face that the news was not good.

Madison jumped to her feet as soon as she noticed the surgeon. "How is my mother?"

Dr. Edwards knew there was no easy way to tell Madison that her mother was gone. "Madison. Please, sit down."

As she sat, Madison started to shake.

Dr. Edwards began, "Madison. Your mother had massive internal injuries. One rib had punctured a lung, her pelvic bone was fractured, her liver was damaged and several main arteries were damaged. We did all we could, but the bleeding wouldn't stop. I'm so sorry, Madison. We lost your mother during surgery."

Tears were streaming down Madison's face. Debbie tried to pull Madison's head over to her own shoulder, but Madison was still in shock.

Madison looked up to Dr. Edwards as she asked, "May I see my mother?"

Dr. Edwards nodded. "Let's give the surgical nurses some time to clean her up. Then I promise I'll take you to her myself."

Chapter 26

For the next few hours Madison felt as if she were in a fog. People were hugging her, crying with her and trying to console her. She knew many of her co-workers had been gathered around her. Ray, Susan, George and Charlotte Davis all arrived at the hospital after receiving the call from Debbie. No one could believe that Rosemary was gone.

After about an hour Dr. Steve Edwards led Madison into a private area so she could say goodbye to her beloved mother.

As Madison sat beside Rosemary's still body and held her cold hand, she wept and whispered, "Why did this have to happen? You were such a wonderful person, always loving and kind to anyone around you. Things like this shouldn't happen to good people. How am I going to get through this without you?"

Steve and Debbie gave Madison a few minutes to be alone then entered the area.

Debbie was the first to speak. "Madison. We have to let the nurses take her away now. I can help you make the arrangements with a funeral home if you would like."

Madison was still in shock. "We never talked about her final wishes. It seemed too early to discuss death and burial. I would appreciate your help. You were her best friend."

Debbie was touched by Madison's request. "I know the owners of one of the funeral homes. It's a family business and they have been friends with our family for years. I can get you the contact information."

Later that day arrangements were made for Rosemary's body to be transported to the Sullivan and Sons Funeral Home the following morning.

Sunday afternoon Debbie drove Madison to meet with Kyle Sullivan to make the final arrangements. Madison selected a traditional service with an oak coffin. The viewing dates and times were set and Father Adam Daniels was contacted to conduct the service. Madison made an appointment for Monday morning to visit the cemetery to select her mother's final resting place.

Those few days were difficult for Madison. She had so many decisions that needed to be made almost immediately. She had to contact the local newspapers to publish the obituary. Debbie and Charlotte helped her write a loving tribute to her mother. It struck her while writing that there was much information about her mother she did not know. Rosemary had never known her father, so Madison just listed Ellie as Rosemary's mother. She wasn't sure what year Ellie had died, or in what city.

Madison kept hearing Rosemary's last words. "You must return to the beginning." She had to get through the next few days before she could concentrate on Rosemary's instructions. She fully intended to find the priest who supposedly held answers to questions Madison didn't even know.

Madison was faced with the decision of what clothes she should give the funeral director for Rosemary to be viewed in. She selected her mother's favorite blue dress. She cleaned the gold pendant necklace and made sure Kyle Sullivan was instructed to place it around Rosemary's neck. After all, Rosemary had promised Madison she would wear the hearts always. Madison felt her mother would want to be buried with the necklace that had been Madison's last gift to her.

On Wednesday afternoon a funeral service was held for Rosemary Elizabeth Cavanaugh. The number of friends, neighbors and co-workers that attended her mother's funeral service amazed Madison. Rosemary had been well liked both at her job and in her church community. When the priest asked if anyone would like to speak, several of Rosemary's friends took the opportunity to tell what Rosemary meant to them, and what a wonderful person she had been. It was a certainty that family and friends would miss Rosemary greatly.

Ray Davis was the last from the congregation to speak. He ended his emotional speech with, "On several occasions Rosemary told me how lucky she felt to have met me in that New Mexico diner many years ago. What I never told her was that our family was equally lucky. Rosemary and Madison became beloved members of our family and we were blessed to have known this wonderful woman."

Ray turned toward the open coffin in which Rosemary now lay, and with tears in his eyes said, "Rosemary, you can be assured that we will continue to love, protect and watch over your daughter. I promise you that."

In the front row, Madison was having a hard time controlling her sobs. Megan was holding her hand and Debbie, seated directly behind her, put her hands on Madison's shoulders. Everyone was heartbroken for the young woman who had just lost her mother.

After the committal at the cemetery, the Davis family held a small meal at the diner for any of Rosemary's friends who wished to attend. Madison was appreciative of all they had done for her.

Megan spent the first few nights after Rosemary's death at Madison's apartment so that her friend was not alone. As Madison was preparing to leave from the diner, Megan hugged her and asked, "Do you want me to stay with you tonight?"

Madison felt the need to be alone so she replied, "No. Thank you for offering. I just want to sit quietly and reflect on my own memories of my mother. I think I'll stay in my old room at Mom's house. I will feel close to her there. I'll be fine."

Madison knew that as the only child, her mother's house would be hers if she chose to stay there. Madison was wise enough to know that she shouldn't make any big decisions immediately. She needed time to consider all her options and make the best decision for herself.

Chapter 27

It was on the floor of her mother's bedroom that Ray found Madison sitting the next morning, Thursday. The bedroom was just as Rosemary left it that past Saturday morning. The blue and yellow plaid quilt was neatly pulled tight to the pillows. Photos of Madison were proudly displayed on the cream colored walls. The room seemed to be waiting for Rosemary to return; an event that would never happen.

Madison had opened Rosemary's cedar hope chest and was quietly going through her childhood keepsakes that Rosemary had saved so lovingly. She was holding a pink baby blanket monogrammed with a large "M" when Ray walked into the room.

"I don't mean to intrude, but the door was unlocked and you must not have heard my knocking. I wanted to check in on you," Ray said to Madison.

Madison looked up at Ray and replied, "I'm fine. I was just going through some of my mother's things."

Ray looked down and said, "You were wrapped in that very blanket the first time I met you. Your mother wasn't traveling with many extras that night, but she made sure you were snuggled warmly in that blanket."

Madison smiled at the thought of her mother's protectiveness. "Ray, did my mother ever speak of her family or of my father or his family?"

Ray thought back to those early years with Rosemary. "She mentioned that her mother died when she was young and that she spent many years in foster homes. I recall that Rosemary's mother had been from a small town in California. To be perfectly honest, the only comments she made when asked about your father suggested that she was protecting you from something bad. I always assumed she chose not to talk about it because it hurt her too much."

Madison decided to confide in Ray about her mother's last conversation.

"Before my mother's surgery she told me she was sorry for not telling me the whole truth. She said something about my needing to start back at the beginning. She gave me the name of a priest in Deming, New Mexico. She said he held information that would help me. But I'm not sure what she was sorry about, or what I need to find."

While Ray was still digesting what Madison had just told him, Madison's cell phone rang. She reached across the floor to answer it.

"Hello", she managed to say in a quiet voice.

"Madison. It's Debbie. How are you doing today?"

"I'm okay Aunt Debbie. Uncle Ray is here with me now. He stopped in to check on me. I was just going through some of my mother's mementoes."

Debbie seemed to hesitate before she spoke. "Madison, Steve and I would like to speak with you sometime soon. Would it be okay if we brought you lunch and visited with you today?"

Madison would have preferred some time to be alone, but she knew Debbie and Steve were just acting out of concern.

"Yes, that would be fine. Will you be here around noon?"

Debbie seemed relieved with Madison's receptiveness. "Yes, we should be there between twelve and twelve-thirty. We'll bring sandwiches and a salad. Ask Ray if he will still be there."

Madison handed the phone to Ray. "Aunt Debbie wants to know if you will be here for lunch."

Ray took the phone and spoke to his sister. "Debbie, this is Ray. What's this about lunch?"

Debbie told Ray her and Steve's plan then added, "Ray, what Steve has to say to Madison may not be easy. Could you please stay for Madison's sake?"

Ray looked down at Madison, who had returned to looking at her baby items and seemed lost in her own thoughts.

"Sure, I can still be here. I need some time to check things out around the house. I want to make sure everything is working fine for Madison."

Debbie was happy to hear her brother's answer. "We will see you in a bit."

Ray disconnected the call and handed the cell phone back to Madison. By then she was holding a single pink baby bootie in her hand.

"I wonder what happened to my other bootie."

Chapter 28

At twelve-fifteen Ray answered Madison's front door and ushered Steve and Debbie into the small dining room that was painted coral with white woodwork. Ray had helped Madison clear the oak table and set four place settings.

Debbie brought an assortment of half sandwiches from the large paper bag and placed them on a platter in the center of the table. Madison took the lid off a large pasta salad and started to pass it around the table.

"I really appreciate you bringing lunch but I don't want you to think you have to fuss over and worry about me. I'll be okay," Madison said as everyone started to eat his or her lunch.

The foursome chatted about various trivial things while they ate. When everyone was done eating, Debbie suggested they move into the living room. Ray made himself comfortable in the large tan recliner in the corner of the room, while Madison sat on one end of the pastel colored floral sofa with Debbie on the other end. Steve sat in the matching floral chair which faced the sofa.

Debbie was the first to speak. "Madison, I know your mother said some odd things to you in the emergency room after her accident. You mentioned them to me and seemed genuinely confused. Since you and I were both listed by your mother on her medical forms, I hope you don't mind, but I confided in Steve about her last conversation with you. I thought maybe the trauma of the accident might have caused Rosemary to be incoherent."

Madison replied, "Of course I don't mind your confiding in Dr. Steve. I was on the same thought line, but she just seemed so clear at that moment and spoke with such urgency."

Debbie reached for Steve's hand and nodded to him.

Steve hesitantly began to speak. "Madison, I know you have been through a great tragedy and have been left with what seems like a lot of confusion. I don't mean to add to that, but I may be able to shed some light on your mother's last statements."

Madison could tell Steve wasn't sure how to continue. "Dr. Steve, please if you can help me to make sense of her last words, I would certainly appreciate it."

Steve took what seemed to everyone to be an extra deep breathe. "Madison, I don't know quite how to begin. I want you to let me step back from knowing Rosemary as your mother, and let me relate to her as my patient in my operating room."

Madison nodded as she said, "OK."

"My patient was a woman in her late forties who had suffered trauma from an automobile accident. She had severe internal injuries and bleeding. In exploring my patient's organs to assess the damages, I made mental notations as a surgeon always does. A surgeon tries to assess his patient's overall health prior to an accident. In this case, my patient's organs indicated a fairly healthy woman. Next, I tried to assess any medical history of surgeries or procedures. This was where something stood out as not ordinary for the woman I knew as your mother."

Madison was hanging on Steve's every word, trying to follow the conversation as a trained medical nurse.

Steve reached over and put his hand on Madison's knee before he continued. "I assessed something from your mother's body as I explored her abdomen for bleeding. The female patient on my operating table showed no physical signs of having delivered a child, and may never have even been pregnant."

Madison wasn't the only person in the room to be shocked by Steve's last words.

Ray's eyes opened wide as he started to contradict Steve. "That can't be. I brought Rosemary and little Madison across the country when Madison was only a few months old."

Steve tried to provide some thought to the situation. "Madison, is it possible you were adopted? Maybe Rosemary assumed your care as an infant after a family member or close friend was unable to. Any number of circumstances could have brought you and your mother together."

The room went quiet, but Ray was the deepest in thought as he tried to remember every detail of his first encounter with Rosemary and her infant daughter.

After a few minutes, Ray said, "Madison, I have always said that Rosemary indicated she was protecting you when I gave her a ride from New Mexico that night. Maybe something had happened that your birth family wasn't able to safely care for you. Maybe they entrusted you to Rosemary to raise and protect as if you were her own child."

Madison's mind was going in several directions. She tried to concentrate on what had been presented to her.

"Maybe this priest in New Mexico that Mom mentioned helped with my adoption, or placement. Maybe he knows who my birth family is," Madison said with hope.

Steve tried to stick to the facts. "Do you have a copy of your birth certificate? Maybe that will give us some information."

Madison got up from the sofa and walked into her mother's bedroom. She knelt beside the still opened cedar chest and pulled out an envelope labeled "Important papers". She returned to the living room and opened the envelope. Among the papers inside, she was able to find a birth certificate and a baptismal certificate with her name on them.

Madison almost chuckled as she read the baptismal certificate. "It appears I was baptized by a Father Francis Gomez in New Mexico. That's the same priest Mom mentioned after the accident. The baptism was in September, when I would have been only a few weeks old. Rosemary Cavanaugh is listed as my mother but there is no notation of a father."

While Madison was still holding the baptismal certificate, Steve reached over and took the birth certificate from her lap. He looked it over with great detail.

"This birth certificate also lists Rosemary Cavanaugh as your mother, with father marked as unknown. But what is odder is that although it lists your date of birth as July 14th, the certificate was not filed until January of the next year. I've come across this type of thing when there was an unattended birth and for one of several reasons the parents did not report the birth until much later."

Debbie, who was taking in everyone's reactions, was the first to realize another fact. "If your birth certificate was not filed until January, you and your mother were already here in North Carolina. Why didn't she report your birth until after she was here? And yet it appears you were baptized in September in New Mexico as Madison Rose Cavanaugh."

Madison was even more confused and needed some time to think. "I don't want to seem rude, but would you mind if I asked you all to leave. I would like some time to digest what we have just discussed. I assure you I'll be fine alone and I promise to call each of you later tonight. I just really need to be alone right now."

Debbie saw the look in Madison's eyes and understood her request. She stood up and started to walk to the dining room to clear the table.

Madison sensed Debbie's intentions and said, "Don't worry about the table. It will give me something to do later and the leftover sandwiches you put in the refrigerator earlier will take care of my dinner needs."

Debbie motioned to Ray and Steve and they headed toward the front door. As they all gave Madison a farewell hug, she thanked them again for checking on her and bringing food.

Steve paused as he started to step outside the door and hesitantly made one more suggestion. "Madison, I don't quite know how to make this offer, but, here goes. I have a colleague who runs a laboratory that is not associated with our hospital. If you wish, I could ask him to run a quick DNA test on samples from you and your mother. I could ask him to report whether there is any family relationship between the two of you. I actually still have a tissue sample from Rosemary's surgery. It's up to you, but if that is something you want to pursue, you can give me a swab from your mouth, or your toothbrush. I would ask my friend to do this as a favor, not as an official report."

Madison was still processing it all in her mind when she replied, "Thanks Dr. Steve. I'll think about it and let you know. It might just be the way I have to start in order to solve this mystery."

Chapter 29

Once she was alone, Madison broke down. If what Dr. Steve said was true and Rosemary was not her birth mother, how could she have not known? She felt stupid for not ever questioning her origins. Suddenly it felt as if her entire life was built upon a lie. How could she be certain about anything now?

There were so many scenarios flowing through Madison's brain that she could not focus on any one of them. Maybe her true birth parents were out there somewhere. Maybe they had sent her away to protect her years ago and had been desperately searching for her ever since. For all these years she assumed she had no reason to search for her father. Maybe that wasn't the case at all.

Or, maybe, her parents were dead, like Rosemary, and she was truly alone in this world. Maybe her biological parents thought she was dead so they were not even looking for her. All those thoughts were too big to get a handle on. There had to be someone somewhere who could help her find the truth.

Madison returned to Rosemary's bedroom and continued to look through the articles in the hope chest. The pink blanket monogrammed with her first initial "M" and the lone pink bootie seemed to have been her first possessions. The earliest photos in her mother's old albums were of Rosemary and Madison in George and Charlotte Davis' home. Many were taken that first December when they had arrived from New Mexico when Madison was five months old. Why were there no photos of her at an earlier age? Madison remembered once asking Rosemary that question. When she was a child, all her young friends had photos from when they were newborn, but Madison did not. Rosemary stated that she had to leave many personal belongings behind when they left New Mexico and was never able to return for them. Young Madison had no reason not to accept her mother's word as the truth.

In her entire life, Madison never doubted Rosemary. She never questioned her explanations. She never pushed the subject of who her father was. Rosemary was such a wonderful mother. Why would any good daughter question her?

She looked again at the baptismal and birth certificates. These were her starting points. She had proof that Father Francis Gomez baptized her in Deming, New Mexico. This was the same priest whom, on her deathbed, Rosemary managed to name and urged Madison to find. He was the person Madison would locate and hope that he could give her information regarding her family.

Madison knew that she had to find the answers as soon as possible. This was not something she wanted to do over the phone. She would put in for a personal leave of absence Monday at the hospital. Madison needed to travel to New Mexico and meet Father Gomez in person. She had to return to where she came from that December so long ago, just as her mother said.

Madison also made up her mind regarding Dr. Steve's offer. She walked into the bathroom, took a cotton swab from the cabinet and swirled it around the inside of her cheek. She obtained a new zippered plastic bag from a kitchen drawer and placed the swab in the bag. She would drop this by the hospital tomorrow morning. She had to start by learning the truth, no matter how much it hurt.

Chapter 30

Every Sunday for as long as they could remember, the Davis family left the diner in the capable hands of their employees and closed the shop for repair business. They gathered at George and Charlotte's home for a mid-day meal as an ever-growing family. It was also tradition that Rosemary and Madison held an open invitation for the meal. After all, they were considered family.

On this particular Sunday, just three days after Dr. Steve delivered the shocking news to Madison, Debbie wanted to make sure Madison was planning on being there. She phoned Madison mid-morning, after giving her a chance to sleep in.

"Madison. How did you sleep?" Debbie asked when a solemn Madison answered the phone.

"I'm sure you'll understand when I say haven't had a good night's rest in about a week. My mind just keeps racing with 'what-if' situations since our conversation on Thursday. That, and being here alone in my Mom's home, I just miss her so much," Madison responded.

Debbie got to her point. "I wanted to make sure you realized Sunday dinner at my parent's home was still on. We want you to come over. It will do you good to be among family."

Madison couldn't help but find that ironic, "Family. I sure don't know much about who my family is, do I?"

Debbie tried to reassure her. "You don't need blood to be family, Madison. We have considered you and Rosemary to be part of our family for almost as long as you've been alive. And you don't have to give birth to a child to be a mother. We may not have all the answers right now, but the one thing I know is that Rosemary was your mother. She loved you more than life itself. She provided you with a wonderful life. Whatever she did all those years ago, she did out of love for you."

Madison felt ashamed of her comment. "I know Aunt Debbie. I'm just so confused at the moment. I need to find answers and I'm starting today. I would love to come for dinner. I thought maybe your parents might remember something from when Rosemary – I mean my mother – first arrived here in Asheville. My life is such a big mystery now; I might as well start with the here and now and work my way backwards. I'll see you soon. Thanks for calling."

When the call ended Debbie knew she needed to head over to her parents' home. If Madison was going to question George and Charlotte, they should know why. She would have to explain the newfound mystery to them before Madison got there. She called Megan to make sure she was home at the apartment in her parents' house. Debbie might as well include her daughter in the conversation. She was sure Madison would confide in Megan soon enough.

Chapter 31

An hour later Debbie walked in the door to Charlotte's kitchen. Megan was already downstairs helping her grandmother prepare dinner.

A surprised Charlotte said, "Good morning, Debbie. Aren't you up and about early? Dinner isn't for a couple more hours. I assumed you'd arrive later with Steve. Is everything alright?"

Debbie knew her mother could sense when there was a concern in the family. "Well, Mom, I need to talk to you and Dad before dinner. I want Megan to hear what I have to say as well. Is Dad in the living room?"

Charlotte then realized that her sense of trouble had been correct. Sometimes she felt her instincts were a curse.

Charlotte answered her daughter, "Yes, he's watching TV. I'll go get him."

Debbie quickly said, "No. Let's join him in there. It might be more comfortable. Can the food be left for a few minutes?"

Charlotte paused then said, "Yes, everything will be fine. I'll just lower the heat on a couple things."

When his wife, daughter and granddaughter entered the living room, George Davis knew something was wrong. He reached for the remote control and shut the television off.

George pulled his recliner straight and said, "Good morning ladies. I assume you aren't here to watch last night's baseball game recaps with me. What's on your minds?"

Not in their wildest imaginations would George or Charlotte have been prepared for the information Debbie brought to them that Sunday morning. Megan and her grandparents sat quietly, asking no questions, as Debbie unfolded the facts they had presented to Madison the day before.

Megan was the first to speak. "Mom, are you telling me that Rosemary was not Madison's mother? I can't believe that."

Debbie tried to reassure her daughter as she had Madison just an hour before. "Megan, Rosemary was Madison's mother in all sense of the word, except biologically. It appears that Rosemary never delivered a child. That could mean that Madison was adopted, or that Rosemary assumed her care as an infant from a family member, or close friend, who was unable to. I know you all have questions. I have questions too. But you can imagine how devastated Madison is at this moment. She has more questions than any of us. I wanted you to know so that we can all help support her right now. She needs our family to stand behind her. She's feeling like a stranger to even herself. We have to let her know how much we care. We always have and always will. No matter what the answers are that she may find."

Charlotte sat listening intently to Debbie's conversation. She was now deep in thought as Debbie asked her a question.

"Mom, are you OK? I know this is a lot to process."

Charlotte looked her daughter in the eyes and said, "I should have listened to my instincts way back then. I knew something wasn't right. I could sense too much uncertainty, too many nervous moves, and not enough motherly instincts."

Debbie was somewhat confused by her mother's comments. "Mom, what are you talking about?"

Charlotte continued. "It was a feeling I got when Rosemary and Madison first arrived with Ray. You and your Dad remember that December when he arrived home with them in the truck. Debbie, you and Susan were so involved with trying to get them set up with clothing, finding extra baby items, and setting up a room for them to sleep in. You didn't have time to sit back and watch their interaction. I did. I immediately thought that Rosemary was not a natural at motherhood. I tried to brush it off. It takes some women longer than others to bond with their babies. However, Madison was five months old. The bond should have been made by then. The stranger thing was that the bonding did happen soon after their arrival. It happened right before my eyes in the first week they lived here. It was undeniable that within a few days Rosemary was in love with her child and completely at ease. I just told myself that this was the first good home environment they had been in. I thought Rosemary was finally able to relax, feel safe and enjoy her baby."

Debbie tried to follow her mother's reasoning. "So you don't think Rosemary loved Madison when they first arrived? Do you think that maybe they hadn't been together very long at that time?"

Charlotte tried to put her feelings into words. "I think she was very fond of the baby when she arrived, she just wasn't as motherly as I expected. It was like she wasn't used to having a child to care for. By five months, a mother knows the difference between a hunger cry and a wet diaper cry. Let's say Rosemary was still fumbling with the baby. She didn't seem to know what baby foods Madison liked the best. She didn't even have a stuffed animal with her. I remember buying a little teddy bear for Madison on my first shopping trip after they arrived. Just little things that could be explained away, but now may mean something. It's possible that she had just adopted Madison, or had only recently assumed her care."

Debbie thought about the certificates Madison had found in Rosemary's chest.

"Madison has a baptismal certificate from September that lists Rosemary as her mother. That would have been three months before leaving New Mexico. That certificate indicates they had been together at least that long."

Charlotte was still trying to make sense of the facts and her instincts. "All I can say is that I felt as if Rosemary and Madison had not bonded as mother and daughter until after they arrived in our home. Maybe Rosemary was just too nervous as a new mother and needed to get away from something, or someone, in

New Mexico. Once she did that, we can all agree that she excelled at being a mom."

Debbie was thinking of Madison. "Mom, I think it's best if you keep your feelings just between us for now. I don't want Madison to feel like Rosemary didn't love her at any point in her life."

George finally spoke. "I agree with that. Rosemary and Madison are part of our family. I love Madison as much as I do my own grandchildren. Let's hope there is a logical explanation for all of this and she finds it soon. We have to stand behind her and help her all we can."

Megan added, "Maybe I'll ask her if she wants company. I could spend the evenings at her place and even stay overnight if she would like. Maybe I can help her find the answers she's searching for."

Debbie was proud of her daughter. "That would be a nice gesture. I'm sure she would appreciate the company, but don't be surprised if she still needs some time alone. This is a lot for her to process."

Megan nodded. "I understand. I just want to help her all I can."

Debbie had one more thing to tell them. "Steve offered to have a DNA test done privately to see whether Rosemary and Madison are related in any way. Madison dropped her sample off to Steve on Friday. The test results should be back next week. She may not mention it until she has the results."

George and Megan nodded in understanding and Charlotte looked at the clock on the wall and said, "Well, I best get back to the kitchen or we won't be eating on time. Thank you, Debbie, for telling us all this before Madison arrives. I had no idea she was going through so much right now. It must be hard enough on her to lose her mother, but to have so many unanswered questions. My heart goes out to her."

Chapter 32

Dinner at the Davis home was excellent as always. The women were experienced cooks. Conversation during the meal was kept light. Ray and Susan had new baby pictures of Claire's little Erica. Megan was happy that the school year was about to wind down. Steve mentioned that his son Jason had been offered a job in Atlanta, Georgia.

After helping to clear the table, Madison finally brought up the subject everyone had tiptoed around during dinner.

"I know you are all aware of the sudden confusion regarding my mother and where we came from. I have made a decision."

Susan Davis, who had been filled in on the story by her husband, Ray, was the first to interrupt. "Madison, you have been through a really rough week. Why don't you take some time? You shouldn't make any decisions hastily."

Madison seemed determined. "Aunt Susan, I've thought about what waiting would gain me. I can't see any advantage in doing so any longer. The answers I need are hopefully with a priest in New Mexico. The sooner I contact him the sooner I will have the answers. My mother wouldn't have mentioned Father Francis Gomez's name to me if she weren't sure he could help me."

Ray, who had been trying to place the Father's name since first hearing it, suddenly found the answer. "Madison. I knew I had heard Father Gomez's name before. I just couldn't place it. I just remembered. About a year after Rosemary and you arrived here, your mother gave me an envelope just before I left for a cross-country trip in the truck. She asked me to mail it from my farthest destination point. The envelope was addressed to a priest. His name was Father Francis Gomez. Rosemary must have read the question on my mind when I looked at the envelope. She explained that it was an annual holiday donation to a church where she had found shelter when she needed it most. She said she didn't want anyone at the church to know where she was living. That was why she asked me to mail it from the road. The same thing happened the next December and after that I never saw or heard his name again until this week."

Madison felt as if she had been handed another piece to the puzzle, but had no picture to reference to know how the pieces went together.

Madison's voice was determined as she said, "I plan to ask for a personal leave tomorrow at work. As soon as that can be arranged I plan to drive to New Mexico and meet with Father Gomez face to face. I looked for churches in Deming, New Mexico and found the address of the only Catholic Church in town. Saint Gabriel's church will be my first stop."

Megan hated to see her best friend in such confusion. "Madison. I'd like to come with you. School will be out and I have the summer free. Let me help you and keep you company on the long drive across country."

Before Madison could answer Ray jumped in, "You girls cannot head across the country alone. I won't allow it. Let me take some time and I'll drive us all out west. After all, I know the roads better than either of you. Besides, the trip might trigger my memory of some facts I may have forgotten long ago."

Madison was grateful for the offers. She thought a few minutes before she responded, "I would really appreciate the company. Can the three of us manage in my little car?"

Ray had a better plan, "We could take my SUV. We'd have plenty of room for three and any luggage you ladies have to take along. I know women never travel light."

Finally there was a chuckle in the room.

Madison seemed to relax a little with a plan established. She was anxious for Monday so she could talk to Anne Hart, the

Elaine LaForge

Supervisor of Nursing at the hospital. Madison was hopeful that Anne would understand and grant her the time off.

Across the room Steve was thinking of how he could help Madison. He knew Anne Hart quite well from all the years they had worked together. He would make a call to Anne later that evening and pave the road for Madison's request. Steve wanted Anne to understand the entire situation.

As if she knew Steve was concentrating on her, Madison said, "I submitted a sample to Dr. Steve on Friday. He offered to help me with a DNA test on myself and my mother. The results will establish how, or if, we are related. I will let you all know as soon as we get the results."

Steve replied, "I believe my friend, who works in a private lab, should have an answer for us by mid-week."

86

Chapter 33

First thing Monday morning, Madison went to find Anne Hart in her office. Madison had gone over her speech several times in her head since the weekend. She only hoped that Anne would understand and grant her request. Madison tapped on the half-opened door to get Anne's attention.

Anne looked up from her paperwork. "Madison, please come in. I want to again offer my condolences for the loss of your mother. I know the two of you were very close. You must feel quite lost."

Madison knew she had the opening she needed. "Anne, thank you so much for all you have done. I received your sympathy card and the flowers you sent from the nursing staff were lovely. I appreciate all my friends here at the hospital. I was wondering if we could discuss a private matter."

Anne, who had received a call from Dr. Steve Edwards the evening before, acted as if she didn't know what Madison was about to say. "Yes, of course, Madison, please feel free to shut my door. Come in and sit down."

Madison closed the door slowly and walked to the padded leather chairs in front of Anne Hart's desk. She sat down and began to speak.

"Anne, some information has come to light after my mother's accident that requires me to travel out west to where I was born. Some questions have arisen regarding additional family that I may need to find to notify of my mother's passing. I was wondering whether you could grant me a leave of absence. I realize it would be without pay, and I would understand if you couldn't guarantee my position when I return. I'm not even sure how much time I would need. I would hope that just a few weeks would be enough."

Anne Hart had done her homework that morning looking into Madison's employment record.

She replied, "Madison, I completely understand that you need some time after this tragic event. If you feel there are family members you need to find, by all means, you should go. I noticed that you have two weeks of vacation and one week of personal time built up. As the Nursing Supervisor, I am authorized to grant a week with pay to any employee with extenuating circumstances. I certainly feel this falls into that category. Therefore, I could grant you up to four weeks in which your pay would continue. If after four weeks, you feel additional time is required, we could revisit the unpaid leave request."

Madison could hardly believe what Anne was saying. Four weeks with continued pay to find the answers to the questions her mother left her with. This was far better than she ever dreamed the conversation would go.

Madison smiled as she said, "Anne, thank you so much. This is very generous of you. I assure you four weeks should be plenty of time for me. I appreciate your understanding. When would this time begin?"

Anne was also prepared for that question. She had rearranged the staff's schedule for the current week and beyond.

"You may start as soon as today if you wish. I have you covered for this week and will post the next two-week schedule mid-week. You are free to make your travel plans any time."

Suddenly, it felt real to Madison. She was about to travel back to where she was born and speak to Father Gomez as her mother urged her to. She even held out hope that she would be able to locate a biological family member. She didn't know whether to be excited or terrified.

Madison brought herself back to the moment. "I will go home and start my plans. I'll stay in touch with you and let you know when I will be back to work. Again, thank you. I only hope I have as good of luck in finding what I'm looking for."

Madison stood and started to offer Anne her hand. Anne quickly stood and walked around her desk. She opened her arms and Madison stepped into them for a warm embrace. Anne understood more than Madison knew and hoped the young woman in her arms would find the answers that would bring her peace.

Chapter 34

The next few days were busy for Madison, Ray and Megan. Madison was busy getting both her mother's house and her apartment in order so they could be left empty for a few weeks. She put a hold on the mail and paid both sets of utilities in advance. Madison knew she would have to make a decision on what to do with her mother's property, but not until after she returned from this trip. For now, she considered that to be the least of her concerns.

Madison went through her mother's old photo albums again. She wanted to take with her photos of Rosemary as a young woman and herself at the earliest age possible. She might need the photos to trigger someone's memory of her mother. She also wondered if she would need to use her own baby pictures to compare to the baby pictures that someone might have of a long lost child. Madison would cross all those bridges, as she needed to in time. For the immediate future, she had to concentrate on finding Father Gomez. She placed the photographs in a large envelope with her baptismal and birth certificates.

Megan wrapped up her classroom requirements and made sure that her grandparents were well supplied with groceries and their medications. She knew her mom and Aunt Susan would be near, but everyone had plenty on their plates and she wanted to do what she could to help.

Ray made arrangements at the garage for his lead mechanic to assume the management of the shop for a couple weeks. Alex Gardner had been a trusted employee for over ten years and Ray was confident he could manage without any trouble. Matt and Susan could help with any emergencies.

By Wednesday Ray and Madison had an itinerary planned out for their trip. Over lunch at the Hungry Drivers' Diner they laid out their plan to Megan, Susan and Debbie.

Since Ray was the more experienced driver, he explained the routes to the group. "It's a fairly simple route. We can take I-40 west out of Asheville all the way to Albuquerque, New Mexico. Then we take I-25 south to Las Cruces and I-10 west to Deming."

Debbie asked her brother curiously, "How many days do you see this trip taking?"

Ray shrugged as he answered, "Well, if I were still driving my rig, I'd say two long days. But since I have two young ladies in my SUV, I have planned out three days with a moderate number of hours. We should be able to cover roughly six hundred miles each day. That allows for the girls to get their beauty rest and provides us plenty of time for pit stops and meals."

Megan laughed. "Now, Uncle Ray, we promise to get up before ten each morning so we can hit the road early."

Ray knew Madison was taking this trip seriously. "I would hope we could be on the road by seven each morning and drive at least until dinner time. I'd like to make it to Little Rock, Arkansas the first night. The second day should get us near Amarillo, Texas. That leaves a shorter third day so we can have time to look around Deming, New Mexico before the sun sets."

Susan pointed out, "If you plan to leave tomorrow, Thursday, that would have you arriving in Deming on Saturday. Do you plan to go to the church to speak with Father Gomez that day?"

Madison was the first to respond. "Aunt Susan, I thought if we could locate the church on Saturday, we could check what time services are on Sunday. I could attend mass that morning and hopefully meet the Father after the service and set up some time to speak with him first thing Monday."

Megan didn't want her best friend to be alone. "Madison, don't forget I said I'd go to mass with you. I want to be by your side each and every step of this journey."

Madison was grateful to have such a good friend. "Yes, Megan, I still intend for you to be with me. I might get nervous trying to explain to Father Gomez why I need to speak with him privately."

The group agreed to use the afternoon to finish packing and get a good night's rest. Ray would be picking the girls up in the morning from their respective homes.

Chapter 35

Later that Wednesday afternoon, Madison received the call she had been waiting for. Dr. Steve Edwards had the DNA test results and wanted to discuss them with her. As she had a few last minute errands to run, she offered to stop by the hospital about four o'clock.

Steve looked up from his desk when Madison knocked on his opened door. "Come in, I was glad I caught you before you left. Please have a seat."

Madison sat down in a chair facing Steve's desk. She was nervous and fidgeted in her seat. Steve noticed her anxiety and tried to reassure her.

"Madison, I have the results from the lab. I thought we could open them together if you would like."

"I'd like that. I'm not sure what to hope for, but at least it's a start at finding the truth."

Steve slowly opened the large envelope and pulled out the analysis his colleague had prepared. He placed the summary cover letter so that they could both read it. It stated that the DNA results found no biological relationship in the two samples provided.

Steve was the first to speak. "Madison, do you understand the results?"

Madison had tears in her eyes as she spoke. "Yes, they prove that not only was my mother not my mother, but she was not related to me in any manner."

Steve stood, walked around his desk and sat in the chair next to Madison. He placed his hand on hers.

"This does not mean she wasn't your 'mother'. From what I've learned, Rosemary raised you as her daughter for as long as anyone can remember. There are a host of possible scenarios. As we discussed earlier, you may have been adopted, or your parents may have died and left you in Rosemary's care. She may have been your Godmother. She may have been your biological mother's best friend, a friend she entrusted her young daughter to for some yet unknown reason."

Madison began to fold up the letter and report to replace them into the envelope. "At least I know this much now. I'm determined to find all the answers, the true answers. I guess this was the first one. If I'm not Rosemary Cavanaugh's daughter, I need to find out who I am."

Madison stood and was placing the envelope into her purse, when Steve placed his hands on her shoulders.

"I hope this news didn't upset you too much. I think you were prepared for the outcome, but it still must be a shock. I wish I could do more for you."

Madison raised her arms and gave Steve a gentle hug.

"I'll be fine. Thank you for being honest with me. I appreciate knowing the truth. I will take these test results with me to New Mexico. You never know when I might need to produce my own DNA profile."

Steve watched as Madison turned and left his office. He thought she was the bravest and most determined young woman he knew. He only hoped that she would be able to find all of the answers she was searching for.

Chapter 36

The road trip went quite smoothly. Ray's daily distance calculations turned out to accommodate everyone. By four in the afternoon on Saturday, the threesome drove into Deming, New Mexico. The first thing they did was to locate a familiar chain hotel and acquire two adjoining rooms on the second floor. They all needed a break from sitting in the vehicle, so they took time to unpack their luggage and walk around the hotel.

Their hotel rooms consisted of the basic set of double beds, a small round table with two chairs set in a corner and a large flat screen television positioned on top of a long, low dresser which had two sets of three drawers. They immediately opened the terracotta and brown designed drapes and turned on the air conditioning units, setting the temperature dial to the coldest setting. It was New Mexico in June, after all.

When they climbed back into the SUV, they went in search of Saint Gabriel's Catholic Church. They located the street easily and found the church on a corner lot. The sign outside stated that mass would be held the next morning at both nine and eleven.

Madison made her decision. "I think we should attend the eleven o'clock mass. That way Father Gomez will not be rushed to prepare for the next service."

Megan agreed. "That's a good idea. Eleven o'clock it is."

Ray had an idea. "Ladies, let's see if the small diner where I met Rosemary and you, Madison, as a baby, is still in business. If I remember correctly, the food was pretty good."

Madison was curious for nostalgic reasons. "Uncle Ray, that's a great idea. I'm sure the food can't hold a candle to the Hungry

Drivers' Diner, but I'm game to try it out. After three days of fast food, I'm ready for a home cooked meal."

Ray turned the SUV in the direction of where he remembered the diner to have been and soon they were on the outskirts of town.

Ray gestured and said, "I think it should be just up here on the right."

Megan was the first to see the sign. "There it is, The Deming Town Line Diner. That must be the place."

Madison chuckled. "Not too original with their name, are they?"

Ray smiled and was happy Madison could find a little humor in the day. "Let's park this little rig and get us some dinner."

When they entered the diner Ray spotted a corner booth near a window that faced the parking lot. He motioned the girls in its direction. The diner was not as modern as the Hungry Drivers' in Asheville, but it was neatly decorated, appeared clean and was filled with heavenly aromas. The booth had black and white vinyl seats and the tabletop was white Formica with red and black speckles.

As they were reaching for the menus standing on the end of the table, a middle aged waitress approached. Her nametag read Naomi. Her straight dark hair streaked with gray was hooked back with combs, her height average and her weight a little on the plump side. Her features showed she was of Native American heritage.

Naomi greeted them with a welcoming smile. "Good evening folks. May I start you off with something to drink?"

Megan was the first to answer. "Yes, I would love a large cold cola. We've been driving for three days and I tried to limit my beverage intake."

Naomi made a note of the order and said, "So, you're not from around here? Are you passing through, or is Deming your final destination?"

Madison was quick to speak up. "We hope Deming is our first stop in unraveling a family mystery. I'd like a large cola as well, thank you."

Naomi was intrigued with Madison's statement and said, "A mystery, huh? I just love a good mystery. I wish you luck in solving it. If you need any local assistance, I've worked in this diner since my parents bought it back when I was a teenager. I know just about everybody in town. I'd be happy to help you."

Ray was the last to speak. "Thank you, Naomi. We really appreciate your offer. I'll have a cup of decaf coffee please."

Naomi nodded and said, "I'll be right back with those. Take your time looking the menu over. Tonight's special is pot roast or a hot roast beef sandwich with mashed potatoes."

Before she read the menu, Madison dug into her purse and pulled out a photo of her mother that was twenty years old.

As she held the photo, she said, "Naomi appears to be about my mother's age. If she's lived in this town her entire life, and claims to know everybody, maybe she will remember my mother. It doesn't hurt to show it to her."

When Naomi returned with the beverages, the group had decided on their orders. Ray ordered the pot roast dinner and the girls chose the hot sandwich special.

After Naomi had their orders written down, Madison held the photo of Rosemary so that their waitress to see.

"Naomi, would you possibly remember this woman? This was taken twenty years ago and she would have been a few years younger when she lived in Deming. Her name is Rosemary Cavanaugh."

Ray added, "I actually met the lady in the picture right here in this diner twenty-eight years ago come this December. Do you by chance remember her?"

Naomi studied the photo carefully before she spoke. "I don't recognize her, and the name doesn't sound familiar. I'm so sorry. She may not have been a regular. We have a lot of people passing through. Plus that December, twenty-eight years ago, I was home with my newborn son. I took a few weeks off after his birth."

When Naomi left the table, Madison sighed. "We knew it wouldn't be that easy. I can't expect that the first person we run into will recognize my mother."

Naomi soon returned with their meals. Everything smelled wonderful.

After she set the plates on the table, Naomi commented, "Just in case you need a contact, my son, the one who was born twenty-eight years ago, works for the local newspaper. He covers the local news. His name is Ned; Ned Tuttle with the *Deming Daily*. He might be able to turn your mystery into a human-interest story, or help you run a personal ad if you get to that point."

Ray could tell Madison was mulling the idea over in her head, so he responded. "Thank you, Naomi. We'll make a note of his name as a resource. For now I think we'll just keep this private and see where the leads we have take us. But you never know, we might be calling on him in a few days."

Ray chuckled after Naomi was out of hearing range. "I bet that woman thinks I'm looking for the lost love of my life. Someone I met and last saw right here in her diner. If she helps me locate her, she gets free publicity."

Madison had to smile at Ray's storyline. "Well, she's got part of it right. You did meet her here."

They eagerly dug into their delicious meals. As Madison had pointed out earlier, three days of fast food had left them starved for a home cooked meal. They even indulged in dessert when Naomi returned and suggested her special strawberry shortcake with ice cream.

The threesome returned to their hotel rooms quite satisfied and ready for a good night's sleep. The next morning the girls planned to attend mass at Saint Gabriel's and would hopefully be able to speak with Father Gomez. Madison knew that would be a very emotional conversation for her.

Chapter 37

On that Sunday morning in Abilene, Texas, Graham Meriweather lay extremely weak in his bed. He knew he was losing the battle for his life. His instincts told him something was wrong with his homecare situation. The latest private nurse seemed to lack the experience to deal with his medical condition. Julie Collins was a kind young woman. She listened to his life stories and fluffed his pillows occasionally, but seemed to provide him with his medication on an erratic schedule.

Graham tried to remember when it was he had last seen his physician. Dr. Simon Haskins had seen him through his kidney transplant and the years of treatments that followed. It was not unusual for Dr. Haskins to treat Graham in his home.

"If only I could get to a phone", he thought to himself. It seemed as if everyone caring for him wanted to make sure he didn't have contact with anyone outside the house. The telephone in his room had been removed and he was certain his cell phone was nowhere within reach. He had become far too weak to get out of bed and make his way to the hallway, let alone get down the stairs and out the front door. He needed his nurse's assistance to walk to his private bath.

As if she had been reading his mind, Nurse Julie Collins appeared in his doorway. Julie could be very pleasant at times, but that didn't make up for what Graham felt was her inexperience as a private nurse. Hiring a different nurse was another subject he wanted to discuss with Dr. Haskins.

"Good morning Mr. Meriweather. Are you feeling like some breakfast this fine morning? May I fluff your pillows? I will get your morning pills ready for you," she said as she walked across the room.

Graham seemed to gain a bit of strength in his voice as he said, "Good morning Julie. It's good to see you today."

Maybe he could manage to get help from this young girl after all. "Yes, I would like some toast and coffee, please. Do you think you could bring me the newspaper and my cell phone? I would like to check my voicemail at the office. I feel like I've been out of touch far too long."

Nurse Julie didn't seem to acknowledge Graham's later request. "I'll ask the cook to prepare your breakfast. I'll bring it back up shortly. Your stepmother has given strict orders that you are not to have any stress related to your work. I'll try to get the newspaper for you when I return with your breakfast."

Graham cringed at the word "stepmother". Patricia Meriweather was no stepmother to him. She was a gold digger who latched onto his father years ago and made sure Oliver thought the world of her so she would be included in his estate. Graham eventually saw through Patricia's fake demeanor, but Oliver never did.

Patricia played the dutiful wife during Oliver's illness right up to his death. She was quite shocked to learn that she had to share the trust fund with Graham's new family. That meant only a quarter of Oliver's assets would become hers, rather than half.

The direction Graham felt his health was going at the moment, Patricia would soon get the entire trust fund, which was what he suspected she wanted all along. With Patricia nearing eighty years of age, and Graham having no direct heirs, the remainder of the trust would eventually fall into Patricia's son Preston's hands.

Julie returned twenty minutes later with a tray containing a plate with two slices of whole-wheat toast with butter and a small pot of coffee. The aroma of the coffee smelled good to Graham. He hadn't felt like eating for days. He hoped that his light meal would agree and stay with him. Julie reached for the pills from the tall dresser.

"Here you go sir. I'll watch and make sure you take all your pills", Julie said as she laid the pills on his tray.

Graham looked at the pill, then hesitated. "Julie, it just seems like these pills aren't doing me any good lately. I may have to ask Dr. Haskins if he could prescribe a different medication. Please make an appointment for Dr. Haskins to come to the house."

Julie replied, "Sir today is Sunday. I won't be able to contact the doctor's office until tomorrow. I'm sure you'll start feeling better soon."

Changing the subject, she added, "I was able to find a couple sections of the paper. I put them under your plate."

Graham was astounded to learn that it was Sunday. Where had the days gone? Without his work, his phone, or even a newspaper, it was difficult to keep track of time.

"Thank you for the newspaper. I will enjoy reading it with my breakfast. Please make a note to contact Dr. Haskins first thing tomorrow."

As Julie Collins turned to leave the room she said over her shoulder, "Yes, sir. I'll make a note to do just that."

What she actually meant was that she would report to Mrs. Meriweather that her stepson wanted to see his doctor. Julie had also been given strict orders not to contact any of Graham's physicians on her own. She would ask Patricia Meriweather to have the doctor's office contacted. She needed this job. She could certainly not go against an explicit order from her employer. After all, she was only an LPN, not a registered nurse.

Julie had been working in a clinic downtown when Mrs. Meriweather approached her and offered her this lucrative opportunity. Julie often wondered why such a prominent woman was visiting a low-income clinic on that day. Probably doing some volunteer or charity thing she mused to herself.

As Julie was leaving the room she bent to pick up the napkin that had fallen from Graham's tray. That was when Graham noticed the outline of a cell phone in Julie's left side pocket. At that moment, Graham started to plan how he could get his hands on that cell phone. He was starting to feel as if his life depended on him contacting the outside world. He felt as if he had become a prisoner within his own home.

Chapter 38

On that same Sunday morning in Deming, New Mexico, Madison and Megan awoke at eight o'clock. They met Ray in the hotel lobby for a quick cup of coffee and Danish. The girls returned to their rooms to shower and dress for church.

Ray would drive them to the church, but not attend the mass. He wanted to walk the neighborhood around the church. He was curious about where Rosemary may have lived all those years ago. When he met her, she had no vehicle, so it was possible she lived near the church. As he had so many years ago, he again wondered how she had gotten to the Deming Town Line Diner that night. It was too far for her to have walked, especially carrying a baby. Someone must have given her a ride. That someone might know where she had come from.

At ten-fifteen, Madison and Megan walked through the parking lot and climbed into the SUV.

Madison took a deep breath as she buckled her seatbelt and said, "Here we are. This could be the start to finding the answers I'm looking for. Let's go."

Madison and Megan were walking into the church at ten forty-five. They were taken by the beauty of the small town church. Stained glass windows that were eight feet high lined both sides of the sanctuary. A wide aisle lined with a burgundy runner rug separated two rows of oak pews. At the front, behind the altar was a large white cross hanging on the wall.

The girls chose to sit in a pew five rows from the back. Madison wanted to watch the people and be able to linger after the mass so that she could speak to the priest.

Music started to come from the large pipe organ at the front right side of the sanctuary. Candles were lit and the priest walked onto the raised altar area.

Madison's heart sank as she heard the not-quite-yet middle-aged priest announce, "Good Morning. My name is Father Patrick Finney. I've met many of you over the past few weeks, but for those of you unaware, I've been assigned to this parish after the departure of Father Francis Gomez. I hope that I will be able to provide you with the same kind of spiritual inspiration as Father Gomez did for forty years."

Madison had a hard time staying focused on Father Finney's words during the mass. She kept thinking to herself that she was too late. Father Gomez was gone, and with him went any information that her mother thought she could obtain. She felt Megan's hand touch her own as a friendly consolation.

When the service ended, Megan was the first to speak. "Madison, this doesn't mean the end. You should still speak with Father Finney. Maybe he knows someone else who may have been at the church when Rosemary was here in Deming."

Madison nodded, unsure of what she might be able to learn. After the majority of the congregation had left the church, the girls headed toward the door and Father Finney.

As Madison approached the priest, he said, "I don't believe I have seen you and your friend before. Are you new to our church?"

Madison's voice was soft as she replied, "We just arrived in town. I was actually hoping to speak with Father Gomez. My mother recently passed away and she mentioned his name shortly before she passed. I'm quite disappointed he is no longer with us."

Father Finney's lips started to form a slight smile. "Oh, when I said he had departed, I should have said retired. Father Gomez is still very much alive and well. He moved to Las Cruces a few weeks ago to a retirement community. Father Gomez is seventy-eight years old, but if you met him you'd think he wasn't a day over sixty. He decided to spend his final years serving the Lord in a different way. He will be working with the elder care facilities in Las Cruces to provide services and communion to those unable to get out to a church."

Megan watched as Madison's face lit up with renewed hope.

"Father Finney, you have made my day. Would you be able to give me Father Gomez's contact information? I desperately need to speak with him to fulfill my mother's last request."

Father Finney reached into his pocket and pulled out what appeared to be a business card.

As he handed it to Madison, he said, "Father Gomez had these printed up. He knew many of the parishioners here would want to keep in contact. His new address is listed there. He didn't have a phone number yet when these were printed."

Madison took the card and said, "The address is fine. I would rather meet face to face anyway. My mother's situation may be difficult to discuss over the phone. Thank you so much, Father."

Father Finney placed a hand on Madison's shoulder, "Bless you my child. I hope Father Gomez is able to help."

Madison and Megan walked toward the vehicle where Ray was waiting for them. Madison flashed the card toward Ray and said, "It looks like we take another road trip tomorrow. Father Gomez is now living in Las Cruces."

Chapter 39

Late that Sunday afternoon, an email was sent from Graham Meriweather's laptop computer. The message was sent to Graham's business partner, and cousin, Harrison Meriweather. It stated that Graham had decided to take some more time off. He would not be at work the next morning. The message outlined some personal reasons for his absence and was signed "Graham".

As the tall, thin, dark haired man pressed the send button, he chuckled to himself. "There you go Graham. You are taking a few more days off. No one will bother you after that tearful message."

As the mysterious man signed off the laptop, he thought to himself how simple it was to assume Graham's identity. After all these years, Graham still used the same password on his computer and other electronic accounts. Olivia. What a touching tribute to his lost daughter. The man wondered whether Graham still held out hope that Olivia was alive and well somewhere in the world.

Again the man chuckled, "If only you knew what I know. You'll see your precious daughter again soon. In the afterlife, that is."

Chapter 40

Monday morning in Abilene, Texas, Judy Rockwell entered the Meriweather Corporation headquarters. She flashed her ID at the security desk, smiled and said, "Good morning Charlie. How was your weekend?"

The elderly gentleman, in a blue uniform that had been lovingly pressed by his wife, waved to Judy.

"It was great Ms. Rockwell. We spent some time with the grandkids, spoiled them, and send them back to their parents. I just love being a grandfather. And how are you this fine Monday morning?"

Judy Rockwell was the type of woman who was friendly to all fellow employees of Meriweather without concern of their rank. She knew Charlie Armstrong had been with the corporation almost as long as she had. He took his job seriously and was always professional. He also never turned down a sweet offering. That was why she dropped a small bakery bag with a fresh chocolate muffin on his counter as she passed.

"Well, Charlie, I had a very relaxing weekend. Danielle and I went shopping. I suppose I've mentioned that I'm going to be a grandmother myself in a few months."

Charlie smiled as he lifted the muffin from the bag. "Yes, Ms. Rockwell, you've mentioned it a few times. I can relate to how exciting that news can be. Thanks for the muffin. You have a good day."

Judy headed for the bank of elevators. Her office was on the twentieth floor and faced the east. Judy Rockwell was a dedicated administrative assistant to Graham Meriweather. She started working for Graham's father, Oliver, when she was in her early twenties. She was happy to be working for the son of a man she greatly admired. Graham had many of his father's qualities; he was an honest, admirable boss who had been quite generous to Judy over the years.

Judy was a few years from retirement, and though she enjoyed her job, she was looking forward to having more free time, especially now that her only child, her daughter Danielle, was expecting her first grandchild. Judy had been widowed almost five years. She and her daughter were very close and she was hoping to spend many years with her grandchild.

Judy unlocked the main door to the office suite. It appeared that Graham Meriweather was not in the office again this morning. Judy had become worried about her employer. She knew he had been under a great amount of stress during different times of his life, but these last few months he seemed less focused on his work. In fact, he had not been in the office for a few weeks. She knew he scheduled a couple weeks of vacation and she hoped he had been able to relax on his trip to Mexico.

It was common for Mr. Meriweather to travel to Mexico at least once a year. Though he never stated it, Judy always thought he went looking for his lost daughter. With his trip over, Judy expected to see him in the office this week.

While Mr. Graham Meriweather was away, Judy capably handled the office and conferred with the other Mr. Meriweather, Mr. Harrison Meriweather, on any urgent matters. Judy felt Harrison Meriweather to be more of a strategic businessman than Graham. Graham often let his emotions and concerns for the employees sway him when it came to difficult business choices. Judy thought it was a wise thing that the two men ran the corporation together both bringing their unique strengths to the table.

During the past few weeks Judy had actually been Harrison Meriweather's administrative assistant as well. Emily Turner, Harrison's assistant, required surgery and was out of the office.

With Graham gone for a few weeks, Judy saw no reason to hire a temporary to fill Emily's spot. Judy knew that hiring a temp usually meant you had to oversee the work anyway, why not just cover the position herself.

Judy was preparing for the day when Harrison entered the office. "Good morning, Judy. I hope everything is well with you today."

Judy looked up from her computer and greeted her employer. "Good morning, Mr. Meriweather. Yes, I'm just fine today. I was a bit surprised not to find Graham here this morning. I thought he might have returned."

Harrison Meriweather's face took on a serious look as he spoke. "Judy, I received an email message from Graham yesterday. He states he will not be back to the office for an undetermined number of days."

Judy's surprise was reflected in her voice. "Oh, I hope nothing is wrong, sir."

Harrison knew that Judy had been Graham's faithful assistant through many difficult times. He knew that she, of all people, would understand.

"Judy, you know this is the start of the most difficult time of the year for Graham. A few weeks ago would have been Lydia's birthday. What would have been Olivia's birthday is approaching fast. Then the anniversary of Lydia's accident is upon us. I think Graham is taking it extra hard this year for some reason. But he adamantly requests his privacy during this time. I feel we have to honor his wishes."

Judy wished there was something more she could do for her employer. She also knew that there was a line between employer and employee that she shouldn't cross when it came to personal matters. She would help Graham by maintaining his business affairs to the best of her abilities.

"Yes, sir, I understand. Let me get you the files you need for your nine o'clock meeting."

Chapter 41

In Deming, New Mexico, Monday morning dawned with blue skies and plenty of sunshine. The local weather predicted temperatures rising into the upper nineties.

Madison and Megan met Ray in the lobby again for coffee and a complimentary breakfast. Since they had decided to make a day trip to Las Cruces, they did not need to check out of their rooms. They had every intention of returning to Deming that evening.

On the drive to Las Cruces, Ray could tell that Madison was nervous. He tried to make light conversation, but most of his attempts failed. Finally he said, "Madison, when we get to Father Gomez's, do you want me to wait in the car? I'll be happy to accompany you, but I want to know what your wishes are."

Madison had been thinking for some time about how she wanted the day to play out. After hearing Ray's question, she made up her mind.

"I would like you both to come with me. We are in this endeavor together. And besides, Uncle Ray, you may have information about the night you met my mother that might help Father Gomez remember her."

Ray was secretly relieved at Madison's response. He felt nervous about letting her speak with the priest alone. There was no way to predict what Father Gomez may have to say about Rosemary Cavanaugh. He didn't want Madison to receive any startling news without his being in the room to comfort her if need be.

The road signs stated they were only five miles from Las Cruces. It was mid-morning and the sun would soon be directly overhead. The vehicle displayed an outside temperature of eighty-five. It was going to be a warm day indeed.

Megan made a suggestion as they approached the outskirts of town. "Can we stop at a convenient store and get a bottle of water? I'm already thirsty and I'd like to have a drink in my bag for during our visit with Father Gomez. I would like to use the restroom as well."

Madison agreed with her friend. "Yes, let's stop and take a break before we locate where the Father lives. I could use a drink as well."

Just then Ray spotted what appeared to be a clean, modern gas station with a convenience store area. He put his turn signal on and they pulled into the parking lot.

Chapter 42

While Madison, Ray and Megan were stopping for a beverage, Father Gomez was looking out his front window. He received a call from Father Finney the previous evening. Father Finney told Father Gomez about the two young women hoping to speak with him after the morning mass. Father Finney stated he gave them the address where Father Gomez now resided and hoped it was not a mistake in judgment on his part. Father Gomez reassured the younger priest that it was fine to give out his contact information.

Now, waiting for a knock on his door, the elder priest wondered what these young women wanted to speak to him about. Father Finney stated that one of the women mentioned the recent death of her mother. Maybe the mother had been a former parishioner. Maybe the young woman simply wanted to notify him of her mother's passing. Maybe it was as simple as that. Or, maybe, it would turn out to be much more complicated.

Ever since he came across the envelope entrusted to him so many years ago, Father Gomez felt as if something were about to happen that would relate to its contents. Since he had no idea what the contents were, he had no way of knowing whether the something would be good or bad. He could do nothing now, except wait.

His wait soon ended. He saw a dark SUV pull up in front of his small retirement home. Not wanting to act as if he were expecting company, Father Gomez waited a few seconds after he heard the knock to answer his front door. When he opened the door, he found a middle-aged man accompanying two young women, who he estimated to be in their late twenties. None of the three looked remotely familiar.

Madison quickly sized up the tall, elderly man who greeted them. His gray hair made him look distinguished, and his dark eyes seemed to search her own. She immediately felt trust for Father Gomez.

Madison was the first to speak, "Good morning. Are you Father Francis Gomez?"

Father Gomez was quick to acknowledge, "Yes, that's me. How may I help you?"

Not knowing quite how to start, Madison nervously said, "Father, my name is Madison. My mother recently died in a terrible car accident. Her last words to me included your name. She begged me to find you. I was wondering if you could help me determine why."

The priest sensed a longer conversation was about to begin, longer than what should be discussed at one's front door.

"I will certainly try to help you if I can. Why don't you please come in and have a seat?"

Ray motioned for Madison and Megan to enter the Father's living room area and waited for them to take a seat. The room was very plain with dark furniture. The girls sat on a tan loveseat. Ray then sat in a straight back chair across the room.

Embarrassed, Madison gestured toward Megan, "Father Gomez, I'm terribly sorry. I didn't introduce you to my friends. This is Megan Davis and her uncle, Ray Davis. Besides my mother, the Davis family has been the only family I've ever known. Megan and Uncle Ray insisted on coming with me to find you."

Father Gomez nodded to Megan and walked toward Ray's chair. Ray stood and the two men shook hands. Then the Father sat in a comfortable looking brown chair facing the loveseat.

Father Gomez looked at Madison and said, "It is nice to meet you all. You know who I am. Madison, you didn't mention your last name, or your mother's name. In my profession, one has to be quite good with names. Maybe I will recognize your mother's."

"My last name is Cavanaugh. My mother was Rosemary Cavanaugh."

Ray noticed Father Gomez swallowed hard before he spoke. "Rosemary Cavanaugh. Would that have been her maiden or married name?"

"She raised me as a single mother. Cavanaugh was her maiden name, her only name."

The priest studied the young woman before him. She had some common features, but did not bare an overly strong resemblance to the young Rosemary he once knew. He needed to be sure they were speaking of the same Rosemary.

He questioned her a bit more. "I can't be sure that I'm remembering the right woman. Do you mind my asking how old you are? Was your mother from New Mexico?"

Madison smiled as she answered. "Father, I will be twenty-eight next month. My mother would have turned fifty in the fall."

Ray interjected the conversation. "Father, I met Rosemary at a local diner in Deming in December twenty-eight years ago. Madison was just a few months old. I was a truck driver at the time and Rosemary was looking for a ride out of New Mexico. She was initially headed for California, but long story short, I convinced her to travel to North Carolina with me and she made a home there for herself and little Madison. They became part of my family."

Father Gomez seemed puzzled as he spoke. "My dear, I did know a Rosemary Cavanaugh many years ago. However, twenty-eight years ago, Rosemary did not have a baby. The young woman I knew was single with no children. We must be speaking of different people. I'm so sorry."

Madison reached for the papers she had brought from her mother's belongings. Her voice was shaky and she felt on the verge of crying as she spoke.

"Father Gomez. Please hear the rest of my story. There seems to be a great deal of mystery surrounding Rosemary, the woman I knew only as my mother. Based on medical evidence, I have recently discovered I am not her biological daughter. Therefore, I can only assume that I was adopted, or left in her care by my true birth parents. I have a baptismal certificate signed by you and dated September twenty-eight years ago. It appears you baptized me when I was only a few weeks old."

The priest took the certificate from Madison and read it over and over again.

"This can't be right. It is certainly my signature, but I never baptized an infant as Rosemary Cavanaugh's daughter. Please wait here while I get something that might help clear this up."

With that Father Gomez stood and left the room.

Chapter 43

Madison and Megan just looked at each other when the elderly priest left the room. Madison wondered whether Father Gomez was going to be able to shed some light on her situation. Maybe he was right. Maybe they were talking about two completely different women. But why would her mother have mentioned his name and where she could locate him?

When Father Gomez reentered the room, he was carrying a manila envelope that showed signs of age and a single sheet of paper.

As he sat down he started to read from the sheet of paper. "Dear Father Gomez, Something has come up suddenly tonight that causes me to leave. There is a family issue that I must attend to in California. I hate to leave without saying goodbye to all of you. I truly appreciate what everyone here has done to help me over the past few years. Please tell Sister Mary Louise how much she means to me. I will miss her dearly. I like to think of myself as a much better person for having stayed here. Since I must leave on such short notice and so late at night, I had to borrow some items from the rummage sale. I hate to admit that I had to borrow fifty dollars as well from the donation jar. Please trust and believe me when I promise to repay you with more than I have taken. There is one last thing. I don't know whether I will ever be back this way again, but I am leaving this sealed envelope in your trusted care. Please do not open it unless I return, or until someone comes to you asking about me specifically by name. Thank you again for all your kindness. I hope you will always remember me fondly as Sister Mary's Rose."

Father Gomez's eyes were filled with tears as he finished reading the note left so long ago.

"The Rosemary Cavanaugh I knew left me this note on a December night twenty-eight years ago. I never knew what the urgent family matter was. Maybe you were it. Maybe she had to leave to assume your care.

"Over the next few months, I never heard from her. However, the next December I received an envelope with a single hundred-dollar bill in it. There was no note and no return address. The same thing happened the next year. I remember noting that the postmarks were different each year. At the time I wondered if it might have been Rosemary repaying the church for the money she borrowed just as she had promised."

Ray smiled as he confirmed the priest's assumption. "I mailed envelopes for Rosemary on two consecutive Decembers. I was still driving my truck across the country and she asked me to mail them from different cities. I never knew what was inside the envelopes, and I only recently remembered that they were addressed to you."

Madison was curious about the ending of the note. "What did she mean by Sister Mary's Rose?"

Father Gomez smiled as he explained. "When Rosemary came to St. Gabriel's church Sister Mary Louise Lopez was our most senior nun at the time. Sister Mary Louise quickly bonded with Rosemary and took the teenage girl under her wings, so to speak. She lovingly referred to Rosemary as 'her Rose'. Thus, the rest of us called her 'Sister Mary's Rose.'"

Megan was fascinated by all the mystery. "Father, you never opened the envelope? Were you never curious as to what was inside?"

Father Gomez answered proudly. "No, I never thought it was my place to open it. I respected Rosemary's wishes. When I was packing up my office in Deming a couple of months ago, I came across it for the first time in several years. I debated at that time whether to entrust the envelope to Father Finney, or retain it and its secrecy. I'm glad I held on to it. Since the envelope is labeled 'For M', I assume it is for you, Madison."

As the priest handed the faded envelope to Madison, she felt nervous. Inside the envelope she was holding could be all the answers she had come to find. Her hands were trembling as she tried to open it. The glue had dried somewhat over the years and the flap released easily. Madison's hands were still trembling as she pulled out the contents. Another sheet of paper held a note in the same handwriting. A smaller piece of paper, seemly torn from a larger sheet, bore a shorter note in scrawling penmanship.

Megan noticed that her friend's trembling hands, looked into her watering eyes, and offered, "Madison. Would you like me to read you the note?"

Madison was again grateful for such a good friend. "Yes, if you don't mind. I'm not sure I could get through it. Thank you, Megan."

Megan reached for the larger note and began to read. "My Dearest Baby M, First I should tell you that since I'm not sure what the 'M' stands for, I plan to call you Madison. When I was a little girl my mother would tell me stories of her family who lived in a small town in California called Madison. She always associated family and Madison together. She lost her family when she was quite young and never returned to her hometown. Since I found you, I consider you my family, and thus I shall name you 'Madison'.

"Now to explain how I found you. It is December 14th and Saint Gabriel's Church has its life-size nativity set in the side lawn. Since I live in the small apartment in the basement of the church, I have the responsibility of shutting off the floodlights that shine on the manger scene each night at eleven o'clock. Tonight when I stepped outside, I heard a small cry. Unable to locate the origin of the cry, I started to walk around the lawn and the cries led me toward the manger set. That was when I heard a somewhat louder cry and saw your tiny feet wiggling above the straw in the actual manger.

"Someone carefully took the doll that represented the Christ Child out of the manger and laid it near the Virgin Mary statue. Someone placed you, a living, breathing precious baby into the straw bedding. I found you wrapped in a soft pink blanket monogrammed with the initial 'M'. When I opened the blanket, you were dressed only in a tee shirt and diaper and were wearing only one pink bootie. I looked in the grass and could not locate the matching bootie. You must have lost it in your travels this evening.

"Tucked into the top of your diaper was the enclosed note. I feel I was meant to find you and keep you from whatever danger this note references. Fate brought us together and I will always protect you. Since you are in danger here, we must leave New Mexico tonight. I have packed us a bag and gathered a few things from within the church that we may need on our journey. I sincerely hope that tonight is just the beginning of a long and loving life together for you and me. I already love you, Baby Madison."

When Megan finished reading there was not a dry eye in the room, and no one spoke for several minutes.

Chapter 44

At last, after wiping her eyes with a tissue she retrieved from her purse, Madison spoke. "She just found me. Who leaves a baby alone outside in December? Was I just abandoned? Where is the other note she references?"

Megan handed Madison what appeared to be part of a receipt of some kind that a few words had been scrawled on the back of. Megan noted the printing on the other side. "This receipt may lead us to the person who wrote the note. It looks like whoever wrote it was in a hurry."

Madison started to read, "Please help. She is in danger. I cannot protect her. Please help Baby M."

Ray was the first to speak. "Someone placed this baby, you Madison, in that manger for safety. You weren't abandoned; you were put there for protection. Someone cared about you so deeply that they had to take a risk and leave you hidden and alone. Luckily someone like Rosemary found you and made you a part of her life."

Megan was puzzled. "Why wouldn't she call the police? Why assume the responsibility of an infant?"

Father Gomez, who was deep in thought, answered Megan. "At that time, Rosemary was just building faith in herself. She hadn't been able to trust many people in her life. She probably didn't want this small child to be placed in the same foster care system she endured. She must have felt capable of loving you enough to leave everything she knew behind and start over with you as a family."

Ray reminded the group. "When I met Rosemary that December night, she said she was looking for a ride west. She may have been thinking of going to her mother's hometown of Madison, California."

The Father interjected. "Rosemary's mother told her that her entire family was dead, there was no one left. Maybe that was why you were able to convince her to travel on to North Carolina with you, Ray."

Megan was trying to make sense of what they had just learned. "So, where does that leave Madison now? How do we find out where she came from and who her family is?"

Madison remembered something Father Gomez had said earlier. "Father, you mentioned a Sister Mary Louise. If she was close to my mother, maybe she spoke to her before she left that night. Is Sister Mary Louise still living in the area?"

"Yes, Sister Mary Louise Lopez is still living in Deming. She shares a home with another Sister. However, I don't believe she knows anymore than what is contained in these notes. The day after Rosemary left Sister Mary Louise was just as perplexed as the rest of us. I'm sure if she knew anything, she would have spoken up at that time. But if you want more insight on the young woman Rosemary was, you should definitely take some time to talk with the Sister. I'm sure she has many fond memories she would love to share."

Trying to stay with the evidence, Ray asked the Father, "How do you explain the baptismal certificate Madison has with your signature?"

Father Gomez had been thinking about that since he had first been shown the certificate. "I think I have an idea about that. As an assistant in the church, Rosemary often helped prepare the certificates prior to the Sunday baptisms. It was not unusual for me to sign a few blank forms prior to the services. I relied on Rosemary to complete the personal information with the help of the parents. She may have taken a signed, blank form to use as false identification that you were her child."

Madison was quick to take the Father's assumption one step further. "Could a baptismal certificate be used to obtain a

subsequent birth certificate? The birth certificate I found wasn't
filed until January of the following year. Maybe she used the
baptism papers to secure the birth record based on what Dr.
Steve referred to as an unattended birth."

Father Gomez pondered that idea. "It's possible. There is
a form that's used when a birth occurs at one of our homeless
shelters. Rosemary would have been familiar with that form and
the requirements to obtain a birth certificate. She could have
taken that form from the church office that night as well. That
could be how she obtained your birth certificate. Rosemary was
probably quite desperate to make you appear as her daughter,
both emotionally and legally."

Megan turned the conversation back to her concern of
learning who Madison was. "Remember the waitress in Deming,
Naomi? She said her son worked for the Deming newspaper.
Maybe he could help us look for missing children during that
time period. Someone certainly would have reported their baby
missing."

Madison was excited about her friend's idea. "Megan, that's
a great idea. Maybe we could also search the birth records in
Deming for baby girls born that prior July."

Megan suddenly looked at the note Rosemary had addressed
to 'Baby M' and said, "Rosemary stated in this note that the date
was December 14th. Madison's birthday is July 14th. Does anyone
else think that is too much of a coincidence?"

Ray was quick to follow Megan's thought, "It would seem
that Rosemary randomly gave you a birthday. She would have
had no way of knowing your true birth date. She probably felt
you were about five months old, which would have meant you
born in July. She picked the fourteenth as the day of the month
since you came into her life that day. If we check birth records,
we should check that entire summer."

Madison smiled. "That's right. I might be younger than I
think I am."

Megan was quick to remind her friend, "Or older."

Everyone laughed. With the next step planned, they all seemed to relax a bit.

Ray wanted to show the Father their gratitude. "Father, it seems we've taken a lot of your time this morning. It's probably past your normal lunch hour. Why don't you let us take you out for lunch? Since we're new in Las Cruces, I'll let you recommend a good spot."

Chapter 45

Father Francis, as he requested to be called, selected a quaint soup, sandwich and salad deli for the group to lunch at. It was located in a small strip mall, which also housed a dry cleaner, a popular bakery and a Mexican take out place.

As the foursome enjoyed their lunch selections, Father Francis asked Madison to discuss her and Rosemary's life. He was curious to learn how the young woman he had known had lived the rest of her life. He was happy to learn that by most respects, Rosemary led a happy life and provided a loving home and childhood for Madison.

Ray asked the Father for the contact information for Sister Mary Louise. He felt that Madison would benefit from speaking with the Sister and gaining insight into Rosemary's earlier life. Father Francis gave Ray what he asked, but also offered to make the first contact with Sister Mary Louise. He wanted to help jog the Sister's memory before Madison met with her.

Madison and Megan decided that their first call when they returned to Deming would be to Ned Tuttle at the *Deming Daily* newspaper. The young ladies were anxious to show Ned the notes Father Francis had given them and see if he would assist them in digging into the archives of his newspaper.

After a much-needed relaxing lunch the group left the deli and headed for their respective vehicles.

Madison approached Father Francis with tears in her eyes. "Father, I can't thank you enough for the information you have given me. I feel I've taken the first step in finding out where I came from and who my biological family is. I'm so grateful you kept the envelope my mother gave you so many years ago. After this much time, many people would have thrown it away."

Father Francis modestly replied, "I guess I just had faith that someday, someone would come asking the right questions. I only hope that these notes bring you peace and closure, not more pain. Keep in mind that it appears you were in danger as an infant. Someone may still wish you harm. Please be careful in your search."

Madison placed her arms around the priest's neck and gave him a hug. "I promise to be careful. I'll keep you informed on what I find. You deserve to know where these papers lead me. Thank you again."

Megan put her arm around Madison's shoulders as they walked to the vehicle. She was trying to comfort her friend the best she could. Ray was more observant of their surroundings. He could not help but notice a middle-aged Latino woman staring at the girls as they walked across the parking lot. He tried to convince himself that she might be staring out of concern, noting how Megan was hugging her friend. In any event, it was time to return to Deming. He climbed into the SUV and started the engine.

Chapter 46

On that Monday morning, Nina Perez was running her normal errands for the Baxter family. After dropping the children at their summer camp, Nina made stops at the post office, Melissa's favorite grocery store, and the dry cleaners to pick up Bryce's shirts from the prior week. The last stop was located in a strip mall that also housed her favorite bakery. She decided to treat Sarah and Colby to a special afternoon snack. She also thought it would be nice to have a fancy dessert for herself and Hector. Nina had been feeling down the last few weeks, perhaps a sweet splurge was in order.

It was after leaving the bakery and she was walking across the parking lot to her car, that she noticed the group of four that left the nearby deli. The group consisted of two gentlemen, one middle-aged and the other more elderly, and two young women appearing to be in their late twenties. One of the women appeared to be consoling the other. It was the one being consoled that caught Nina's attention. She bore a significant resemblance to someone from her secret past. Nina could not help but stare. She was embarrassed when the middle-aged man noticed her. She quickly turned away.

Seeing this young woman made her realize why she was feeling so gloomy of late.

"The secrets I'm keeping are coming out to haunt me," she thought.

Nina's grandmother used to say that there was a time in life to keep a secret, and there was a time in life to let a secret set you free. Nina realized the time was nearing to set herself free from her past. She would have to confide in Hector soon. She just had to find the right moment.

Chapter 47

To the east of New Mexico, in San Angelo, Texas, Catherine Wallace was catching up on her correspondence. There were several notes and cards she had put off writing. Catherine always fell into a lethargic period after visiting her daughter's grave on the first of June each year. She seemed to stay that way until after the middle of July. Even after more than a quarter of a century, it was difficult to let the days pass marking her daughter and granddaughter's birthdays knowing there would never be another celebration for them.

This year Catherine was determined to not let her depressed mood last as long. She began writing notes to old friends and addressing cards to others who were celebrating milestones of their own. She then came to Graham Meriweather's name on her to-do list. Catherine decided, while visiting Lydia's grave, to send Graham a short note. She assumed he would also be feeling sad during this time. She wanted him to know he was not alone. He was not the only one remembering dearly departed loved ones.

After Catherine wrote what she felt was a kind, heartwarming note, she addressed the envelope to Graham's office. She stamped her pile of outgoing mail and set them aside.

"I'll drop them at the post office tomorrow morning", she thought.

Chapter 48

Promptly at nine o'clock on Tuesday morning, Ned Tuttle met Madison, Megan and Ray in the lobby of the *Deming Daily* newspaper office. Madison had phoned the paper late the previous afternoon upon their return from Las Cruces. When she mentioned meeting his mother, Naomi, Ned was quick to accommodate a meeting.

Madison made the introductions and Ned shook hands with his new acquaintances. He was smiling as he said, "I must say I'm intrigued by what little information you gave me over the phone yesterday. I hope that I can be of assistance. Let's go into my office. Please follow me."

Ned's assistant had arranged four chairs around a conference table and had placed a pot of coffee, four cups and an assortment of individual juice bottles in the center. Ned motioned for the group to take a seat and help themselves to the refreshments as he shut his door.

After everyone was settled with his or her beverage choice, Madison pulled the envelope Father Francis Gomez had given her from her bag. Before she opened it, she gave Ned a short bit of background.

"Ned, my mother was in a serious car accident a couple of weeks ago. On her way into surgery, and literally on what turned out to be her deathbed, she told me she was sorry for not telling me the truth. I had no idea what truth she was speaking of, and assumed she was delirious from her injuries. Sadly, she did not survive the surgery, and I was never able to question her further.

"However, the surgeon who operated told me that the woman I knew as my mother could not have been my birth mother. In fact, it has been proven with DNA testing that she was not even related to me. Before she died, my mother told me to find a Father Francis Gomez, here in Deming. She felt Father Gomez would be able to help me find the truth."

Ned was quickly caught up in the mystery Madison was unfolding for him. "Father Gomez from Saint Gabriel's church? He recently retired from the parish."

Megan smiled as she interjected. "Yes, we found that out this past Sunday during mass. Father Finney was gracious enough to tell us how to reach Father Gomez."

Madison continued, "We visited Father Gomez yesterday in Las Cruces. He remembered my mother and was able to provide us with more information. Unfortunately, his information only brings more mystery. It seems that Rosemary Cavanaugh, that is my mother's name, disappeared into the night in December twenty-eight years ago."

Ray was quick to help Ned understand. "That December night was when I met Rosemary. At that time in my life, I was an over the road truck driver. I was traveling through Deming on my route to California. I actually met her at the diner your mother works at. Rosemary was looking for a ride and I offered to help her out. She had an infant, Madison, who was only a few months old."

Ned nodded, but became confused when Madison continued. "Yes, I was with her at the diner. However, Father Gomez says Rosemary did not have a baby in her care at the time she was living in his church. Rosemary left this envelope for the priest that night and the information within it was never revealed until yesterday when I opened it."

Ned was hanging on Madison's every word when he said, "I'm more than intrigued now. What is in the envelope? Does it tell you who you are?"

Chapter 49

Madison took one piece of the puzzle at a time from the envelope.

"This is the note Rosemary left to Father Gomez. As you now know, he did as she asked. He kept the envelope sealed, until I showed up on his doorstep asking questions about Rosemary Cavanaugh."

Ned read the letter to himself. "She mentions a family issue. Can you contact her family in California to find out what happened?"

Ray was the first to respond. "Rosemary has no known family in the area. Her mother apparently spoke of a family in California, but told Rosemary everyone there had died. Rosemary's father died before she was born and her mother died while Rosemary was still a child. She was placed in foster care for several years. I think that possibly Rosemary planned to travel to California in hopes of finding some long-lost family members, but with no place to start, there was little hope. Rosemary eventually traveled with me back to North Carolina and made a life for herself and Madison there."

Ned was fascinated with the story. "So we have a young woman known by the priest not to have a child, and yet that same woman is found at the diner with an infant in her arms looking for a ride out of town."

Madison was surprised at how simple a statement Ned had turned her life's mystery into. "Yes, that would be the basic situation. Here is what the envelope Rosemary left with the priest contained. It appears she found me, apparently abandoned in the church's nativity setting, with a note asking for help to protect me."

Ned read and reread the notes from the long-sealed envelope. He was trying to imagine the series of events as they took place on that long ago December night.

He tried to make sense of it. "Let's try to put what we know in sequence. Someone places an infant into the manger setting on St. Gabriel's church property. A note is left with that infant indicating she is in some kind of danger and asking the finder to protect that infant."

Ned continued, "Then a young woman working and living within the church goes out to turn off the lights and secure the church doors hears a baby's cry. The cries draw her to the manger where she finds a baby girl with a note of distress literally stuffed in her diaper. Since she once was a child in need of protection, she feels an immediate connection and is determined to do whatever it takes to protect her newly found charge. To her it must have seemed as if she had been given a new purpose for her life."

Ray seemed to like Ned's appraisal. "We all agree that Rosemary was doing what she felt was the right thing at the time. I feel that once she committed to caring for Madison and referred to her as her daughter, she couldn't stop. If she had told anyone the real story, she most certainly would have lost Madison. Once that mother-daughter bond was made, Rosemary was determined to preserve it at all costs."

Madison agreed. "What I need is to find out who wrote that note and attached it to me before they left me in the manger that night. That person was also protecting me. That person might be part of my family, or at least know who my family is."

Everyone was deep in thought when Madison spoke again. "Ned, I don't know where to start. I was hoping that you might have an idea. Working at a newspaper, you must come across stories similar to mine in nature; people searching for lost family, former girlfriends, classmates from high school. Do you have any advice for me?"

Ned thought carefully before he answered. "Yes, we have had our share of human interest stories that have reconnected family members and college sweethearts. Your story, however, also contains an element of danger. If the person who wrote the note that was found with you was writing the truth, you were in danger that night. Since you were so young at the time, I might wonder whether you had been a victim of child abuse. Ray, you were probably one of the first people to see Madison after Rosemary found her. Did you notice any signs of abuse? Did she have any bruises, or seem neglected in any way?"

Ray thought long and hard before he answered. "No, I have to say that Madison always seemed like a happy, contented baby. She certainly was not malnourished, and I never saw a bruise. Rosemary didn't seem to have the right size clothing and I remember thinking Madison needed a heavier jacket for the time of year. Now, with what we have learned, we realize Rosemary was not left with many clothing options. We learned from Father Gomez that she took what she felt she needed from the church's shelter donations."

Megan had been thinking as well. "Maybe the person who left Madison at the church was the one being abused. If that person were a woman, she may have felt it was only a matter of time before her abuser turned on Madison. The note says they could not protect her. Maybe the person had been able to protect Madison up until that night. Maybe they felt something horrible was about to happen."

Ned responded to Megan's ideas. "That's a lot of maybes, Megan, but you might not be that far off base with your assumptions. I would tend to believe that it was a woman who left you in that manger, Madison. The careful placement, the fact you were wrapped in a blanket with a note attached all point to a female touch. I have a hard time speculating whether that woman was your mother, or someone else trying to protect you."

Madison agreed. "Yes, I too feel quite certain my protector was a woman. Where do we start in order to determine exactly who she was?"

Ned had been giving that some thought as well. "We have a research assistant in our archives department. Her name is Jackie Potter. Let me talk to her and see if she can research reports of missing women and children in the area around the time Rosemary found you. I doubt this woman would have reported you missing if she was trying to protect you. However, if this woman also ran away, there could be a missing persons report on her. Let's hope Jackie can dig up some names to follow up on."

Madison felt a ray of hope shine within her. "Thanks Ned. That sounds like the perfect place to start. I'd be happy to meet with Jackie as well if I could shed any more light on the mystery surrounding me."

Ned's mind was already ten steps ahead of the current conversation. "Let me get Jackie up to speed on the information you have given me and then I'll set up time for all of us to talk. Do you have a cell phone I can contact you on?"

Madison was happy to provide Ned with her contact information. The group parted company just after noon. Ray suggested to Megan and Madison that they go back to the local diner for lunch. He wanted a chance to talk to Madison to make sure she wasn't regretting any of the decisions that had been made that morning.

Chapter 50

Over a leisurely lunch of homemade chicken soup and grilled cheese sandwiches, Ray broached the subject with Madison.

"Are you sure you want to pursue all of this? None of us knows where this will lead. There is always the chance that the answer you get won't lead to a happy ending."

Madison had been thinking the same thoughts so she was prepared with her answer. "I know I'm taking a risk, but I feel it's a risk worth taking. My mother protected me the best she could. She certainly gave me all the love and support any mother would give to their daughter. If she hadn't wanted me to eventually know the truth, she would not have left the envelope with Father Gomez. I think she wanted to tell me the truth over the years, but probably could never bring herself to in fear that I would resent her in some way. I could never resent her for changing her whole life to revolve around me and my well being."

Ray knew that Rosemary would have been touched with her daughter's statement. "Madison, you truly amaze me. You have grown into such a wonderful, mature young woman. Rosemary had every right to be very proud of you. I'll be here at your side for as long as you need me."

Megan wiped a tear from her eye and added, "Me too. I want to help you solve this mystery and be with you on what I see as a great adventure."

Madison too was choked up. "I'm so lucky to have such great friends as my family. My mother could not have found a better family to be befriended by. I have certainly been blessed since she found me that night. She was my guardian angel that night and for the rest of her life."

As they were finishing their lunches Naomi Tuttle arrived early for her shift. She spotted the trio in their booth and walked over.

"Good Afternoon, how are you fine people today?" she asked.

Madison was quick to answer the cordial greeting. "We are just fine. We spent the morning with your son, Ned, at the newspaper. He was quite interested in my mysterious story. I think he might be able to help me, or at least point me in the right direction."

Naomi smiled as mothers do when their children are complimented. "I just knew he wouldn't be able to pass over a great story like yours."

The conversation turned more casual and the group decided to take a break for the afternoon and explore the town and its unique shops. Naomi was happy to make suggestions on her favorite spots.

Chapter 51

Wednesday morning Madison's cell phone rang before they left the hotel room for breakfast. It was an excited Ned Tuttle.

"Madison. I'm glad I caught you early. I was wondering if you could meet with Jackie from archives and me later today. She was very intrigued with your story and is anxious to get started on her research as soon as possible."

Madison felt as if her great adventure, as Megan had called it yesterday, was about to begin.

She replied to Ned, "My schedule is wide open. What time do you want us to come by?"

Ned responded, "Jackie wants to search the archives on her own this morning. She said she should have data for us to review after lunch. Could you be here about one o'clock?"

Madison was happy to get started. "One o'clock sounds great. I'm sure Megan and Uncle Ray would like to join us if that is okay."

Ned was secretly hoping to see Madison's friend again. He might be highly interested in Madison's story, but it was Megan who had caught his eye.

Trying not to sound overly anxious, he replied, "I'm sure Jackie won't mind. It seems they have made the journey this far with you, I'm sure you want them along for the long haul."

Madison and Ned exchanged farewells and she turned to Megan, who was just emerging from the bathroom dressed and ready for the day, "That was Ned. He wants us to meet again today at one o'clock. Jackie hopes to have some research done by then for us to look over."

The girls met Ray for breakfast and they discussed the appointment and what hopes they each had for the day. They spent the rest of the morning writing down everything Ray could remember from that December so long ago. Madison made her own list of facts about Rosemary and was sadly amazed at how little she knew of her mother's background. Rosemary's faded birth certificate that Madison had found among her mother's papers listed Rosemary's mother as an Ellie Cavanaugh and father "unknown". The town of birth was listed as Sunshine, a small town south of Deming. It wasn't much to go on, but Madison would follow up with the town records while she was in the area.

Chapter 52

Ned was waiting for them in the lobby of the newspaper when they arrived fifteen minutes early. He seemed to be filled with as much anticipation as was Madison and her friends.

"If you'll just follow me this way, I'll take us back to the Archives Department. Jackie is waiting for us", Ned said as he motioned to a doorway on the right side of the lobby.

Madison, Megan and Ray were led into a large room that contained shelves reaching from floor to ceiling on the three perimeter walls of the room. Each shelf was crammed with what appeared to be old newspaper editions, file storage boxes labeled with a month and year and file folders full of loose papers. To Madison it seemed as if they had just found the proverbial haystack in which they needed to find a single needle.

In the center of the room long tables were set end to end with multiple computer terminal access points. Table lamps were placed near each computer with ample surface space on which to spread out one's research. Sitting at the center computer terminal was a woman who appeared to be in her early forties with medium length dark brown hair. Her hair was pulled back and secured with a large barrette allowing her natural curls to fall down the back of her head, reaching just beyond her shoulders. As Jackie Potter stood to greet her guests, Madison could sense warmth immediately from the woman's dark brown eyes.

Jackie extended her hand toward Madison. "Welcome to Archives. I'm Jackie, as you might have guessed. I assume you are Madison, our woman with a mystery."

Madison shook Jackie's hand. "Yes. That would be me. I don't believe I've ever had as many questions as I've encountered in the past month. I hope your research will be able to provide me with some answers."

Ned captured the conversation as he motioned to Megan and Ray. "Jackie, this is Megan Davis. She is Madison's best friend, also from North Carolina. Ray Davis is Megan's uncle and the first known person to have met Madison with her mother, Rosemary, here in Deming, over twenty-seven years ago."

Madison explained to Jackie, "I hope you don't mind that my friends are with me today. Ray has been like an uncle to me for all these years. I truly want him and Megan with me as I search for the truth."

Jackie smiled as she responded. "I'm glad to have your friends involved. I find that the more people involved in the research, the more information can be drawn from the data. Ray might be able to provide details that he may not even remember at this moment. Shall we get started?"

Jackie and Ned arranged five chairs in a half circle so that everyone had a view of the computer monitor and could see Jackie as she displayed documents.

Jackie explained where she had started her research, "I wanted to take a look at who Rosemary Cavanaugh was before the night Ray met her. I was able to confirm her birth record recorded in the town of Sunshine that lists Ellie Cavanaugh as her mother and her father as unknown. Digging further back I discovered that Ellie Cavanaugh was in a shelter at the time Rosemary was born. I was unable to find any information until almost six years later when a death record was recorded for Ellie Cavanaugh. The cause of death was listed as a drug overdose. After her mother's death, Rosemary was placed into the social services system and spent the next twelve years with various foster care providers. I realize most of this is what you have probably known for years, but at least we are able to confirm Rosemary's early life's story."

Madison nodded. "Yes, my mother described her childhood as difficult due to her mother's problems and that she was quite lonely and unattached at her foster homes. She never mentioned the church or Father Gomez until the day she died."

Jackie was doing her job as a research assistant as she asked, "Madison, if you don't mind my asking, what mention was ever made by Rosemary of your father. I'm sure as a child you must have been curious."

Madison was a bit ashamed as she replied. "There was never much discussion on that subject. I asked at a young age and my mother simply said she did not know who he was. I realize now she was telling the absolute truth. As a young child, I imagined a mysterious stranger who would someday appear to claim his daughter. As I approached my teen years, I surmised one of two scenarios. One was less than honorable with my mother having multiple boyfriends and not being sure who had fathered her child. I certainly did not want to imagine my mother as merely a fun loving young woman who did not take relationships seriously, so I quickly moved on to my second scenario. In that one, I feared that my mother had been raped by an unknown assailant and because she was such an honorable and moral person, had given birth, loved and raised her child alone."

Ned seemed amazed with Madison's thoughts. "You and your mother must have had a very special bond. Because of that, this must come as even more of a shock to you."

"Yes, I was shocked the day of the accident with losing my mother and even more shocked a few days later to learn she was not my birth mother. Finding the note she left for me, though, proves what a kind and loving person she was. She didn't just find me. She wrapped her whole life around me. She did as the desperate writer of the note attached to me requested. She helped and protected me."

Jackie tried to get the group back on point. "Your mother sounds like a great person. After I confirmed her information, I searched the records for missing children in the surrounding counties. I was unable to identify any baby girls ages four to eight months that were reported missing that December. I want to expand my search to all of New Mexico, but that could take some time."

Megan was disappointed that Jackie was unable to find a missing child record that matched her description. She asked Jackie, "With that said, where do you suggest Madison go from here?"

Jackie was quick to answer. "I do have one idea."

Chapter 53

Madison was anxious to hear Jackie's idea. "Please tell us. Yesterday I felt like we had a good start, but now I feel we have hit a brick wall. I need to find answers."

Jackie continued, "My idea has two parts. First, I think you should take out a personal ad in our newspaper, and some others in nearby towns. I would suggest you print, word for word, the message left with you that night in the manger. After those words, your ad would continue with something like 'Looking for the person who wrote these words twenty seven years ago' and provide a phone number for people to call."

Ray was the first to express concern. "Don't you think Madison would be inundated with a mass of crank calls?"

Jackie shook her head as she continued. "That is where the second part of my idea comes in. I would like you to meet a good friend of mine, Larkyn Belanger. Larkyn is a very discreet private investigator. I think it would be best to have a middleman, so to speak. The phone number in the personal ad would be to a cell phone purchased specifically for your case. Larkyn would answer any and all calls, take the information and sort out the crank calls. Hopefully she will also be able to identify any caller who may have valuable information, or be the person who actually wrote that note. I know this must sound like a long shot, but I feel it's your best first step."

Madison was calculating the plan in her head. "Do either of you think there is a chance that the person who wrote that note and left me in that manger is still living locally?"

Ned spoke up first. "I believe there is a good chance the person is still within our publication's reach. When I first heard the words from the note, I had a vision of a desperate mother. I saw a woman, possibly in danger herself, who was trying to protect her infant daughter. She must have been distraught enough to believe leaving her daughter alone in the night was better than the alternative. A woman like that would want to know how her daughter's life turned out. She may have stayed in the area, or returned here, to try to find her child. This woman may even be a communicant at the very church she left you. She would never dare ask, but has probably always wondered what became of the child she left in the manger that night. A woman like that would remember her exact words from that note even after all these years."

Madison was near tears. "Wow. I hadn't thought of it in those terms. If there is a chance this woman has never given up looking for me, I want to do everything I can to find her. She should know that I had a safe and happy life."

Jackie was eager to continue. "Great. Let's draft how we want personal ad to read. Do you have the actual note with you?"

Madison pulled the small piece of paper from her purse and handed it to Jackie. "I seem to carry it everywhere with me these days."

Jackie copied the words exactly into an electronic document. The group decided to continue the ad with the phrases "Do these words sound familiar?" and "Looking for the person who wrote this note many years ago."

Jackie explained she would contact her friend Larkyn Belanger that afternoon and between them a cell phone number would be established and added as the contact number. It was decided that the ad would run in the *Deming Daily* and the *Las Cruces Herald*. They would run the ad on Friday, Saturday and Sunday.

Just as the group was about to disband, Madison's cell phone rang.

"It's Father Francis", she announced to the group.

"Hello, this is Madison."

Father Francis was concerned when he asked, "How are you Madison? Have you made any discoveries yet?"

Madison explained her meetings with Ned and Jackie and told the priest when her personal ad would run in the newspapers.

The Father commented, "That sounds like an excellent place to start. I wish you all the best, Madison. The reason I called was to tell you I was able to contact Sister Mary Louise. She would very much like to meet you and answer any questions you might have about your mother. She is free tomorrow, if you have time in the morning."

Madison was beaming as she answered. "I'm open all day tomorrow. I would love to have the opportunity to speak with the Sister. Did she say what time would be best?"

"She said if you could be at her place about ten she would have tea ready for you."

Madison and Father Francis confirmed the address and directions before ending their conversation.

Chapter 54

While Jackie Potter was discussing her research data with Madison, the head teller of the Albuquerque National Bank greeted a familiar tall, thin, bearded man.

"Good Afternoon Mr. Horne. How might I assist you today?" Everett Sherman asked formally.

This particular customer never seemed to want to engage in idle conversation. "I would like to access my safe deposit box. May I sign in?"

Everett Sherman had known Mr. Horne for several years. He knew that the man made a visit to his safe deposit box approximately once every six months. He spent a few minutes in one of the bank's private rooms with his property and then returned the box to its rightful position. Everett also noted that this customer had always paid cash on each visit for the continued rental of the deposit box.

Mr. Horne and his visits had long intrigued Everett. He often fantasized over what might be contained in Mr. Horne's box. Everett had envisioned his customer to be everything from a recluse millionaire hiding his wealth in cash to an explorer who was keeping a priceless treasure a secret from the rest of the world. The fact that Mr. Horne sported a toupee that had long ago seen its better days, had an unkempt beard, always wore what appeared to be the same long raincoat and sported extra large glasses, made him even more irresistible to Everett's imagination.

Everett jolted himself back to reality and quickly ushered Mr. Horne into the safe deposit area of the bank.

Only once Dennis Horne was sure he was alone in the private room did he open the narrow, oblong box. He lifted from inside several stacks of hundred dollar bills and fanned the stacks in front of his face. He enjoyed the sound and smell of money. Reaching into the bottom of the box, he emerged with a beautiful ruby and diamond necklace.

Dennis Horne sneered as he held the necklace and read the familiar inscription etched on the gold, "To my darling Lydia. Thank you for the most precious gift, our daughter, Olivia. Love Always, Graham."

Chapter 55

Thursday morning promptly at ten o'clock Madison arrived at the duplex residence of Sister Mary Louise Lopez. Ray offered his vehicle to Madison so that she might have a private meeting with the Sister. He and Megan felt Madison might need some time alone with the woman who may have known Rosemary the best while she lived at Saint Gabriel's in Deming.

A petite, small framed, white haired woman greeted Madison a minute after she rang the bell. Sister Mary Louise appeared to be in her middle eighties, but was able to maneuver herself about without assistance. She bore a smile on her wrinkled face and Madison could see a gentle kindness in the woman.

"Hello. You must be Madison. Please come in. I have been quite curious to meet you ever since Father Gomez called."

Madison entered the Sister's home slowly, taking in the warmth of the room. Warm that was generated by both the morning sun shining through a large picture window and from the soft colors. On the Sister's living room walls were displayed many photos and paintings.

"Thank you for seeing me, Sister. I assume Father Gomez explained the reason for my visit to New Mexico. I have come to learn about my mother, Rosemary Cavanaugh. I understand you knew her quite well."

Sister Mary Louise motioned for Madison to sit on a pale blue and yellow floral loveseat. She sat in an upright matching chair facing a rectangular coffee table.

"Yes, Madison, the Father briefly explained your situation. I must say I was as surprised as he was to learn Rosemary had a daughter."

Madison was quick to correct her. "To be honest, I was raised as Rosemary's daughter, but after her death, it was proven that I am not biologically related to her. My mother's dying words to me were to start back here, in Deming, at what she referred to as 'our beginning'. At the time I had no idea how much of a mystery 'our beginning' would turn out to be."

Sister Mary Louise reached to the center table and poured steaming hot tea into two delicate china cups. As she handed Madison her cup of tea, she also slid a packet across the table.

"I was able to find a few photos of Rosemary last evening that I thought you might like to have."

Madison set her teacup and saucer back down to examine the packet. As she pulled the photos out she smiled as she recognized a younger version of the woman she loved so dearly. She took a few minutes to look at the fifteen or twenty photos and had to wipe a tear from her cheek.

Sister Mary Louise sipped her tea in order to give Madison some quiet time.

"Most of those were taken at church events over the years that Rosemary worked and lived with us," the Sister explained.

Madison, anxious to learn more details, asked, "Sister, would you please explain how my mother came to work and live at Saint Gabriel's?"

Sister Mary Louise's mind went back in time as she recalled. "When your mother was about fifteen she was placed with a foster family that attended Saint Gabriel's on a regular basis. These foster parents were a bit older than usually desired for foster parents of teenagers. But these parents had a wonderful track record of being loving caretakers of many youth over the years. You have to also realize that Rosemary had been in several foster homes prior to this and most of them had not worked out well for her. I believe the social worker felt your mother would do better with more mature parents and in a home where there were no other children. The natural children of this couple were adults at that point, out of the house and starting families of their own. The couple was able to provide Rosemary with an established home without rivalry from other teenagers."

Sister Mary Louise paused and then continued. "Anyway, Rosemary started to attend Saint Gabriel's with Gary and Jean Stewart. I wasn't sure at first whether Rosemary felt pressured to attend church with them, or came out of curiosity. Whatever the case, she soon seemed happy to be a part of the congregation. She volunteered to set up for our fundraisers and served meals during the summer at our affiliated homeless shelter. Rosemary always seemed more comfortable among older members of the congregation than within the youth group. Maybe her troubled early years made her mature beyond her true age."

Madison could easily picture her mother doing the things Sister Mary Louise described.

"My mother worked for over twenty years in North Carolina in an elder care facility. She managed the activities and schedule with great success for the entire center. Caring for the older generation must have been almost a natural talent for her. Are the foster parents you mention still living in the area?"

The Sister said sadly, "No, I'm afraid not. Jean had a major stroke soon after Rosemary graduated high school. Gary did everything he possibly could to care for her at home, but in the end Jean was placed in a long-term care facility in Santa Fe. Gary and Jean's daughter Linda lived in Santa Fe and she felt having her mother closer would make things easier. Gary put the family home up for sale and made plans to move closer to his wife and daughter. Since your mother was turning eighteen at about the same time, she was about to be dropped from the foster care services. That was how Rosemary came to live at Saint Gabriel's."

Madison commented, "I had wondered how her transition to actually living at the church had come about."

Sister Mary Louise explained. "There were two small rooms with a private bath in the basement of the church. No one had lived there for a few years. When I realized that Rosemary would have nowhere to live, I approached Father Gomez with an idea. Since the church recently lost its part time secretary I suggested that Rosemary be hired into that position and that additional responsibilities be added to the role in order for her to work full time. I noted that if the church were to offer her a place to live as part of her compensation, there would be very little added financial burden. The Father was skeptical at first, but agreed to a trial basis of time."

Madison was quick to interject. "It must have worked out if she were still living at the church four years later."

"Yes, I am happy to say that my idea was as good for the church as it was for Rosemary. Your mother was eager to take on more and more tasks within the church. She actually came up with great ideas of her own that allowed Saint Gabriel's to offer more services to the community. Our church's success and growth is due in part to Rosemary Cavanaugh."

Chapter 56

Madison could have listened for hours to Sister Mary Louise tell stories about Rosemary's years at Saint Gabriel's, but she was anxious to talk about the day Rosemary left. As Madison sat her empty teacup on the table she approached that very subject.

"Sister, thank you so much for your insight and delightful stories. I was wondering, though, what you can tell me about the night my mother left Deming with me."

Sister Mary Louise was much more serious as she spoke. "Madison, dear, if you are asking me whether I have any idea who you are, I am afraid that I do not. That December morning when we realized that Rosemary was gone I was probably the most confused person in the church. Your mother was making plans to distribute winter jackets to the needy in the community. She was also scheduled to help serve a hot holiday meal at the shelter before she and I were to celebrate Christmas together. I had invited Rosemary to go with me to my sister's home and share the holiday with my family. I thought your mother was looking forward to the day as much as I was.

"When Father Gomez found the note stating she had to leave for California due to a family emergency, I was shocked. I had never heard Rosemary speak of any actual family other than her deceased mother."

Madison was touched to hear how dearly the Sister felt about her mother. "Did Father Gomez explain to you that my mother left a second note that was addressed to me?"

Sister Mary Louise nodded as Madison continued. "If she found me in that manger setting late at night, do you have any idea who might have placed me there?"

The Sister thought before she answered. "I simply cannot think of anyone in the congregation who would have done such a thing. I have been trying to remember any young lady with a baby who may have been at one of the church's shelters at that time. I'm afraid that after so many years I cannot recall any."

Madison too was quite somber. "I realize it has been a long time and no one will be able to quickly conclude who placed an infant in that manger, but I am determined to learn my identity. I have been working with some people from the *Deming Daily* newspaper and we plan to place a personal ad in upcoming issues of the paper both here in Deming and in Las Cruces in a hope that someone will come forward who is able to help me."

Sister Mary Louise slowly got up from her chair and came to sit on the loveseat putting her arm around Madison's shoulders.

"Madison, the woman you knew as your mother was a very special person. The two of you may have become joined together in life in a very unusual way, but the important thing is that you were joined together. It appears Rosemary raised a lovely young woman and I can see that you loved her dearly. I wish you all the best in your search. I will pray for you."

Madison was close to tears again. "Thank you so much, Sister. I have learned a great deal about my mother today. Everything you have said has only reinforced what a great person she was. I miss her immensely. She told me to come to Deming and start at the beginning. I believe she wanted me to find the truth. I also believe she gave me enough strength to handle whatever I discover."

Just before Madison was about to leave, Sister Mary Louise offered her a slip of paper from her pocket.

"I remembered the social worker's name who handled Rosemary's case when her mother died. She was quite new to the job at that time. She may still be working for Luna County.

Her name was Christine Morgan. I wrote it down for you. It's up to you whether you contact her. She may or may not be able to provide additional information about Rosemary."

Madison took the piece of paper with the social worker's name. "I appreciate all your information and insight. I will indeed try to contact this person. I plan to use any lead I can to help gather more detail about my mother's life."

Madison gave the Sister a warm hug and walked along on the brick walkway back to the street where Ray's vehicle was parked. The midday sky was without a cloud and the temperatures were nearing triple digits. She was thankful when the air conditioning kicked into high gear and cooled the inside of the SUV.

Chapter 57

When Madison arrived back at the hotel she found Ray in the girls' room watching the news with Megan.

Ray was the first to inquire. "How did things go with the Sister? Were you able to learn any new details about Rosemary?"

Madison smiled as she answered. "Sister Mary Louise was very kind in telling me about my mother's teen years. I discovered that it was actually the Sister's idea to have Rosemary move into the church. I'll tell you all the details over lunch. I'm starving. I was so nervous I couldn't eat much this morning."

The group decided it was time to explore a local Mexican restaurant. Over their lunches of fajitas and quesadillas Madison told Ray and Megan all the stories Sister Mary Louise had shared with her.

Ray was glad that Madison had not learned any details that troubled her. "Madison, it sounds like the Sister believed Rosemary was a good person. It seems that she was a young woman who was bright and caring, who just needed someone to care about her. That all goes to prove that in the moment when she found you, all she wanted to do was protect you. I don't believe she ran away with you maliciously, but rather out of a strong sense of responsibility to protect your life."

Madison was suddenly choked up with emotions. "Thanks, Uncle Ray. I appreciate you saying that. This whole morning has been such an emotional time for me. I'm so glad that I was able to talk to Sister Mary Louise. She also gave me the name of the social worker that helped place my mother in foster homes. I plan to call the County Department of Social Services this afternoon to see whether she is still employed there. Maybe she can provide me with some facts from my mother's childhood years."

Megan was a little concerned about her friend. "Madison, it's great that you are learning so much about Rosemary's past. I want to make sure you do not forget that it is your past we came to Deming to discover. Someone out there has to know who that baby was that Rosemary discovered in the manger."

Madison was glad that her friend kept her grounded on the primary mission. "Yes, I realize that. I just need to learn about the past my mother never shared with me. She must have been afraid that in telling me about her past I would somehow have learned she was not my birth mother. I would like to discover the facts about two people's lives in this journey, my mother's and mine."

As everyone was finishing his or her respective lunch, Madison remembered one more thing. "I also had a message from Jackie at the newspaper this morning. She asked if we could stop over about three o'clock this afternoon to meet Larkyn Belanger. She and Larkyn are meeting to finalize the personal ad that will start running tomorrow. I should call her back and confirm, unless you two have other plans."

Megan and Ray said they were at Madison's disposal.

Madison suggested they return to the hotel room for a short rest before driving to the newspaper building. She also wanted time to call Social Services in hopes of locating Christine Morgan.

Chapter 58

Back in their hotel room, Madison quickly freshened up and proceeded to take the phonebook out of the nightstand drawer. In the government listings she was able to find the number for Luna County Social Services. She was glad to see that there was an office located in Deming. As Madison dialed the number on her cell phone, her stomach filled again with nervous jitters.

When a voice answered the phone announcing the office by name, Madison nearly stuttered as she started with her request.

"Good Afternoon. I am looking for a social worker by the name of Christine Morgan. She worked a case many years ago, and I was wondering whether she is still employed by your office."

Madison was shocked when the voice on the other end of the phone replied, "Christine is still with our office. I will transfer your call."

After hearing a single click, Madison soon heard her call ringing into another line. After three rings, a mature female voice answered. "This is Christine Morgan. How may I help you?"

Madison started to ramble, but quickly composed herself. "Yes, my name is Madison Cavanaugh. I have recently learned that you handled my mother's case several years ago when she was a child and into her teenage years. My mother recently passed away and I was hoping to learn more about her past. I have traveled to Deming from North Carolina. Since I arrived I have spoken with Father Francis Gomez and Sister Mary Louise Lopez. The Sister gave me your name. My mother's name was Rosemary Cavanaugh. I know it's a huge assumption to think you would be able to remember one particular case from over thirty years ago, but I am somewhat desperate."

What Madison could not see through the telephone was that Christine Morgan's eyes widen and her mood softened when Rosemary's name was mentioned.

After a short pause, Christine responded to Madison. "I pride myself that I can remember a few details about the majority of my cases from my forty plus year career. However, some cases have left such a mark on my heart that I can remember them as though they just happened. Rosemary Cavanaugh's case was one of those. Your mother's was one of the first cases I was named as the primary social worker. I was just starting my career at that time. Rosemary was such a good hearted little girl. I was determined not to let her become a statistic that fell through the system's cracks."

Madison was stunned to hear Christine's clear recollection of Rosemary. "I was wondering whether I could meet with you to discuss my mother's early years. As I mentioned, she recently died and I am on a discovery journey of sorts to learn about the both of us. If you would be kind enough to meet with me, I could explain in greater detail."

Christine thought for a few moments. She was not in the habit of discussing her clients' cases, present or past, but she could hear a sincere need in Madison's voice. She had often wondered what had become of Rosemary. Meeting with Madison might help both women's curiosities.

Madison was delighted when Christine finally spoke. "I would very much enjoy meeting with you. I'm not sure how much I can help you, but I will dig out Rosemary's case file from our archives to help us both. You mentioned that you were in Deming. Would you be free tomorrow morning to meet?"

"I will make myself free whenever you agree to talk. Should I come to your office?"

Christine felt it would be better not to meet within the less than private space of the social services department. She offered an alternative. "Why don't we meet away from the office? There is a quaint coffee shop and bakery downtown. Would you be able to meet me there?"

Madison smiled. "That sounds like a much better place to meet. Tell me the name of the shop and when you would be able to meet."

Christine checked her on-line calendar before answering. "The shop is called Luna's Sunshine Coffee House. I could meet you there at ten o'clock."

"That sounds perfect. I can't wait to meet and speak with you. Thank you so much for agreeing to see me."

Madison was ecstatic when she ended the call. She crossed the room and hugged Megan.

"This woman remembers my mother's case. Isn't that amazing? After thirty years, Rosemary is still remembered by so many people."

Megan tried to share her friend's enthusiasm. "That is wonderful news. Let's just keep our fingers crossed that someone remembers writing that note found with you in the manger. Someone out there certainly could not forget about their baby."

Chapter 59

When the trio arrived at the newspaper office, it was ten minutes before three. They asked the receptionist to let Jackie Potter know they had arrived. Before they could settle into the visitors' chairs Jackie came through the glass door leading to the administrative offices.

As she extended her hand to Madison, Jackie greeted the group warmly. "Good afternoon. I'm glad you were able to come in on such short notice. I wanted you to meet Larkyn and finalize the ad before we run with it this weekend."

Madison smiled and said, "I really appreciate all you are doing to help me with this matter. I know this is adding extra work to what I assume is already a busy schedule."

Jackie led Ray, Megan and Madison to a small conference room where a woman was standing beside a white board at the front left side of the room. Larkyn Belanger turned to face the door when she head Jackie enter. Larkyn stood taller than Madison at five feet, ten inches. She had reddish brown hair that just touched her shoulders, green eyes and beautiful bronzed skin.

Jackie was the first to speak. "Madison, I would like you to meet Larkyn Belanger. As I told you, Larkyn is a private investigator and a personal friend of mine for several years."

Larkyn reached to shake Madison's hand. "Madison, it is nice to meet you. Jackie and Ned have explained your situation to me and I must admit that I find the mystery of it all quite fascinating. I hope that I will be able to help you find answers to your quest."

Madison returned the greeting. "I truly hope you can help me discover who I am and where I might have come from. I want you to understand that I fully realize that the answers we uncover could bring me either joy or more heartbreak, but I really need to know."

Larkyn was glad to hear Madison's proclamation. She introduced herself to Ray and Megan and took control of the meeting.

Larkyn pointed to the whiteboard and said, "Here is the first take at the personal ad we want to run in the papers. Let's look at it once more together and make any changes we agree on."

She read the now familiar words aloud, "Please help. She is in danger. I cannot protect her. Please help Baby M."

Larkyn continued, "As you all know, those are the four sentences contained in the note attached to baby Madison. I agree we should start the ad with these lines. They might catch the attention of the original author. Then I would phrase the rest of the ad like this.

"Do these words sound familiar? Did you write this note many years ago? Baby M wants to know who she is. No judgment will be made. Baby M is just looking for answers. Please call 800-555-5546.

"I have set up a disposable cell phone with that number. I will take all the calls and filter them as needed. You should realize that we might receive numerous calls that will provide no leads whatsoever. Many will just be crank calls. Others may seem promising at first, but will not pan out. I have filtered calls on several other cases and know what to look for. I assure you that I will not let a legitimate call get filtered out."

Madison was feeling as if she were on the edge of a cliff. Should she jump off the edge, take the plunge, or turn away and run back to the safety of her mother's quiet little house in North Carolina? She took a deep breath and hoped she would never regret not turning back.

"I like the message. Using Baby M as the messenger of sorts personalizes it. I think that if someone in your reader population has been looking for Baby M for more than twenty-seven years they will be compelled to call the number."

Megan and Ray agreed that the ad sounded good and hoped it would get the attention of the right person.

Ray was the realist of the group. "Madison. There is a chance that whoever wrote the note and left you at the church is no longer living in this area. That person could have moved or passed away. I hope you realize that Larkyn may not get that one legitimate call we are all hoping for."

Madison took in Ray's concern, paused a moment and said, "Thanks for pointing that out. It is a possibility I have set my mind to deal with. This trip, all the people I have met who knew Rosemary and the publication of this personal ad may not reveal my heritage. But I will never regret having made this trip or met the people. It has already been an enriching week in my life. I'm ready for whatever the rest of this journey brings."

Megan, who was sitting in a chair next to Madison at the conference table, reached over and put her arm around her friend's shoulders and pulled her close. As strong as Madison seemed to be, Megan knew her friend still needed a hug.

Jackie knew there was a deadline for the ad to appear in the next day's paper. She brought the group back on track by saying, "Now that we agree on how the ad will read and know what results we can expect from it, are there any other questions?"

Madison felt encouraged by the meeting. "I believe I'm ready to move forward. Ned and Jackie thought the ad should run tomorrow, Saturday and Sunday to reach the most readers. Larkyn, are you ready to take calls as early as tomorrow?"

Larkyn took a deep breath and answered, "I have tested the phone line, and have a tape recorder ready to record promising calls and a notebook ready to log all the calls. The cell phone will display the caller ID information, unless blocked. In some of my past cases, legitimate callers have made their first contact from a pay phone or a public location. They do not want to be identified until they can check out the person they are calling. It's usually a good sign when a caller wants to check out the number, just as we want to check out the callers."

Jackie stood up and said, "I will take this over to the classified department and make sure it's placed on the page in an easily spotted location. It helps to work at the paper sometimes. You know what they say, 'location, location, location.'"

Everyone laughed at Jackie's light remark and stood to leave. Madison went to shake Larkyn's hand and thanked her again for taking the case. Ray, Megan and Madison then headed back to their hotel room hoping that the next day would bring answers to all their questions.

Chapter 60

Friday dawned as the first cloudy day since Madison arrived in New Mexico. She hoped that the dreariness of the morning was not a sign of any news that she might receive that day.

Luckily Madison had nothing to worry about when it came to the weather. By the time she was showered, dressed and ready to leave for the coffee house to meet Christine Morgan, the sun was shining and blue sky abounded. Madison was a bit nervous about the meeting, but equally excited to be meeting a person who had known Rosemary as a young child.

Madison pulled Ray's SUV into the parking lot of Luna's Sunshine Coffee House at ten minutes before ten that morning. She was about to walk toward the coffee house door when she noticed a petite, gray haired woman taking a folder from the backseat of her vehicle. As the woman, in a tan colored linen business suit, turned in Madison's direction their eyes met. Madison was the first to speak.

"Hello. Would you by chance be Christine Morgan?"

The older woman's face broke into a broad, welcoming smile. Her blue eyes were warm as she answered, "Yes, I am. You must be Madison Cavanaugh. It is so good to meet you. Shall we go in a find a table?"

The two women headed for the entrance and Madison opened and held the door for Christine. The inside of the coffee house was decorated with earthen colors. Various shades of tan, green and terracotta were used on the walls, floor and tabletops. The smell of freshly brewed coffee and warm oven-baked sweet rolls filled the air. The place was not overly crowded at this mid-morning hour. They were able to secure a small table in a sunny, quiet corner of the establishment. A waitress who appeared to be about seventeen took their orders and recommended the sweet roll special of the day. Neither woman could resist after inhaling the sweet aroma.

Christine started their main topic of discussion by saying, "I'm happy to say that I was able to locate your mother's file in the archives. Although I like to think I can remember cases, reading the file brought many more details back to me. I'm not sure what information you are looking for, or where you want to begin. I, however, would like to begin by telling you how sorry I am for the loss of your mother."

Madison was not sure whether telling Christine the full truth would prevent her from sharing information about Rosemary, so she kept her reply simple. "Thank you. It was a tragic accident that took my mother's life. I was not prepared for that sudden of a loss. As I said on the phone, my mother left some unanswered questions regarding her past, as well as my own. I have traveled here to try to learn where we both came from. I think learning as much as I can about my mother's early years will better help me put the pieces of her life's puzzle together."

Christine touched the red-rope folder she had laid on the table beside her. She was quiet as she spoke. "Our case records started when Rosemary, your mother, was about two years old. Ellie, Rosemary's mother, was staying at a homeless shelter. One of the workers placed a call to Social Services because the then-toddler Rosemary seemed somewhat neglected. I was assigned to the case and visited the shelter hoping to locate and talk to Ellie."

The young waitress in a golden yellow uniform, whose nametag read 'Lisa', carried a tray to the table containing a cup of coffee for Christine, a small silver tea pot and an empty cup with a tea bag for Madison. She also brought two plates with warm sweet rolls drizzled with icing.

After the women thanked Lisa, Christine continued. "On the first day I stopped into the shelter, Ellie was not there. A worker told me she often stayed a few days, and then was not seen for a few days before returning. I left my card and asked to be called the next time she and the baby were in."

Madison had just swallowed her first bite of roll before she asked, "How long was it before you met them?"

Christine took a moment to enjoy a bite and a gulp of her coffee. "About a week later I received a call. I was able to get away and arrived at the shelter just after lunch had been served. Ellie and Rosemary were pointed out to me. They were in a far corner of the room at the end of a long table. Ellie was feeding Rosemary a cookie from their meal tray.

"As I approached I could tell Ellie was a bit nervous. I introduced myself and said that I was checking in on the welfare of young mothers with infants in the community. I asked what her name was and how she was doing that day."

Madison could sense Christine's concern from her voice. "You must have met with a wide range of people during your career. Where would you put Ellie on that scale?"

Thinking a moment, she answered, "I could tell immediately that Ellie was a caring, loving mother. I had watched her feeding Rosemary the cookie and there was no rush, no frustration. Ellie appeared patient with the child and careful not to give her more than she could handle in her little mouth."

Madison nodded and Christine went on describing her first encounter. "Ellie was hesitant to tell me her name, but very pleased to introduce her daughter. During the next few minutes I was able to discover that Ellie had delivered her baby at another shelter and that the baby's father had died prior to the birth. Ellie explained that her parents were dead and there was no one to help her."

Madison added, "That is how my mother always described her mother's lack of family. She said Ellie had mentioned coming from a small town in California, but that her family had been tragically killed in an accident and she was left an orphan."

Christine referred to the file. "Yes, Ellie eventually mentioned that she had come from California. She never gave up the first name of the baby's father. Over the next few weeks I was able to interact with Ellie in a very positive way. I found a group home for single mothers that had an opening. Ellie was thrilled to move into a place where she and Rosemary had a private room. I arranged for her to attend parenting classes and found a part time job that provided childcare."

Madison smiled, "It sounds like Ellie owed you a lot for getting her life back on track. If she had so much going for her, how did she slip back into drugs?"

Again Christine referred to the file. "It appears that Ellie was able to maintain the life I helped arrange for about two years. She left the group home suddenly. No one knew exactly what had happened. I did not hear from Ellie for over a year after that. Then one day she called my office number. She told me she had done a bad thing, had fallen back in with the wrong crowd of people and was scared for her daughter. I agreed to meet her, but insisted she come into my office. She would not hear of that. She feared people there would take her child. I finally relented and met her at another shelter.

"When Ellie walked in, I hardly recognized her as the same young woman. Her hair had not been washed or brushed in days; her clothing was dirty and stank of alcohol. She did not bring Rosemary to the meeting. I believe she knew that if she had, I would have had no choice but to remove the child from her care."

Madison felt so badly for what Rosemary's mother must have been going through at that time. "Were you able to help her again?"

"No, I'm afraid not. Ellie said she wanted to get clean again and we even set another meeting time and place. Unfortunately, she never showed up to that meeting."

"Were you able to find out why she didn't meet with you?"

Christine reflected sadly, "Two days after we should have met Ellie left me a message again. She said she was ill. She left an address in the message. As soon as I picked up the message, I drove to the address. It was a vacant building on the outskirts of town. I called out, but Ellie didn't answer. I had taken another social worker with me for assistance. We broke up and started to search the building.

"I was the one who found her. In a corner, under a blanket, Ellie lay dead from an overdose. Lying across her chest, sound asleep, was Rosemary, who was almost six years old by then."

Madison was deeply moved by what she just heard. "My mother never mentioned that she was with her mother when she died."

Christine explained, "That was something we never told the child. We were able to pick her up without waking her. When she woke up later at social services, she was far too young to understand more than that her mother was gone. I am not aware whether the fact that she was with her mother at the time of her death was ever divulged to Rosemary."

Chapter 61

As the two women finished their sweet rolls, Lisa refilled Christine's coffee cup. Both sat in the stillness for a few minutes reflecting on the story that had just been told.

Madison was the first to break the silence. "I assume that is how and when my mother ended up in foster care."

Christine began to tell of Rosemary's life after Ellie's death.

"Yes. She was placed in an orphanage while the state searched for any living relatives. Unfortunately we had little to go on, so after a few weeks, Rosemary was legally declared a ward of the state. She was then placed in a state facility for children until an adoptive family could be found. Another piece of bad luck was Rosemary's age. Most couples are looking for infants or toddlers. Rosemary was just old enough to fall out of the desired age range. From all we could figure, she had never been to school. Her social skills were below average. She had not interacted with many children over the years."

Madison remembered her mother telling of the several foster homes she had spent time in. "My mother told me her younger years were very difficult. She said she was moved from home to home within the system. Was that correct?"

Christine gave a quick smile. "Yes, she was placed into several foster homes over the course of eight years. Most were with foster parents who took in several children at the same time, sometimes while still raising their own. It seemed Rosemary did not do well in a group environment."

Madison remembered her conversation with Sister Mary Louise. "She apparently finally found a foster home she fit well in, right?"

Christine nodded. "The Stewart household was a great fit for your mother. Their children were grown and out of the house. Jean Stewart was not adjusting well to what we now call 'empty nest syndrome'. Jean and Gary applied to be foster parents and I immediately thought of Rosemary. Since she was a loner and the Stewarts were more mature, I thought the combination might just work out. Rosemary bloomed in that home. She had her own bedroom and private bath. Jean was a homemaker, so she taught Rosemary to cook and sew simple things. Rosemary spent her teenage years very happy in their home.

"It was a tragedy when Jean had a stroke and had to be moved into a facility. But by then Rosemary was too old for the system. I heard later about her move into the church and her position there. I was very happy to know she was settling in."

Madison commented, "I have spoken with both Father Gomez and Sister Mary Louise since I arrived here. They both spoke fondly of my mother. I believe the time she spent working at the church led her into the career path she took."

Christine was curious. "What career did your mother choose?"

Madison was quite proud as she spoke. "My mother started working in an elder care facility and worked her way into the directorship of the home's activities. She was very happy helping others and making their lives as full as they could be."

"You said you were here from North Carolina. How did Rosemary end up on the East coast, if you don't mind my asking?"

Madison took a deep breath. "Well, that part of the story will take another pot of tea for sure." She raised her hand to catch the waitress' attention.

While the two women sipped their hot beverages, Madison related the story that was now her life's mystery. She hoped that Christine would not think ill of her mother for the choices Rosemary had made all those years ago.

It took a few moments after Madison was done for Christine to absorb what had just been recounted.

"I am completely astonished at that story. Not that I am judging Rosemary in any way. I am amazed that you have been able to find out as many details as you already have after all these years."

Madison was thankful for that as well. "It is as if at every door I knock, I find another piece of the puzzle. My problem seems to be putting all the puzzle pieces together in the right order to solve the bigger mystery of who I am. I admit to putting a lot of hope in the personal ad that will run in the newspaper for the next three days. If the ad does not bring someone forward, I might be at a dead-end."

Christine tried to add encouragement. "I certainly wish you all the luck in the world. If you have come this far, I believe you will find what you need to know. I only wish I could help you more."

As soon as she said that, Christine grabbed her handbag from the floor and opened it.

"I do have something for you, though. These photographs were in Ellie's old file. I can't imagine why my office would need them now, but I made copies for the files. I would like you to have these originals. They were found among Ellie's personal belongings after her death. Since Rosemary was so young, they were probably put in the file for safekeeping. They should have been turned over to Rosemary when she was older. Maybe they will help you in another way."

Madison slowly took the photos from Christine's extended hand. The first photo showed Rosemary at about a year old sitting on Ellie's lap. Rosemary had never been able to show Madison a picture of her mother. There were a couple more of the mother and child that appeared to be when Rosemary was a little older. The last photo in the bunch was a group shot. On the back someone had written, "Mom, Dad, Beth and me".

Madison questioned Christine. "Who is Beth?"

Christine shrugged. "We were never able to identify the family in that photo. Ellie mentioned that her parents were dead, but she never mentioned any siblings. I always felt Beth must have been Ellie's younger sister, but was never able to substantiate my guess."

Madison clutched the photos to her chest. "Thank you so much. My second mission in life is to find any family Ellie may have left behind in California. I certainly have my work cut out for me, but these photos may help more than we realize at this moment."

Christine glanced at her watch and announced that she had to be getting back to her office.

"I am so happy I got to meet you and hear about Rosemary's life. Again, accept my condolences at your loss. I can see in your eyes and hear in your voice that you and your mother were exceptionally close. I hope you find answers that bring you peace."

As she handed Madison a business card with her cell phone number on the back, she added, "I would very much like to hear how things turn out for you. Feel free to call me anytime."

Madison was genuinely touched with Christine's caring personality. "Thank you for all you have told me today. I especially appreciate the photos. Even if I find no further answers, I will treasure them always. I will be sure to call you and let you know how things turn out."

After Christine insisted on paying the bill, they exited the café and headed for their vehicles. Christine was the first to outstretch her arms for an embrace. Madison hugged the older woman warmly and they parted, each with tears in their eyes.

Chapter 62

At her office, Larkyn Belanger was taking calls that were coming into the special cell phone set up for Madison's case. So far the calls had not provided any leads. Larkyn was hoping for a miracle, but sure of one thing. Many calls would come into the line over the next few days.

She was about to go out for a quick sandwich when Madison and Megan walked through her front door. Madison had not been to Larkyn's office before so she took a moment to take in the room. It was a small street front office with vertical blinds at the wide front windows. There was a waiting area inside the door with a small davenport and four padded chairs. On a center coffee table laid various magazines to occupy the waiting clients. There was a coffee pot and disposable cups on a small table on the left side of the room. A door led to a private room where Larkyn met with her clients. The furniture in that room consisted of an old wooden desk and several metal filing cabinets. Two padded leather chairs were positioned in front of Larkyn's desk.

Larkyn motioned for Madison and Megan to join her in the inner office and to take a seat.

Madison seemed nervous when she spoke. "I apologize for just stopping in, but I was a bit anxious to see if you had received any calls this morning."

Larkyn responded, "Yes, I received a few calls. I am sorry to say that none of them appear to be valid leads. A couple of calls were looking for Baby Mike and one lady thought we found her lost cat."

Madison tried to hide her disappointment while Megan comforted her. "Madison, I'm sure Larkyn comes across this often in her cases. There will be many calls and only a few will develop a lead or two, right Larkyn?"

Larkyn agreed. "That is so true. I also find that the true leads come from calls a few days after the ad has appeared in the paper. Those people are nervous about calling, not sure whether they want to identify themselves or are afraid of self-incrimination. I realize all this waiting feels like an eternity, but we have to hold out hope that sooner or later someone will call with information that will help us."

Madison felt a little better, but realized she was probably keeping Larkyn from her lunch. "I bet we interrupted your lunch plans."

Larkyn smiled. "I was just been thinking of going around the corner to the deli for a sandwich. Could I interest you two in joining me?"

Megan was the first to jump at the invitation. "That sounds great. I am starving. Maybe we can even get Madison to share the information she got from her meeting with Rosemary's social worker this morning."

Larkyn's interests were peaked. "Yes, I can't wait to hear. Let me grab my purse and lock up on the way out."

Chapter 63

Madison knew that the weekend would consist of two very quiet days unless Larkyn received a call with detailed information. On Saturday morning she was trying to decide how to occupy her free time when her cell phone rang.

She looked at the caller ID hopeful that it was Larkyn with a lead. She was mildly disappointed to see Ned Tuttle's name appear on her display.

"Good morning, Ned."

Ned's return greeting sounded as though he were in a very good mood that morning, "Hi, Madison. I know you are waiting for good news, but I was wondering whether I might interest you and Megan, and Ray, of course, to a movie and dinner. It might be good for all of you to give your minds a break."

Madison smiled just hearing Ned's enthusiasm. "You know that might be just what we need. Let me check with Megan and Uncle Ray. Can I get back to you in a few minutes?"

On the other end of the call, Ned Tuttle was practically beaming at the thought of having dinner with Megan Davis. He almost stuttered as he answered, "Yes. That would be great. You have my cell phone number now. I'll be waiting to hear from you."

In their hotel room, Madison waited for Megan to return from the lobby with the coffee and hot tea she had gone for. As soon as Megan knocked on the door, Madison opened it and took her steaming cup of tea from Megan's left hand.

Madison was smiling when she asked, "Megan, guess who just called to ask you out on a date?"

Megan almost choked on her coffee as she asked, "A date? What are you talking about? There's nobody here who wants to take me on a date."

Madison was nodding her head as she teased her friend. "Oh, yes there is. Ned Tuttle called to see if the three of us would like to have dinner and maybe see a movie tonight. He says he just wants to help us kill time waiting for the right call to come in, but I think he wants to see you again."

Megan was blushing. "Are you serious? Ned wants to have dinner? We don't know many people here in Deming, and we do have to eat. I guess we could accept. What do you think?"

Madison was laughing. "What do I think? I think you want to see Ned again too. I have to say he seems like a very nice person and has certainly provided a lot of help to me."

"Where does he want to go? We should call Uncle Ray's room and see if he is up to it."

Megan picked up the hotel phone on the small desk and pushed his room's number. Ray Davis answered on the third ring. Megan explained Ned's offer to her uncle.

After a couple minutes she hung up the phone and looked at her friend. "He says he will bow out of this one. He thinks us 'young people', as he calls us, will have more fun without an older tag-along."

Madison could have predicted Ray's response. He was giving his niece some time to get to know this young man who genuinely seemed interested in her. She smiled to herself at his gesture.

"Good. Then it's settled. I'll call Ned back and set a time. What do you feel like eating tonight?"

Megan only took a moment to answer that question. "You know we have had Mexican and a variety of sandwiches and pizza this week. I was thinking of a juicy steak and salad, how about you?"

Madison agreed. "That sounds perfect. Ned must know of a good steak house in the area. I'll call him right now."

Madison made the call to Ned. He suggested the location of a good place to eat, and they set a time to meet.

Chapter 64

While Madison, Megan and Ned were dining and enjoying a comical movie, Larkyn Belanger was answering the cell phone that had been set up. Each time it rang, Larkyn crossed her fingers that the caller would be able to shed some light on Madison's identity.

She received calls until midnight on Saturday and started again at six o'clock Sunday morning. A call at two o'clock Sunday afternoon started out hopeful.

Larkyn answered on the second ring, "Hello."

The caller immediately started crying into the phone. "You found my baby, didn't you? I knew I would find her someday. Where is she?"

Larkyn tried to calm the female caller. "If you could calm down I need to ask you some questions."

The woman calmed a bit. "Okay, but I want my baby back."

Larkyn tried to ask her questions. "How long ago did you lose your baby?"

The answer dashed any hope Larkyn was starting to have. "Last month. I lost her last month. Some lady took my little Marcy from me. She said she was with Social Services, but I think she was a baby thief. She is probably trying to sell my little girl. I want my baby back. Do you have her?"

Larkyn told the woman the truth. "No, I do not have your baby. I can assure you that the ad is not related to your child. I am sorry."

The woman hung up.

Larkyn had dealt with a few calls similar to the one that just disconnected over the last forty-eight hours. Not a single lead had come of any of the calls. But she was not giving up. The Sunday edition reaches more readers than any other day. Somewhere out there, someone would come forward. Larkyn Belanger was not about to give up hope.

Chapter 65

On Monday morning Nina drove Sarah and Colby to their summer day camp. Melissa had signed the children up for a four-day per week program that included a variety of activities in a six-hour period. Both children were enjoying the time. When Nina arrived back at the Baxter home, she started on her daily housekeeping chores.

After putting some laundry in the washing machine, Nina decided to pick up the kitchen counters. Bryce was notorious for spreading the entire Sunday newspaper out over the counters as he read the whole edition, especially the sports section. The children would read the funnies with him and Melissa would grab for the Arts and Theatre section.

Nina decided to pour the last cup of coffee left in the morning's pot into a fresh cup and take a short break. Never able to stop working entirely, she started piling the newspaper neatly. The Classified section was folded so that the Personal Ads were visible.

Nina thought to herself, "There's something I can read while I sip my coffee. I enjoy imaging about the people writing these ads."

Several ads were placed by lonely couples desperate to adopt a child. There was an older gentleman looking for an elderly woman companion. There was a baby photo with a notation that made the reader guess who was turning fifty.

Nina was about done when a phrase caught her eye. "Baby M". Her heart started racing and her hands were shaking as she folded the newspaper in order to read the full ad.

Her voice was soft as she read the words to herself. "Please help. She is in danger. I cannot protect her. Please help Baby M." Nina was unable to read the rest of the ad due to the tears flowing from her eyes.

Nina was trying hard to wrap her mind around what she had just read. Those words, they were her words. After all these years, who would publish them now? Nina re-read the words and was able to finish the entire ad. She reached for the phone and pushed the on button. Suddenly her mind grasped the consequences of her making the call, but what else could she do?

Nina thought immediately of Mrs. Jackson. Melissa's mother was an attorney. She would be able to help her. Quickly she dialed the office number she had memorized many years ago.

Jillian Jackson's secretary, Carol Storms, answered the phone. "Good Morning. This is Attorney Jackson's office. May I help you?"

Nina was tongue-tied at first, but managed to answer. "Good Morning, Carol. This is Nina Perez. Is Mrs. Jackson in the office? I need to speak with her. It is an emergency."

Carol Storms had worked for Jillian Jackson for almost twenty years. She knew which callers should be put straight through to her boss, even if it meant interrupting a meeting. Nina Perez was one of those callers.

"Just a moment Nina, I will put you right through to her."

Carol placed Nina's call on hold long enough to buzz Jillian.

"Mrs. Jackson, Nina Perez is on the line. She says it is an emergency."

Jillian Jackson was a woman of average height and weight. Her auburn hair was cut short and was now streaked with lighter tones that came naturally with age. Her blue eyes opened wide when she heard Carol's words. Jillian only needed to hear the name 'Nina' and the word 'emergency' to make her heart jump into her throat. She quickly grabbed her receiver and pushed the blinking light signaling the call on hold.

"Nina, what's wrong? Are Sarah and Colby okay? Is it Melissa?"

Nina realized the panic she had just caused. "Mrs. Jackson, your family is fine. I am sorry I frightened you. I am the one with the emergency. I think I might be in big trouble. Could I speak with you, please?"

Jillian Jackson took a moment to calm her heartbeat. She was relieved her family was fine, but knew if Nina Perez said she had an emergency, she was not exaggerating.

"Yes, of course, Nina. Do you wish to speak now? Can you tell me what the problem is?"

Nina was still upset, "No, Mrs. Jackson. I cannot talk about this over the telephone. Could I come into your office? I really need your advice. I would like to see you today, if possible."

Jillian looked at her calendar. She didn't have any appointments until three o'clock.

"Nina, I have some open time from now until three this afternoon. Are you able to come downtown to my office?"

Nina almost rushed through her answer. "Yes. I will drive there right now. I really appreciate this. I just didn't know who else to call."

Jillian was reassuring when she spoke. "Nina, try to calm down. I'm sure you, of all people, are not in trouble. Whatever it is, I will help you deal with it. Will Hector be with you?"

Nina was shaking her head. "No, Mrs. Jackson, Hector does not know about this. I cannot tell him yet. Please, promise me, you will not tell him."

After hearing Nina's reply, Jillian was even more concerned with Nina's problem. "You have my word, Nina. I will keep anything you tell me confidential. Now, please, drive carefully. I will see you soon."

After the call ended, Carol stepped into Jillian's office doorway and asked, "Is everything okay? Nina has not called in such a long time. I hope nothing is wrong with your grand-children."

Jillian looked up from her desk. "No, thank you, Carol, Nina assures me my grandchildren are just fine. Nina actually has a personal problem she wants some advice with. She will be arriving soon. Would you please see to it that we are not interrupted while she is here? She sounded quite upset. I cannot imagine what could be wrong."

Carol knew her employer thought a great deal of Nina Perez and her husband, Hector. "Yes, of course."

Looking at the clock, Carol asked, "Would you like me to send out for sandwiches for you and Nina. It looks like you might not have time to get out for lunch."

Though food was the last thing on Jillian's mind at the moment, she accepted Carol's offer.

"That would be great. Would you please order a tuna salad sandwich for me and a turkey on wheat for Nina? If I remember correctly, that is her favorite."

Jillian's mind was trying to find a reason for Nina's sudden call. She wondered what kind of a problem Nina could have that she would not want Hector to know about. Jillian knew she would learn the answer soon and only hoped that she would be able to help Nina as she promised.

Chapter 66

At the Meriweather residence in Abilene, Texas, Julie Collins approached Patricia Meriweather in the elder woman's study.

Julie was hesitant as she knocked on the open solid oak door. "Mrs. Meriweather, may I speak with you?"

A white haired woman in her early eighties turned her slender body toward the doorway of the room. As usual, Patricia Meriweather was dressed in an expensive suit. Today the color was a mint green. Gold bracelets dangled from her thin wrists and diamond studs glistened from her ears.

She spoke quietly when she replied. "Yes, Julie, how may I help you?"

The nervous young woman began to speak. "It is Mr. Meriweather. He's asking when Dr. Haskins will be visiting him. I was under the impression that the doctor had visited Mr. Meriweather a couple weeks ago during the evening. However, Mr. Meriweather does not remember the visit and is asking again for his physician."

Patricia was polite, but firm. "My step-son is having trouble remembering events from day to day. I'm sure it is not unusual for him not to remember the visit. I told you what the doctor said the day after the appointment. Graham's health is failing and there is not much at this point that can be done. Everyone, including Graham, has agreed that no extreme measures are to be taken and that he wants to rest comfortably at home, rather than in a sterile hospital room."

Julie was not sure she agreed with the current line of treatment, but she was, after all, only the employee.

"Yes, Mrs. Meriweather. I just thought you could possibly call Dr. Haskins again so that Mr. Meriweather could be reassured and less stressed over this issue."

"Fine, I will make the call later today. Maybe Dr. Haskins will have time to drop in this week. I will try to arrange a time when you are on duty as well. Would that make you both feel better?"

Julie felt as if she were being patronized, but nodded. "Yes, that would be good of you. I, or should I say we, would appreciate that."

Julie Collins then turned and walked up the stairs to her patient's room. It was almost time for his next medication.

Chapter 67

Jillian Jackson's office was in a large office building near the courthouse and other government offices in Las Cruces. Nina had been to the office a few times during her tenure with the family. She was able to find a parking space on the second floor of the nearby parking garage and walked briskly across the busy street to the office building entrance.

Once inside the revolving doors, she headed for the elevators. She pressed the 'up' button and immediately a door to her left opened. She stepped inside the large, empty box and pressed the button for the seventh floor. When the elevator doors opened, she stepped out and to her right. She was facing double glass doors that had been stenciled with the names of several lawyers within Jillian Jackson's firm. After Jillian's name, were printed the words, 'Senior Partner'.

Nina pushed on the heavy glass entry door and entered a waiting area. She told the receptionist sitting behind a circular counter that she was there for Attorney Jackson. The young receptionist pointed her in the direction of Jillian's office. Nina knew the way and walked directly into Carol Storms' office area.

Carol Storms was just a few years from retirement. Her gray hair hung to her shoulders. She was a short woman with a slightly stocky build.

Carol looked up and smiled. "Good Morning Nina. I have not seen you for several years. How have you been?"

Nina tried to relax. "Hi Carol. I have been fine."

Carol knew from Jillian's brief conversation after her call that Nina might seem upset.

"Attorney Jackson is waiting for you. Let me show you the way in."

Carol tapped on Jillian's closed door, opened it slightly and announced Nina's arrival.

Jillian stood and walked from behind her desk. She reached her hand out to take Nina's.

"Hello Nina. Please come in. I took the liberty of having Carol order us sandwiches. They have just arrived. Would you like something to drink?"

Nina looked into Jillian's caring eyes. "I am not sure I can eat right now, but thank you. Maybe a cup of coffee would be good."

Jillian nodded to Carol, who understood and quickly left to obtain two cups of coffee.

Jillian put her arm on Nina's shoulder and led her to a comfortable chair that faced her desk. She said softly, "Nina, please have a seat. As soon as Carol brings our coffee, we can talk. But first, I want you to know that you can tell me anything. I will keep everything just between us, attorney-client confidentiality. I am sure this problem is not as big as it seems once you share it with me and let me help you."

Nina sat down slowly into the leather chair. She looked at the credenza under the large window. Lovely family photographs were framed and arranged across the top. She smiled realizing she knew everyone in the photos and even remembered some of the treasured moments.

Nina commented to Jillian, "You have such a lovely family, Mrs. Jackson. You are a blessed woman. Hector and I have enjoyed working for you and your family all these years. You have all made us feel appreciated and cared about."

Jillian was moved by Nina's words. "Thank you Nina. Please, call me Jillian. Here is Carol now. Thank you, Carol. Would you please close my door on your way out?"

Carol Storms set the cups down in front of the two women and exited the room. She quietly closed the door as she left.

Jillian sat down behind her desk and positioned a new legal pad and her best pen within her reach. She looked at a very nervous Nina.

"You can start whenever you want, Nina. If possible, you should start at the beginning so that I can record everything as it happened. Take your time. I have asked Carol to make sure we are not interrupted."

Nina's hands were shaking as she placed them on the thick sheet of glass covering Jillian's desk. It appeared as though she was trying to use the desk to steady them.

Nina was on the verge of tears as she started, "The beginning? It all started so many years ago. I was just a teenager. Jillian, I have never told anyone this before. I am so scared that I am in big trouble now."

Jillian tried to reassure Nina by touching her hands gently. "Nina. From the look in your eyes, this is something you need to tell someone. You can tell me. I will help you with whatever you need."

Chapter 68

With that reassurance, Nina Perez told Jillian Jackson her life's story. There were many tears and some heavy sobs along the way, but after almost two hours, the story had been told.

Jillian's face was as sober as it had ever been when Nina ended her revelation. There were no words she could find to convey how her heart felt. She knew what Nina needed. Jillian laid her pen down; her legal pad nearly filled, and gently pushed her rolling chair back from her desk. She quietly moved to the front of her desk and sat down in the matching leather chair next to Nina. She reached for the Mexican woman whom she had known for over twenty years and pulled Nina's head over onto her own shoulder. Together the two women held each other and wept.

After a few moments, Jillian held Nina by the shoulders, looked deep into Nina's eyes and said, "I do not want you to worry. If everything you have just told me is true, and I want you to know that I do not doubt your word in the least, you have done nothing wrong. However, it would seem we have some work ahead of us to make this all end well. I need to go over my notes again and come up with a plan."

Nina felt immensely better than when she walked into Jillian's office. The old saying that baring your soul is good for your spirit was true.

Nina wiped the last of her tears from her cheeks and said, "Jillian, thank you for listening. I hope this does not make you think less of me. I didn't know what I should do next?"

Jillian herself was not sure of that either. "Nina, I think you were a brave young woman. I admire the courage you had all those years ago and even more for the courage you had today in coming to me with this. For now I do not think you should mention any of this to anyone."

Nina, feeling relieved from years of holding such a secret, questioned Jillian. "Not even Hector?"

Jillian was quite sure of her instinct. "I am afraid not even Hector. From what you have told me someone could be trying to find the truth or attempting to lure you out. I think the fewer people who know would be better.

"I will make some calls and meet with people who can help. I will not mention specifics, just generalizations of our conversation. I want to get some prospective on how deep and wide this goes."

Jillian looked at the sandwiches still sitting on her desk. "Nina, I think we should both try to eat at least a little. Let's try relaxing a few minutes and have our lunch."

Nina had to agree. She was finally feeling as though she could eat.

Twenty minutes later Jillian opened the door and motioned for Nina to walk through the doorway first. Nina turned and hugged Jillian again.

Jillian reminded her, "Do not worry, Nina. I will call you tomorrow. Go home. Drive safely and try to relax."

Nina tried to smile. "Yes, Mrs. Jackson, I mean, Jillian, I will. I have just enough time to pick up your grandchildren from day camp and get them home in time to start Melissa and Bryce's dinner. I cannot thank you enough for seeing me so quickly. Thanks too for all your kind words."

Jillian watched Nina Perez walk away from her office. She knew that Carol was staring at her with the greatest of curiosity.

Jillian turned to Carol and rattled off instructions. "Please see if Linda in Research is available now. I will need time with Evan Gibson first thing tomorrow morning. Can you clear my calendar for tomorrow? You might have to clear things for the entire week."

Carol was stunned by the requests. "Yes. I will call Linda right away. You need time with Evan Gibson from the District Attorney's office? Has Nina done something wrong?"

Jillian knew that as her administrative assistant she would have to explain everything to Carol soon, but for today, she wanted to absorb the tale told by Nina before sharing too much too soon.

She replied, with more shortness than usual, "Yes, Evan from the DA's office. No, Nina has done nothing wrong. I just need some advice from him. After I have compiled things, I will explain everything to you. Thank you for understanding."

Jillian turned and went back into her office, again shutting the door. Carol started spinning her Rolodex to find the numbers needed to make the calls her boss had just asked of her.

Chapter 69

As scheduled, Madison, Ray and Megan met Larkyn Belanger at one o'clock on Monday for lunch at a delicatessen three blocks from Larkyn's office. Madison wanted an update after the personal ad had run for the past three days.

As the group entered the deli, Larkyn waved to them from a corner table for four that she had secured.

Larkyn greeted Madison with a warm hug and said, "Hi. I just got here and thought I would grab a table while there was one available. We can order at the counter and they will deliver to the table."

Ray told Megan what he wanted and said as he gave Megan a fifty-dollar bill, "I will sit here and hold onto the table. You ladies get whatever you want, lunch is my treat today."

Megan grabbed the crisp bill from her uncle's hand quickly and smiled. "You heard him, ladies. Let's go order something really good."

Madison and Larkyn laughed as they followed Megan to the line of customers waiting to order. They studied the menu that was written on a large chalkboard with multi-colored chalk that hung high over the counter. The selections all sounded delicious and it was a difficult decision for the young women. They were still contemplating their choices when they reached the head of the line. Madison was the first to rattle off her order, followed by Larkyn with Megan last with her own and Ray's orders.

After paying, the trio headed for the beverage dispensing area to fill their cups before returning to the table where Ray was sitting.

As she set her drink on the table, Madison anxiously asked Larkyn, "I just cannot wait any longer, Larkyn. Have you received any calls that may help me?"

Larkyn was truly sorry as she replied. "I'm afraid not yet, Madison. I followed up on a few calls this morning, but nothing panned out. I do not want you to worry yet. Remember I told you that it can be the later calls that come with the most helpful information. Someone out there may need a few days to think his or her situation over before coming forward."

Ray wanted to help reassure Madison. "I've been thinking. We all assume that a female wrote the note Rosemary found. That could set the stage for several different current-day scenarios. One I keep coming back to in my mind is that this woman might be happily married with a new family today. Madison, you might have been the child from an abusive relationship that is a complete secret to her current family. In that case, the woman may need much soul-searching before coming forward. She may feel that leaving some secrets buried is the best thing for everyone."

Larkyn was nodding as Ray spoke. "That is exactly correct. We placed that personal ad to not just tug on someone's memory, but his or her heart and conscience as well. Someone who truly cared about you wrote the words in the original note. That person was pleading for help. That same person has to feel the need to come forward. But first they must feel safe in revealing themselves."

Megan was not about to let her friend give up hope so soon. "I think Uncle Ray and Larkyn are right. Within the next few days, I believe a call will come in that not only sheds some light, but clarifies your world."

Madison smiled as she looked at the faces of the people around her who were so desperate to help her find herself. There was no way she could give up hope with these three supporting her.

Their lunch arrived and they engaged in lighter conversation while enjoying superb sandwiches.

Chapter 70

Jillian Jackson was still digesting the information she had received during Nina Perez's earlier visit to her office. She could not fully grasp the series of events and tragedies that had been a part of Nina's life over the past quarter of a century. She was determined to help this wonderful woman end her turmoil and bring peace and closure to what might involve multiple families.

Jillian was startled back to reality by a tap on her closed door. She answered, "Yes, come in."

The door slowly opened and Linda Butler, a legal research consultant, entered the office, shutting the door behind her. She was a middle aged woman who had worked in the legal system during most of her career. Linda had brown eyes and her shiny, dark brown hair was tucked behind her ears and angled down under the sides of her face. She stood five foot five inches and some would say she was full-figured.

Linda started as a legal secretary in a small law firm after two years at a community college where she completed a paralegal program. After seven years she moved to a position as the assistant to a prominent judge in Dona Ana County. Five years later, after taking additional classes at the state university, Linda Butler found her current employment opportunity as a research consultant within Jillian's law firm.

Linda addressed Jillian with admiration. "Carol said you needed to see me. Do you have a case you need my assistance on?"

Jillian, not knowing where to begin, said, "Yes. A client has reached out to me with a very unique situation. I plan on consulting with Evan Gibson from the DA's office, as well as Manuel Escobar from our criminal defense group."

"It sounds like a serious case. How can I help you?"

"First, I must make it clear that this case is not to be discussed with anyone outside the core group of individuals that I select. It is not that I believe you have ever overstepped the values of this firm, but this particular case is quite personal to me. I want to be sure that all my options have been weighed and my plan is in order before going public."

Linda had never divulged proprietary information, but hearing Jillian state the case was personal, she fully understood why the request was being stressed.

"I fully understand. I would never betray any of our clients."

Jillian motioned for Linda to take a seat. She took a deep breath and began to relate Nina's case. As she had instructed Nina, Jillian started at the beginning and concluded with the latest revelation.

When Jillian came to the end of the account of the events she said to Linda, "I think you understand now why I stressed complete secrecy at the beginning of this meeting."

Linda Butler was nearly as shocked as Jillian Jackson had been earlier. "Yes, I certainly do. May I ask how credible you find your client?"

Jillian did not hesitate in defending Nina Perez. "Though I will not divulge my client's name at this time, I believe every word of her story. I have known this woman for over twenty years and have never had reason to question her character."

Linda smiled. "That's good to hear, because this certainly could turn into a very public case."

"I realize that will be inevitable, probably sooner than later. I just want to make sure I have all the appropriate background information. That is why I had Carol call you in. I also want to insure my client has no charges issued against her. That is why I want to consult with the DA's office."

193

Linda was hesitant on Jillian's last comment. "I would not be so sure about that. This client may not have directly been involved in a crime, but she certainly aided in covering it up for all these years."

Jillian's voice was firm as she nodded. "I realize that, but I am hoping that the information my client will be bringing to the table will outweigh any criminal consequences."

Linda hoped the attorney was correct. "How, or where, would you like me to begin?"

Jillian had made notes on her legal pad under Linda Butler's name. She began to read them off. "First, you will need to pull all public and police records, along with newspaper accounts of the case. I'm sure information will be abundant on the internet, but getting the actual police records might prove more difficult. Do you have any thoughts on that?"

"Yes, as a matter of fact, I do. I have worked several times with Detective Samantha Harper from our local police force. Sami, as she prefers to be called, has been able to work with other police departments across the country in order to obtain information. If you agree, I could contact her."

Jillian thought for a moment before replying. "Yes, let's get her onboard. I would prefer to discuss the case in person with her, though. Do you think she could meet tomorrow?"

"I'll call her as soon as our meeting is over."

"Good. I believe we are done here. Carol can help you with setting a time to meet with Sami Harper tomorrow", Jillian said as she concluded their meeting.

Chapter 71

During the remainder of the afternoon Attorney Jillian Jackson made a file documenting Nina's account of events and created a timetable for her own reference. She realized there were a few gaps in the timeline and made notes to herself to question Nina during their next meeting.

Jillian was also able to catch Manuel Escobar in his office. She brought him up to speed on the case and obtained his availability for the next day. Jillian wanted him in attendance when she spoke with Evan Gibson from the DA's office.

Though she knew she stressed to Nina not to divulge any details, Jillian's mind kept coming back to the fact that her daughter, Melissa, and her grandchildren would have to be given a cover story. Nina would need to meet with Jillian and several other individuals over the course of the upcoming days. Melissa would need to make other arrangements for the children's care. She picked up the receiver on her desk phone and pushed the speed dial button for her daughter's home.

Nina Perez was alone in the kitchen when the phone rang. She answered, "Hello, this is the Baxter residence."

Jillian was glad she had caught Nina before she left for home. "Hello, Nina, it is Jillian. I wanted to check on you. I hope you are feeling better since we talked."

As earlier in the day, Jillian's kind voice calmed Nina. "Yes, I am still a little nervous, but you made me feel much better. Thank you again."

"Nina, I am arranging some meetings that you will have to attend this week. I was thinking that you should ask Melissa for a few days off."

Nina was apprehensive over how Melissa would react to the events she had described to Jillian. She also did not want to lie to her employer about why she was unable to do her job.

Nina shared her concern with Jillian. "I am not sure what to say. I cannot say we are going away, because Hector will still be here working. What do you think I should tell Melissa?"

Jillian offered an idea. "Nina, I could swing by on my way home. We could explain to Melissa, together, that you have a legal issue that I am helping you with and therefore you will need some time off. Would you like me to do that?"

Nina felt tears forming in her eyes. "Yes, thank you. I just do not want Melissa to think I am a criminal."

Jillian was smiling in her office as she replied. "Don't worry about that. I will reassure her you are not in trouble with the law. I should be leaving the office in about thirty minutes. Do you expect Melissa home by then?"

Nina nodded in the empty kitchen. "Yes, she should be here by then. I will tell her you are stopping by."

The women said their farewells and ended the call.

Chapter 72

When Tuesday morning dawned in San Angelo, Texas, Catherine Wallace was feeling like a new person. It had been a full week since she had taken ill, but today, looking out at the clear blue sky, Catherine felt well enough to be up and about. As she walked across her and Nathan's master bedroom, her husband appeared in the doorway.

Nathan Wallace was a tall, lean gentleman. His gray hair was thinning with age, but still made him look distinguished. He had strong, brown eyes and bore a tanned complexion, partially obtained from many rounds of golf.

"Good Morning. Are you the same woman that has been hiding out in bed the past week?" he asked with a smile on his face.

Catherine returned the smile. "No, she has left. I am your loving wife who cannot wait to have breakfast on the terrace with you. I cannot believe how much better I feel today."

Nathan had been quite concerned about his wife the past few days. Even after a trip to the doctor and the pharmacy, Catherine just had not recovered as quickly as he hoped.

"You must have gotten that summer flu with a vengeance. It will certainly be good to see your lovely, smiling face and sparkling bright blue eyes across the table from me. I will go put the coffee on and set us up on the terrace table. You take your time getting around. I'll see you downstairs shortly."

Catherine knew that a quick shower would add to her rejuvenation so she headed for their bath. After her shower, she blew her white hair dry and applied just a touch of makeup and lipstick. She appeared on the terrace looking the picture of health, neatly dressed in white Capri pants with a red and white striped blouse in less than half an hour.

Over coffee and bagels with cream cheese and fresh jam, Catherine and Nathan discussed the weather, the news and their two grandchildren. Catherine was excited about the summer vacation plans their family had made for the first week in August. Nathan rented a beach house on Padre Island for their whole family. Luke and his wife Emma would be there, along with their children Holly and Nicholas. Nathan knew that since both grandchildren were in college, this could be the last family vacation for some time.

Catherine pushed her coffee cup aside and said to Nathan, "After I clear these dishes away, I think I will go into my study and call Yvette. I could stand to have my hair done today. I might even get my nails done. Did you have any plans for the day?"

Nathan knew his wife was feeling better. "I need to do a couple of errands. I could drop you at the salon and come back for you, if you like."

Catherine smiled at her adoring husband and said, "That would be great. Let me go call."

Nathan grabbed the plates. "I can take care of these. You go get your appointments set."

Catherine nodded and headed to her study. It had been a week since she sat at her desk. She dialed the salon number and asked for Yvette. Catherine was pleased to be able to get an appointment for eleven o'clock that morning. As she was writing the time in her calendar she noticed the stamped envelopes that had never been mailed. The top card was addressed to Graham Meriweather.

"Oh, dear", she said aloud. "These cards never got mailed. I will take them now and we can drop them at the post office on our way."

Chapter 73

Carol Storms was able to set a meeting for Tuesday morning with all the key players that Jillian Jackson requested. At a quarter to ten that morning, Carol was escorting them one by one into the large conference room which was in the northeast corner of the building.

First to arrive was Evan Gibson from the District Attorney's office. Carol met him at the reception desk and showed him to the conference room. There were windows on the outside walls of the room that provided a view of the city. When Carol reached the door, she found Manuel Escobar and Jillian Jackson already in the room.

Jillian walked across the room and to greet Evan. "Good Morning. It is nice to see you again. Thank you so much for arranging your calendar on such short notice to be able to meet with us. I assure you this matter is quite urgent."

Evan Gibson was in his forties and stood just less than six feet tall, with a muscular build from many hours at the gym. His hair was light brown and his eyes hazel. He shook hands with Jillian as he replied, "Nice to see you again as well. You have had me wondering what this secret matter could be about all night."

"We have a few more attendees to arrive before we can get started. Please feel free to get a cup of coffee and a muffin or some fruit", Jillian offered as she pointed to a rectangular table in the back of the room.

While Evan was pouring himself a cup of coffee, Linda Butler entered the room with Detective Samantha Harper. Detective

Harper, Sami, was in her mid-thirties, an athletic young woman with long yellow-blonde hair and light blue eyes.

After everyone served themselves, Jillian motioned for the group to sit at the large conference table. Carol Storms appeared at the door and asked whether Jillian needed anything else.

"No. Thank you, Carol. I believe we are set for now. Please close the door for us", Jillian replied.

After introductions were made around the table, Jillian began her to relate her conversation with Nina from the previous day. She was careful never to mention Nina Perez's name. She was determined to get immunity papers signed by the DA's office before revealing her client. Each person at the table was still hanging onto Jillian's every word when she came to the end of the facts.

Jillian looked around the table as she concluded, "As you see, a very interesting case has fallen into my lap. Naturally, you can see what a high-profile investigation this will start."

Evan Gibson was the first to speak. "I have to ask whether you believe the facts presented to you by your client."

Jillian smiled. "That question has been asked several times. Yes, based on the character of my client, I truly believe her every word. What I am not sure of is whether the personal ad she has drawn my attention to comes from a credible source."

Sami Harper joined in the conversation. "I would suggest the best way to find out is to call the number. I can get a disposable cell phone from the department that can't be traced. That way we could make an anonymous call to gather information and assure credibility before we go any further."

Jillian knew everyone would be ready to jump on this case. "Before we get too far down that path, I need to assure my client has immunity from any and all charges. I feel my client did nothing criminal. I do not want any DA's office attempting to file charges. Evan, can I get your office to agree with those terms?"

Evan Gibson knew he had to field that question to his superiors. "Jillian, I will take your request back to the office and personally support it. I can only say that I hope the DA agrees with our line of thinking. I believe the information we can gather from your client could solve a twenty-five year old case. However, we have to remember that the legal system in New Mexico is only a piece of your problem. There is another state involved and the Feds will want in on this case as well."

Jillian was ahead of Evan in planning for that when she answered. "Yes, I do realize that. Sami Harper will be contacting Texas and I will personally call the local FBI office. I would like full agreement and closure on my client's immunity by the end of day. I do not want to take any longer than necessary to get to the bottom of this one. Manuel will be the point person for those signed agreements."

Evan nodded his head to Jillian and turned to face Manuel, "I will get back to you this afternoon. If all goes well, I can fax the documents over, or send them by carrier."

Sami Harper addressed Linda Butler when she said, "I will go back to the office and make some calls to Texas. Then, if Jillian agrees, I will bring a disposable cell phone back here this afternoon. Linda and I can make the call and see how much information the person on the other end of the line holds for us."

Jillian thought Sami's idea was good. "That would be great. I just do not want to give out too much information until I have my client protected."

Since it appeared the group knew what their respective next steps were, Jillian adjourned the meeting. "I want to thank you all again for taking the time this morning. I assume we will be working together frequently over the next few weeks."

Chapter 74

Brian McGregor was sitting in his Chief of Detectives office in Abilene, Texas drinking what was probably his sixth cup of coffee. He was looking at his calendar with disbelief that it was the last day of June.

"Tomorrow I will turn the page on this calendar and it will be July again", he thought to himself. Brian McGregor knew that every July, on the anniversary of the birth of her first grandchild, Catherine Wallace would make a call to him. He was saddened to think that yet another year had passed on what was doomed to be an unsolved kidnapping.

As Brian drew closer to retirement he found himself often reflecting on those few cases that were especially hard to leave unsolved. Olivia Meriweather's kidnapping was one such case.

"If only I could give Mrs. Wallace some closure before I retire", the Irish detective prayed in a wishful manner. He could not have known that his very next phone call might be the answer to his prayer.

The loud ringer on his desk phone brought Brian McGregor back from his deep thoughts. He answered on the second ring. "Hello, this is Chief McGregor."

Sami Harper was on the other end of the line, "Yes, Chief McGregor, my name is Samantha Harper. I am a detective in Las Cruces, New Mexico. I would like to speak to the lead detective on a kidnapping case that occurred over twenty-five years ago."

Brian McGregor's interest in the call heightened immediately. "Good morning, Detective Harper. I would be happy to assist you on that. Could you please give me the victim's name?"

"Please call me Sami. The victim's name is Olivia Meriweather. I was hoping that the detectives who worked the case might still be with your police force."

Brian's normally rosy complexion turned pale at the mention of Olivia Meriweather's name.

"Detective Harper, I mean Sami, that is indeed an old case. You are in luck, though, because I happen to have been the lead detective on that case. I'm sorry to say there have been no substantiated leads in many years. May I ask your interest in this case?"

Sami Harper knew that she could not reveal the full depth of her information at this time. She abbreviated the details to Brian McGregor.

"We might have a source with certain details concerning this case. The individual's lawyer is in the process of investigating the credibility of the information and securing immunity for her client."

As passionate as Brian was about the Meriweather case, he did not like hearing the word immunity.

"I hope no one is trying to grant immunity to the person responsible for that baby's kidnapping. I want to see whoever took Olivia Meriweather punished to the fullest extent of the law."

Sami was sympathetic to Brian's emotions and tried to explain. "The source does not appear to be the kidnapper, but rather another possible victim. As I stated, we are still gathering the details. The reason I called your office was to request any case files and details you might be able to share with our office."

Brian was not going to let another police force have this particular case without his direct involvement.

"Sami, I will do you one better. I would like to bring the records to New Mexico personally. Since I was the lead detective, you certainly can't ask for a better resource."

Sami was not fully sure of the reason behind Brian's offer, but she was not about to turn away assistance from someone who had firsthand knowledge of the case.

"Chief McGregor, we would be grateful for your help in this matter. When would you be able to travel here?"

Brian McGregor was already mentally packing his bag as he answered. "I would like to be there as soon as possible. Let me see if I can arrange a flight, or better yet I might just drive over. That way I can bring the case file easier. As you might guess, it's a large file."

Sami Harper gave her contact information and her office's address. The two detectives discussed some additional logistics before ending the call.

Brian McGregor stood up behind his desk as soon as the call ended. He ran his hand across the top of his baldhead in amazement.

As if speaking to her, he said, "Do not give up yet, Mrs. Wallace. I might just have some new information before Olivia's upcoming birthday."

Brian knew he was unrealistic to feel hope for a case that was doomed to end with sadness. However, he, like Mrs. Wallace, wanted closure, no matter what that might mean.

Brian was not a very tall man, standing five foot, ten. His build had become stockier since sitting behind the desk as the Chief for the past fifteen years. His reddish-brown hair had long ago turned white and left him bald on top. He had light blue eyes.

Brian moved across his office and entered the area where his detectives' desks were. He turned right and headed to the desk of his youngest son, Detective Timothy McGregor. When Tim had made detective, one of Brian's old partners, Detective Carlos de Marco was in need of a new partner. Brian had trained and worked with Carlos for several years. Brian knew that Carlos would teach Tim well and be a trusted partner for his son.

As Brian approached Tim McGregor's desk, he felt a renewed energy. "Detective McGregor, how would you like to take a road trip?"

Tim McGregor looked up from the paperwork he was filling out. He was in his early thirties with the same reddish-brown hair his father had in his younger days, but with his mother's green eyes.

The younger Irishman addressed his father, "Good Morning, Chief. Me, take a road trip with you? Is it time for lunch already?"

Brian knew that his son had a great sense of humor and tried to give some back. "No, this would be a trip to investigate a lead in a cold case. Are you up for some time with your old man, I mean your boss?"

Tim knew from his father's tone of voice that there must be credible information to follow up on. He was honored to have the opportunity to work a case with his father.

Chapter 75

Tuesday afternoon Sami Harper appeared back at Jillian Jackson's legal office with a disposable cell phone from the police force's supply. She walked directly to Linda Butler's office in research.

"Linda, I brought over the cell phone we will use to make the call. I was thinking that you could pretend to be someone with information and at the same time gather as much information as you can. I will listen and make notes. With the phone being untraceable, no one will know where the call is coming from."

Linda Butler was slightly nervous over making the call to the number printed in the personal ad, but also slightly excited knowing what could be at stake should this call lead to more credible information.

Sami was delighted to tell Linda about her conversation with Chief McGregor in Texas. "He was very interested in what we have, though I kept the information very generic. He plans to gather up the case file and travel to Las Cruces by tomorrow. I think he is quite anxious to hear more."

Linda reported that others had made productive results as well. "Jillian has assurances from Evan Gibson that our DA's office will sign the immunity agreement. Evan's superior is contacting the Taylor County District Attorney's office in Texas this afternoon to request the same. Jillian is still dealing with the Feds, but feels confident enough for us to make an initial call."

Sami was setting up the phone while instructing Linda, "Do not give out too much information. You should try to question the person we talk to about specific details so we can validate."

Linda and Sami both had their notes from Jillian's meetings on the desk before them. Linda pressed the numbers from the ad. They heard the beeps through the speaker of the phone as the numbers were pressed and then the ringing began.

Chapter 76

In Deming, New Mexico, Larkyn Belanger was finishing a late lunch at her desk. She had not received a call regarding Madison's personal ad since the day before. Larkyn was starting to wonder what her next step should be in helping Madison find her identity. Just as she tossed her empty sandwich wrapper into her trash basket, the special cell phone rang.

Larkyn answered and simply said, "Hello."

The woman on the other end of the call responded hesitantly, "Yes, hello. I am calling regarding the personal ad in Sunday's newspaper."

"Do you have information regarding the message in the ad?" Larkyn asked hopefully.

"I may know the person who wrote those words," the woman said.

Larkyn had created a series of questions to determine the authenticity of the callers. "I would like to ask you a few questions, if you don't mind."

The caller responded favorably, "That would be fine."

"Is Baby M male or female?" Larkyn's first question had a fifty-fifty chance for the caller.

"Baby M is a female."

Larkyn smiled and thought silently, "One down, let's move on to the next one."

Aloud Larkyn asked the next question. "How long ago were the words written?"

The caller wasted no time in saying, "More than twenty-five years ago."

Larkyn's interests were peaked now. She had not gotten to question number three often. "Here is my third question. On what were the words written."

In Las Cruces, Linda and Sami were thumbing through their notes until they found an appropriate answer. "The words were written on a piece of paper the writer found inside the glove compartment of a car."

In Deming, Larkyn Belanger nearly fainted when she heard the answer. The piece of paper Madison had revealed with the note written on was thought to be some form of vehicle registration or rental agreement. This caller might be the one they were hoping to hear from.

Larkyn had paused long enough to worry the caller, who asked, "Are you still there?"

Larkyn answered quickly, "Yes, I am here. I have one more question. Could you tell me where this note would have been found?"

On the other end of the line, Linda and Sami needed some confirmation as well. Linda replied to Larkyn, "I have answered your first three questions correctly. I will state that the note was found near a building. Why don't you tell me what type of building and I'll be the one to verify your answer?"

Larkyn wasn't sure about going along with the caller, but decided it was her best shot at gaining her trust. She did not provide specifics when she said, "Near a church."

Larkyn was even more confident that she was speaking with a reliable source when the caller said, "That's right."

Larkyn needed to arrange a meeting. "Would you and the person who wrote the note be able to meet with me in person to discuss this?"

Linda Butler wanted to ask another question. "Before we meet I would like to ask one more question. Do you believe you are Baby M?"

Larkyn did not want to misrepresent herself or her client, so she replied truthfully. "No, the woman who has the note is a client. I am a personal investigator helping her locate the writer."

Linda had a sudden sense of familiarity in something just said. "What is a personal investigator? Are you with the police?"

Larkyn wanted to calm her caller. "No, I am not with the police. My client has not been involved with the police. I am a private investigator, but I prefer the word personal. I feel it helps my clients trust me with their personal matters."

In her office in Las Cruces, Linda Butler was scrambling for a pen and piece of paper. She quickly wrote four words and shoved the piece of paper so Sami Harper could read it.

"I know this woman!!!"

Sami Harper could not believe what Linda had just written. What were the chances? She made a gesture for Linda to wrap up the call. They needed to talk in private.

In Deming, Larkyn Belanger was worried she had scared the caller off. What she did not know was that she had actually done the complete opposite.

Linda spoke next. "I need some time to speak with my friend. I will have to see whether she is willing to meet face to face. I will call you again."

Hearing the call disconnect, Larkyn Belanger sighed deeply and smiled. She felt better than she had in several days.

Chapter 77

Linda Butler gestured for Sami Harper to follow her out of her office and down the hallway toward Jillian Jackson's large office. Carol Storms was sitting at her desk and Jillian's office door was closed.

Linda addressed Carol. "Is she in? I really need to speak with her as soon as possible."

Carol picked up her phone, pressed the intercom for Jillian and said, "Linda Butler is here. She would like to see you."

Carol placed the receiver back on the phone base and gestured her hand toward the door. "She said to come right in."

Linda did not waste a second in reaching for the doorknob and opening the door. Sami Harper was right behind her, unsure why Linda was in such an excited state.

Linda did not wait to be greeted, and did not take a seat. She blurted out the words she had been holding in. "I know who I was speaking with when we called the personal ad phone number."

Jillian Jackson was quite surprised at Linda's revelation. "Are you sure?"

"I am positive. The woman who answered the ad's phone number was Larkyn Belanger. She is an investigator from Deming."

Jillian was still a little skeptical. "How can you be so sure?"

Linda stated her reasons. "I have worked with Larkyn on a few cases over the years. She makes it a point to call herself a Personal, rather than a Private, Investigator. She thinks it sounds more reassuring to her clients. The woman today called herself a Personal Investigator. Once she announced her profession, I listened closer to the tone of her voice and I'm sure it was Larkyn."

Jillian tried to assess what this meant to Nina's case. "Linda, how would you say this fact plays into my client's case?"

Linda stated firmly. "If Larkyn Belanger took this case; I would bet that the person in possession of that note is legit. I think your client's case just got a whole lot more interesting."

Chapter 78

In Deming, Larkyn Belanger was anxious to report her most recent call to Madison. Though she did not want to get Madison's hopes up without warrant she had a responsibility to her client to keep her updated.

Larkyn used her office line to call Madison's cell phone. After three rings, she heard Madison's voice. "Hello, Larkyn. Do you have news?"

"So much for surprise with call ID", Larkyn chucked to herself.

"Hi Madison, yes, I do have some news. I received a call just a few minutes ago that was the most promising of any call yet."

At the other end of the call, Madison was so excited she reached over and squeezed Megan's arm. The two young ladies were shopping in the local boutiques to pass the time.

"How promising is it?" Madison asked of Larkyn.

"This caller knew the right answers to the first three questions and I went on to number four. When I asked where the note would have been found, this woman turned the question around on me to verify I had the facts. When I said near a church, the woman said that was correct. How promising would you find that?"

Madison gasped and practically squealed with delight. "I would call that VERY promising. Were you able to set up a meeting?"

Larkyn knew she was about to disappoint her client. "I'm afraid not. The woman said she was calling for a friend. I couldn't determine whether that was the truth or not. Anyway, she said she needs a little time to discuss with her friend and said she would call back. No ID was listed on the call, so she was probably using a disposable cell as well."

Madison was a little saddened, but still hopeful. "I have to believe she will call back. If she does, I want to meet her as soon as possible. Can you call me as soon as you hear again?"

Larkyn was nodding as she confirmed, "You know I will do that. I wanted to give you this great bit of news. You have a good day. Hope to speak with you soon."

Madison was not ready to end their conversation. "Larkyn, there's one more thing. Tomorrow is the first of July. You may not know this, but my birthday is the fourteenth. Now I'm not sure whether my birthday is really my birthday. Do you understand? I need to solve this so I know when to celebrate turning twenty-eight."

Larkyn felt such emotion for her client. "Madison, I will do everything possible so that you can celebrate on the right day this year."

Madison felt a little better. "Thank you. Good-bye."

Madison closed her cell phone and practically dragged Megan out of the boutique so she could share her information from Larkyn.

Chapter 79

Before the crack of dawn on Wednesday morning, Brian and Timothy McGregor were in a vehicle headed southwest from Abilene, Texas on Interstate 20. Brian was taking the first shift at the wheel. Once the sun came up, he wanted to be able to review the case file while Tim drove for a few hours.

The men stopped for a break and to get fresh coffee about six o'clock. Tim jumped into the driver's seat at that time. As they drove toward Interstate 10, Brian pulled the first of the case files into his lap and began to review aloud.

"Olivia Meriweather was not quite five months old when she was kidnapped. The kidnapper took her in broad daylight right in front of the Meriweather estate. The problem, Tim, was that the police were not called in until after a ransom drop by the family did not result in the return of the infant."

Tim McGregor was astonished that the police were not involved early on in the case. "Why didn't they contact the police sooner?"

Brian shook his head. "I was never actually convinced why. They gave the usual reasons; that the kidnapper told them the baby would be harmed if they went to the police; that the kidnapper only wanted the money; that they felt capable of handling the situation. We will never know, and they will never know whether calling the police would have brought their baby home."

Tim needed to be well versed on the case before they reached Las Cruces, New Mexico. He continued to listen as his father reviewed aloud the facts of the case.

"On the day of the kidnapping, the new young nanny was about to take the baby for a walk. The baby was in the stroller and they were headed down the front walk to the street. The statements made say that the baby's step-grandmother, Patricia Meriweather, called out to the nanny. She wanted her to come back to the house to get an extra blanket for Olivia. The nanny left the baby unattended in the stroller at the end of the walk. The nanny, one Gabriella Garcia, stated she hurried back to the door for the blanket and when she returned to the stroller, the baby was gone. Gabriella later stated that there was a slight delay when getting the blanket, as the older Mrs. Meriweather dropped it while handing it to Gabriella. The two women both bent over to pick it up. It was assumed that it was at that point the kidnapper was able to grab the baby unnoticed."

Criminals who target children always disgust Detective Tim McGregor.

"The kidnapper must have been watching and jumped at the point when both women were distracted. Maybe he, or she, had planned to grab the baby while the nanny was walking, but an opportunity presented itself earlier," Tim suggested.

Brian nodded. "That was our original thought as well. Within a few hours an envelope was delivered to the Meriweather estate with a crude note put together with words cut from magazines. The kidnapper demanded one hundred thousand dollars for the safe return of baby Olivia. The note also stated not to call the police, or the baby would be harmed. The family was given until the next day at noon to put the money together. It stated another note with instructions would follow."

Tim asked curiously, "Why only one hundred thousand dollars? Even that many years ago, I imagine the Meriweather family could have managed to pay much more than that."

"The meager amount was part of the logic used to identify the prime suspect."

Tim was quick to interject. "There was a prime suspect? Were you ever able to locate this person?"

Brian shook his head. "A few weeks earlier Graham Meriweather had to dismiss the prior nanny. Her name was

Mia Sanchez, a young Mexican woman whom the late Lydia Meriweather had hired shortly after Olivia's birth. It seems the family caught this nanny trying to steal some of Graham's deceased wife's jewelry. It was logical that a hundred grand was a lot of money to a young Mexican woman in those days. She might not have realized how much more she could have asked for. The family felt that she wanted retribution for being fired. That was another reason they initially felt they could handle the matter without police assistance. Graham Meriweather was convinced that Mia Sanchez would never harm his daughter. He felt once she had the cash, he would get Olivia back."

Tim, needing to know more, asked, "So what went wrong?"

"Patricia Meriweather's son from a previous marriage, a Mr. Hamilton, worked within the Meriweather financial establishments. He was able to bring the cash needed to Graham for the ransom drop. He also volunteered to make the money drop, leaving Graham at home in case the kidnapper called with instructions on where to find Olivia. The drop was made, supposedly exactly as instructed in the second note, but no further contact was ever made by the kidnapper. After twenty-four hours, Graham Meriweather called in the police."

"Were the police able to find any leads?" Tim asked.

Brian answered his son's question. "No, unfortunately all leads turned to dead ends. We searched the nanny's apartment and found signs that the baby had been there. We found an empty baby bottle and a small pink bootie with a drop of blood on it. The place was a mess, as if someone had left in a hurry and had no plans to return. We even found the duffle bag that had been used for the money drop. Everything pointed to this Mia Sanchez, but we were never able to locate her. We even contacted the Mexican officials, who were able to find many women with that name, however, none of them turned out to be the right one. It was as if that particular Mia Sanchez disappeared into thin air, along with baby Olivia Meriweather."

Chapter 80

When Julie Collins arrived at the Meriweather estate for work on Wednesday morning, Patricia Meriweather and an older gentleman were waiting for her. Patricia made the introductions.

"Julie, I would like you to meet Dr. Simon Haskins. Dr. Haskins has just examined Graham. I wanted you to meet the doctor, since you are responsible for Graham's care here at home."

Julie extended her right hand and shook the doctor's hand. She thought his hands to be rather rough for a doctor, but decided it was due to age, not his profession. Dr. Haskins appeared to be in his late sixties, had greenish brown eyes, but had lost most of his hair. The doctor stood shorter than Julie had expected.

Julie addressed the doctor regarding her concerns for her patient. "Dr. Haskins, Mr. Meriweather does not appear to have much strength lately. He also seems somewhat depressed. Should there be a change in his medications?"

Dr. Simon Haskins seemed prepared for Julie's questions. "Miss Collins, you need to realize that Graham Meriweather is in the final stages of his disease. He has been fighting, and winning, the battle with his kidney disease for many years. It appears as if the disease is now winning. Mr. Meriweather is adamant about staying in his home for as long as possible. The most important things you can do for him at this point are to keep him calm, comfortable and make sure he takes his medications. I am very sorry to admit that at this point, even with dialysis, it is only a matter of time."

Patricia Meriweather added, "Dr. Haskins has asked whether we would like him to recommend additional nursing assistance at this time. I said that you and I could discuss that matter later today. I am sure you would enjoy a day off now and then."

Julie Collins smiled and nodded. She hoped Mrs. Meriweather was indeed being thoughtful, rather than insinuating that Julie was not doing a good job.

Julie answered, somewhat snidely, "Yes, we should discuss that matter. Maybe you would even like help in the evenings and on weekends. It must be quite a burden on you as well."

Patricia Meriweather led the doctor to the door as Julie headed up the open, winding staircase. When Julie looked back briefly, she thought she saw Mrs. Meriweather give something to Dr. Haskins. Julie wondered whether Dr. Haskins had just been paid for his home visit.

Chapter 81

On that same Wednesday in San Angelo, Texas, Milton Donovan was returning from getting the daily newspaper at the stand on the corner. As he opened the front door he yelled to his mother that he was home. He laid the newspaper on the table and turned the coffee maker on. Gurgling noises soon came from the coffee maker and the smell of fresh brewing coffee filled the kitchen. Realizing his mother had not answered him he headed into the living room.

Milton called out again. "Mother, I just started the coffee. What would you like for breakfast today?"

The door to Milton's mother's bedroom was still closed. He walked to the left side of the living room and knocked on the closed door. There was no answer.

Milton gently opened the door and called to his mother again. As he slid the door halfway open he saw his mother lying on the floor next to her bed. He ran over and found the woman unconscious.

Milton Donovan grabbed the nearest phone and pressed 9-1-1. When the dispatch operator answered, he was quite nervous. "Please help me. My mother has fallen and I cannot get her to answer me."

The operator asked for the address and assured Milton that an ambulance would be on its way immediately.

Forty-five minutes later in the emergency room of the San Angelo Mercy Hospital, Milton Donovan waited for the doctors to tell him what had happened to his mother.

A young doctor walked through the double doors holding a clip chart, and said, "I am looking for Mrs. Donovan's family."

Milton stood up and met the doctor in the middle of the room. "I am her son, Milton Donovan."

"Hello. My name is Dr. Peter Austin. Your mother has broken her hip. She must have fallen while getting out of bed. She will require surgery. Otherwise, her health seems fine. I don't see any problems arising from the surgery. If you would like to come with me, you can see her before we head to the operating room."

Milton was somewhat relieved to hear that she would be fine. "Thank you. How long will the operation take? How long will she have to be in the hospital?"

The young doctor tried to reassure Milton. "She should be in surgery a few hours" he said. "For a woman of her age, she will probably be in the hospital up to a week and then require rehab, possibly as an out-patient, after that."

Milton Donovan did not like the prospect of his mother being in the hospital for a week. He had not been alone in many years. It was an unwelcome thought for him now. Milton's mother helped him to remember his own medications. Missing his daily meds allowed the confusion and delusions to invade his brain. Milton would have to be very careful the next few days to stay on his correct dosages. He was also worried about the medical bills that might pile up. One could say that Milton Donovan was becoming very stressed out.

Chapter 82

Carol Storms arrived at work earlier than usual on Thursday morning. She was setting up the large conference room for her boss, Attorney Jillian Jackson. Jillian had given her a list of the attendees the afternoon before. Carol knew most of the names on the list, but a few were unknown to her. She learned that there would be two detectives from Texas arriving for the meeting. Carol was not sure what all the secrecy was about, but she would learn soon enough. Jillian had also included Carol in the meeting.

By eight-thirty the conference room was ready. Nina Perez was the first to arrive with her husband, Hector. Jillian escorted them into her private office and asked Carol to bring them coffee. Jillian wanted them to stay in her office until all the others had arrived. Carol could tell that Nina was very nervous and her husband seemed somewhat confused.

Shortly after nine o'clock Jillian Jackson stood at the head of the long, rectangular conference table and addressed the seven people at the table.

"Good Morning. I am Attorney Jillian Jackson. I want to start by thanking all of you for your assistance and quick responses to the requests I have made over the past few days. I realize I have asked for a leap of faith on your behalf to believe in the integrity of my client. After today's meeting, I guarantee you will not regret your involvement in this case."

Jillian then introduced each individual sitting at the table and told the others of their respective role in the case.

"Linda Butler works for my firm in our research group. She has been helping to validate the facts given by my client."

"Samantha Harper, better known as Sami, is a detective with the Las Cruces police department."

"Brian McGregor is the Chief of Detectives in Abilene, Texas. With him is Detective Timothy McGregor, also from Abilene"

"Manuel Escobar is a criminal defense attorney from this law firm. He assisted in obtaining the immunity agreements for my client."

"Evan Gibson is an Assistant District Attorney from our Dona Ana County's office. Evan has secured immunity agreements from both Dona Ana County here in New Mexico and from Taylor County in Texas with assistance from the District Attorney in that county, Betsy Littleton."

"Brock Richards is from the local branch of the FBI. He has obtained authorization for federal immunity for my client."

"I have also asked for a court stenographer to be in attendance. I want to be sure to have all details recorded. Today we have the pleasure of having Melanie Duncan with us. Welcome to you all."

At that point, Jillian Jackson used the telephone on the wall to call Carol Storms. She asked Carol to bring her client to the conference room. No one at the table knew quite what to expect, but the sight of a middle-aged Mexican woman had not been anyone's first guess.

Jillian asked Nina to sit at the head of the long table. She motioned for Carol to take Hector to the right side of the table where two empty seats awaited them.

"Ladies and Gentlemen I would like to introduce you to Nina Theresa Garrido Perez. Her husband, Hector Perez is sitting next to my assistant, Carol Storms."

Jillian stood behind Nina and placed a hand on her right shoulder for reassurance as she continued to speak.

"I have asked Nina to tell us the events in her life that have led her to us today. As I asked of her when she first related these events to me, she will begin at the earliest point in time and bring us to the present day. I know that you will have many questions as you listen to Nina. I would ask that you hold all questions until she is finished. I do not want her to lose her line of thought. If you could please make a notation to yourself regarding the event and your question, I promise that we will get to them all before we adjourn today."

Jillian Jackson sat in the first chair on the left side of the table. She wanted to be able to give Nina strength and guidance while she was presenting her amazing account of events. As she reached over and squeezed Nina's left hand, she quietly said, "Everything is okay Nina. You can begin now."

Chapter 83

Nina Perez began to speak in a soft voice, but remembering Jillian's instructions to speak so she could be heard, she quickly raised her voice.

"My name is Nina Perez. I grew up in a small village in Mexico. When I was sixteen, my cousin and one of her friends were in a car accident. My cousin's friend was from the United States and had come to visit my cousin and her family. This friend died as a result of the accident. My cousin was in the hospital for many days. When I went to visit, she asked me to take her purse and other personal items home with me. When I got home, I opened the purse and discovered that it also contained the wallet belonging to her dead friend. Some pieces of this young lady's identification were still in her wallet. She had a social security card and a photo ID. Her photo looked very much like me. We had very similar skin coloring, facial shape and hairstyle.

"I wanted desperately to come to the United States. I wanted a better life than what I had in Mexico. Looking at that photo I saw my opportunity. I thought I could use her identification to get into your country. Then I was sure I could find a job and make lots of money. I was only a teenager, but I had big dreams. Assuming this young lady's identity, I became Mia Sanchez."

At the mention of name Mia Sanchez, Brian McGregor came to full attention. Was this woman at the head of the table the suspected kidnapper herself? Why had everyone granted her immunity?

Nina continued, "I was able to get to Texas by using Mia's identification. However, finding a job was not as easy as I imagined. I ended up in Abilene, Texas working in a homeless shelter. I received meals and a place to sleep in exchange for helping with the cooking and cleaning. Mrs. Lydia Meriweather did volunteer work at this shelter. One day, when she was over eight months pregnant, she became lightheaded and needed to sit down. I went over to her with a glass of water. She thanked me and we talked for a few minutes that day. Over the next week she sought me out and we became friends. Just before she was due to deliver her baby, she asked if I would consider working for her as a part-time nanny. I was thrilled with her offer. I was almost eighteen by then."

Nina stopped to take a sip of water before going on. "I went to work for the Meriweathers taking care of their newborn daughter, Olivia. I was happy with my job and Mr. and Mrs. Meriweather seemed pleased with me. Things went very well until that September. That was when Mrs. Lydia Meriweather was hit and killed by a car. She had been out for a walk. I usually went with her and we pushed little Olivia in her carriage. On that day Olivia had a runny nose and we didn't think we should take her outside. I said I would stay inside with the baby. Mrs. Meriweather liked to get outside, so I insisted that she should go for her usual walk."

Nina wiped a tear from her cheek before continuing. "That was the last time I saw Mrs. Meriweather. She died that afternoon. It was a very sad time. Mr. Meriweather was so depressed over the loss of his wife. He asked me to stay through the night for a couple weeks to tend to Olivia. For the next few weeks I worked many hours taking care of the baby. Olivia was such a good baby. I felt sad that she would never know her mother."

Nina took a deep breath before her next segment. "Early in November things started going bad for me at the Meriweather home. I'm still not sure what happened. One day I reached in my sweater pocket for something and one of Mrs. Meriweather's earrings fell onto the floor. The older Mrs. Meriweather, Patricia, was in the room and picked up the earring. She gave me a very mean look and called for Mr. Meriweather. She told him I was trying to steal his dead wife's things. I swear I do not know how that earring got into my pocket. I said that maybe it fell in when I was dusting the dressers upstairs. Mr. Meriweather had some concerns, but accepted my explanation. It upset me very much to have him think I might have tried to steal from him.

"About a week later I was leaving at the end of the day. Olivia was in her crib and I was hanging up my apron and taking my jacket off the hanger when I heard something hit the floor. Both Patricia and Graham Meriweather were in the room. We all looked down and there on the floor was Lydia Meriweather's diamond necklace. I was so ashamed; not for anything I had done, but for how they both looked at me. Needless to say I was fired that day. I swear to you, someone else must have stuffed the necklace into my jacket sleeve. I could never figure out who would have wanted me fired. Maybe another member of the Meriweather's staff wanted to take over my duties caring for Olivia."

Brian McGregor was making notes on a pad. So far her story matched the information in the police records. The nanny was caught stealing and was fired. Only this woman swears she was innocent. Brian wondered whether another member of the house staff might have been setting her up. He would have to review the list of employees.

Jillian Jackson interrupted Nina. "I think we can take a ten minute break now. Please help yourself to refreshments. Restrooms are down the hall to the right."

Chapter 84

After the short break, Nina Perez began again. "After I was let go from the Meriweathers, I tried to find another job. I had managed to rent a small apartment while I was working, but would not be able to pay the rent without a job. Things went from bad to worse.

"In early December I was on my way back to my apartment with what few groceries I could afford. A tall bearded man in a long trench coat and dark glasses grabbed me and pulled me into an alley. I was scared that he was going to kill me. I tried to scream, but he kept his gloved hand over my mouth. I remember him placing a cloth over my nose. The next thing I remember is waking up on a cot in a room in what I believed to be a basement. There were no windows and the door appeared to be locked from the outside. From the cot I could see a small refrigerator, a hotplate, a few dishes and some cans of food. There was a small door in one corner that was opened enough to reveal a toilet and sink. On a sidewall was the cot I awoke on which had an old pillow and blanket. When I sat up I noticed that next to the head of the cot stood a very old crib. I had no idea where I was, or why I had been taken."

Nina was upset just remembering her ordeal. "I was left alone there for a couple of days. When I finally heard someone unlocking the door, I thought I was being rescued. I was terrified when I saw the same bearded man walk through the door. He was not alone. He was carrying a baby. I immediately realized that he had Olivia Meriweather in his arms. The man practically threw her at me. She was wrapped in her monogrammed pink blanket. He tossed a large grocery bag onto the floor and left. I heard him lock the door and then the sound of his footsteps disappeared.

"I could not believe what had just happened. Who was this Bad Man? Why had he taken Olivia? Why had he left her with me in that basement? I did not understand any of it. When I looked inside the grocery bag I found disposable diapers, baby formula, two baby bottles and some more canned food. Again I was left for a couple of days, this time with Olivia. I fed her and took care of her. Like I said earlier, Olivia was such a good baby. She recognized me. She didn't know to be afraid."

Nina Perez was shaking. Jillian reached over and patted her hand. "You are doing great. If you need a minute, that's fine. Take your time."

Nina nodded, "The next time I saw the Bad Man, he seemed very angry and in a hurry. He told me to pack up the baby; we were going for a ride. While I was gathering up Olivia's things, I laid her in the crib. That was when the bad man did a very strange thing. He pulled one of Olivia's pink booties off her tiny foot. Then he took his pocketknife out and made a quick jab into the baby's heel. Olivia screamed and I jumped. The bad man squeezed her heel until a drop of blood appeared. Then he rubbed the blood off with the bootie and put the bootie into his trench coat pocket. I grabbed the baby out of the crib and held her until she stopped crying."

Brian McGregor was making notes again. This woman knew about the bloody pink bootie. Was her story legit? Or was she a great storyteller?

Nina went on with the events of that night. "The Bad Man told me he had a gun. He carried Olivia and told me if I tried to escape or cry out for help, he would shoot her. I believed he would have done it. It was dark outside. I could not tell where we were. The Bad Man put us into a dark colored car and drove us away. He drove for a very long time. Olivia and I even fell asleep for part of the trip.

"Much later the Bad Man said he needed to gas up the car. He warned me to stay in the car and not to try to get help. He reminded me he had a gun and would use it. The Bad Man pulled into a gas station and parked at the pump that was furthest from the building. He was watching me all the time, but I was watching him too. I saw him walk to the building to pay for the gas. There were three or four other people waiting to pay. He had to wait for his turn to pay. I could see him looking back at the car to make sure I did not move. Just as the Bad Man got to the front of the line, a large white box truck drove in and parked at the pumps between the car I was in and the station. The Bad Man lost his view of me."

Nina was starting to talk too fast. Jillian reminded her to slow down.

"I grabbed up Olivia with her blanket. I looked in the glove compartment for something to write on. I found a piece of paper and a pen. I stuffed them into my pocket. I opened the car door and got out with Olivia in my arms. I used the box truck to hide us then ran into the shadow of darkness from the building next to the garage. I then ran into a short alley and came out onto a side street. I had no idea where I was or what to do. I just kept running. Then I saw the church. It was a large older church that stood on one of the four corners of two intersecting streets. There was a nativity display in the side yard. I thought it was a sign from God. I ran over to the display. I removed the doll representing the Christ Child and laid baby Olivia into that small manger bed. I covered her with her blanket and put some straw on top of the blanket. I remembered the paper and pen in my pocket. I wrote a very quick note and stuffed it into her blanket. I left Olivia Meriweather with the Virgin Mary watching over and protecting her."

Everyone in the room was astonished at this woman's account of the now famous missing Meriweather baby. They were wondering why she had come forward now.

Nina wrapped up her story. "I kept on running, but the Bad Man found me in another alley. I would not tell him where I had left the baby. He hit me until I lost consciousness. The next thing I remember was being dragged out of the backseat of the car. He pushed me over a small bank into a field. Then he kicked me and kept kicking me. I must have blacked out again. I think he thought he had killed me."

Nina's voice calmed a bit as she said, "A few days later I awoke in a small clinic in Mexico. Some farmers had found me and brought me there. The doctor at the clinic thought I would die for sure, but I lived. Until this week, I have never told anyone, not even my husband, this story."

Hector Perez was crying for his wife's pain. He had never loved her more.

Jillian handed out a photocopy of Sunday's edition of the local newspaper. "This is the reason Nina Perez is telling her story today."

After everyone had read the highlighted personal ad, Nina said confidently, "That is the note I wrote. Those are the words that were on the piece of paper I stuffed into Olivia Meriweather's blanket that cold December night."

Everyone read the ad silently. "Please help. She is in danger. I cannot protect her. Please help Baby M." The ad continued with the phone number to contact if the words sounded familiar.

Chapter 85

Looking at the people sitting around the conference table, Jillian Jackson could tell that everyone was trying to process the events Nina Perez had just presented. Jillian thought it was a good time to take another break.

"Ladies and Gentlemen, I realize we have been sitting for some time now, and you have received much information. Before we begin to address your questions, I suggest we all take a twenty minute break."

As the group began to stand and scatter, Hector Perez walked over to his wife. Nina looked up at Hector with tears running down her cheeks.

"Hector. I am so sorry. I should have told you all of this long ago. I did not want you to think I was a bad person."

Hector took Nina by the shoulders and helped her stand to face him. He looked her in the eyes and said, "Nina. I cannot believe you have been carrying this secret for all these years. I know you. You could never do a bad thing. You probably saved that baby's life that night. I am just sorry you didn't feel you could confide in me. I would have helped you deal with this long ago. Maybe it would not have been such a burden for you."

Hector then took Nina in his arms and held her while she cried on his shoulder.

Jillian came over to Nina and Hector and said, "Nina, I can take you to one of our private restrooms. I don't want you to be questioned without my being at your side."

Twenty minutes later, the group had reassembled at the table.

Jillian stood behind Nina as she spoke. "I know you must have many questions. I would like to go around the table so that each person has an opportunity to ask his or her questions."

Everyone nodded and Jillian continued. "I would like to allow the Texas detectives first chance with their questions. Since Brian McGregor led the kidnapping investigation, he should have some long unanswered questions."

Brian McGregor was grateful to be able to ask the first questions. "Thank you, Attorney Jackson. Thank you, Mrs. Perez, for coming forward to tell us your story. Without giving out specifics, you did mention a few facts that were never disclosed to the public, which does give your story credibility. I noticed that you always refer to your captor as the 'Bad Man'. Can you describe him in more detail? Had you ever seen him before?"

Nina Perez did not like picturing the Bad Man in her mind, but she was able to tell Brian McGregor, "The Bad Man is the name I assigned him in my mind all those years ago. I had never seen him before. As I said, he was quite tall. He always wore dark glasses, even when it was nighttime. He wore a hat most of the time, but when he took it off in the car, it looked as if he had on a toupee. He also had a beard and mustache. However, when I was struggling with him in the alleyway, after he caught me, I thought I felt the side of his beard give way. Maybe he used a fake beard to help hide his face. He always had a suit on under a long trench coat."

Brian McGregor was making notes and ready with his next question. "When you came back into the states, why didn't you come forward at that time?"

Nina's eyes filled with tears again as she answered. "I tried to find out what might have happened to Olivia. I went to the library and looked up old newspapers and magazines. The articles all said Olivia Meriweather had been kidnapped, that a ransom was paid and that Olivia was never seen again. I learned that Mia Sanchez was accused of the crime. I thought I would go to jail if I came forward. I never knew whether the Bad Man found her later that night, or whether someone else did."

Tim McGregor was eager to add to his father's questions. "Mrs. Perez. This personal ad refers to Baby M at the end of the note. Why didn't you write the baby's name in your note?"

Nina thought hard before answering. "I started to write Baby Meriweather, but then I had a terrible thought. If the Bad Man had kidnapped her once and threatened to harm her, what would happen if she were returned home? I was afraid he would get to her again and I would not be there to protect her. Then I thought about signing Mia, the name I was using at the time. In the end, I left it with just the letter 'M' as you see it in the ad."

To some at the table Nina's explanation almost made sense, but others were still skeptical of her whole story.

Brock Richards was one of the skeptics. Brock was an African American man in his forties, who had been working as an FBI agent for fifteen years. He was tall with broad shoulders and was not the kind of agent who liked to have unsolved cases.

Agent Richards asked, "Mrs. Perez, as you learned many years ago, your alias, Mia Sanchez, was the prime suspect in the kidnapping. Your lawyer convinced everyone at the table that her client was innocent of any and all crimes, so you have total immunity. Today you tell us a tall man with what was possibly a fake beard and dark glasses was the actual kidnapper. If you will not be able to help us identify this man, why did you come forward at this time?"

Nina could sense Brock Richards' skepticism from his words. She was careful when she replied. "When I saw the personal ad, I realized someone out there is looking for me. The person might be just someone who found my note, or by some miracle, it could be Olivia Meriweather trying to find her way home. I didn't feel I had any other choice that night but to leave her hidden from the Bad Man. Today Olivia Meriweather would be a young woman. If the person who placed this ad is Olivia, I need to find her and tell her who she is. I want to lead her home."

Jillian Jackson was proud of her client. She was addressing the questions with confidence and without fear.

Evan Gibson, from the District Attorney's office, had a question that followed Nina's last comments. "How do we know if the person who placed the ad is legit, or just by chance used Nina's words?"

Linda Butler jumped in to answer Evan. "Sami Harper and I placed a call to the number listed in the ad. Sami brought an untraceable cell from the police force, and I pretended to have information. I was also able to get some information back. The phone number goes to another untraceable cell phone that was answered by an investigator who is filtering the calls for her client. By sheer luck, I believe I know the identity of the investigator. If that proves to be correct, I would bet that her client is credible."

Sami Harper added, "I would like to have Linda call this investigator at her office and try to establish whether her theory is correct."

Jillian Jackson thought that was a good idea. "Linda, why don't you make that call? If you are right, set up a meeting with her client for tomorrow. We can meet in this room again. Most of you will want to return, I assume."

All were in agreement. Jillian could see Nina's excitement. "Nina, I'm not sure it's a good idea for you to meet the investigator's client until we have established what, if any, relationship there is to Olivia Meriweather. Don't worry. If we discover Olivia Meriweather, alive and well, you will be one of the first people we introduce her to. After all, you saved her life."

Though disappointed, Nina Perez understood and nodded to Jillian.

After reiterating the need for secrecy of what was learned that morning and exchanging contact information, the meeting was adjourned.

Chapter 86

Julie Collins was serving Graham Meriweather his lunch in bed about the same time the people in Jillian Jackson's conference room were trying to digest everything that had just been related to them by Nina Perez.

Julie helped Graham sit up and arranged his tray so that he could reach his lunch. She knew that it was unlikely Graham would eat a quarter of the soup and sandwich she had just delivered.

What Julie Collins did not notice was that while she was positioning the lunch tray table over Graham's lap, her cell phone inadvertently fell from her side pocket. Graham Meriweather, on the other hand, did notice.

After he was positioned with his meal, in a weak voice, Graham asked Julie, "Would you mind getting me a cup of coffee? I believe that would taste good with my lunch."

Julie replied in her typical cordial manner. "Of course I will. Let me go downstairs and get that right now. Is there anything else you would like? I'll be gone just a couple minutes."

Graham Meriweather was hoping her couple minutes would turn into a few more. As soon as Graham heard Julie start down the long hallway, he began his attempt to obtain the dropped cell phone. It was a struggle for him to reach the floor and not disrupt his lunch tray. At last, he was able to wrap his fingers around the slim cell phone and bring it up onto his bed. Graham opened the phone and quickly dialed a number from memory. Just as the call was connecting and he heard the first ring, he also thought he heard footsteps in the hall. He quickly closed the phone, disconnecting the call. Once he was sure no one was in the hall, he tried the phone again. This time he had to again hang up before anyone answered, as Julie Collin's was speaking to him from the hall.

"I have that cup of coffee for you", she said as she entered the room.

Graham hid his disappointment that she was back so soon. "Thank you. You can take your lunch break now if you'd like. I'll be fine."

Julie knew that Graham Meriweather was far from fine. He was getting frailer by the day, but as Dr. Haskins had told her earlier in the week, her job was to keep him comfortable during what appeared to be his life's end. She decided to retrieve her lunch from the kitchen.

"How about I get my lunch and eat here in your room with you? It will just take me a few minutes to get it from the kitchen," Julie said as she left the room.

Graham nodded. He knew he only had another few minutes, so he quickly grabbed for the cell phone again. This time he dialed another number, but received a recorded request to leave a message. He whispered as best he could, "Judy, help me." He closed the phone and let it slide back onto the floor.

Julie Collins came back into the room and found Graham with his soupspoon to his lips. She was glad to see him eating today. She sat across the room and ate her own sandwich. When she stood up she patted her side pocket and realized her cell phone was gone. Julie started to panic and then noticed something shiny on the floor next to Graham's bedside. She walked over, bent down and retrieved her cell phone. Julie stuffed the phone back into her pocket. It was then she sneezed. Julie knew that a sick nurse was no good for an already ill patient.

"I might have to take a few days off to shake this cold", she said to herself.

Chapter 87

Judy Rockwell was about to leave her office at noon on Thursday when the mail was delivered. She quickly sorted out Harrison Meriweather's mail and dropped the envelopes into his inbox. She glanced quickly at the pile for Graham Meriweather. She noticed a greeting card type envelope and pulled it out of the pile. The name on the address label read 'Catherine Wallace'. Judy wondered what kind of message Mrs. Wallace would be sending to her boss. She knew they were both still grieving from their losses even after all these years. Judy placed the card on top of the pile for Monday morning. She would try to have it delivered to Graham's home.

Like most businesses, the Meriweather office was to be closed the next day, Friday, in celebration of July 4th, which actually fell on Saturday. Judy arranged to leave early on this day, Thursday, as well. She was spending the long weekend with her daughter. Danielle's husband was a city fireman and would be on duty most of the weekend. She and Danielle planned to spend the time shopping for her upcoming grandchild.

Judy was very excited about the upcoming weekend. She pushed the button on her desk phone to send all incoming calls to her voice mail. She did not want to think about work until Monday morning.

When Judy reached her car, she used her cell phone to call Danielle. "Hi dear, I'm just leaving the parking garage. I should be there in thirty minutes. Do you want me to bring lunch?"

Danielle Miller was in her eighth month of pregnancy. "That would be great, Mom. I'm pregnant, when aren't I hungry?

Would you mind picking me up my favorite at that little deli I love? You know the one, Nellie's"

Judy smiled. "Yes, after all these years, I know your favorites. Add fifteen minutes to my arrival time. See you soon. Love you."

Judy Rockwell started to close her phone when she noticed she had two missed calls. When she viewed the numbers, she found both calls to be from the same number with an ID listing the name of 'Julie Collins'.

Judy said to herself as she closed her phone, "I don't know any Julie Collins. Someone must have dialed a wrong number. If she didn't leave me a message, she must have realized her mistake as well."

Chapter 88

Linda Butler went back to her office after the long meeting in the firm's large conference room. From the clock on her desk she realized it was almost the lunch hour. Linda hoped to catch Larkyn Belanger still in her office. She retrieved Larkyn's business number and placed the call from her desk phone.

Larkyn Belanger was just wrapping up some paperwork and contemplating what to do for lunch when her office line rang. She answered with the proper business greeting. "Good Morning. This is Belanger Personal Investigation. How may I help you?"

Linda was quick to identify herself on this call. "Hello Larkyn. This is Linda Butler from the law firm of Archer, Jackson and Rodriguez. I am currently working on a case for Attorney Jillian Jackson. I believe I spoke with you yesterday. I was wondering if you remember our conversation."

Larkyn remembered working with Linda Butler on several cases over the past few years, but she did not recall speaking with Linda any time recently, certainly not yesterday. She stated the same to Linda.

"I'm afraid you must be mistaken. I have not spoken with you for a few months. Did you leave me a message that I might not have gotten?"

Linda knew she had to lay her cards on the table. Now was the time to confirm her theory.

"I'm quite sure it was you I spoke to. We discussed a twenty-five year old note found at a church. Do you remember our conversation now?"

Larkyn Belanger was near shock and took a few seconds to respond to Linda Butler's reference. "You were the woman calling about the personal ad? Do you know who wrote that note?"

Linda wanted to give herself a 'high-five' for proving her theory correct. Larkyn and she were definitely involved in the same case.

Linda was vague in her reply. "Attorney Jackson's client may have information that could help your client. Our firm would like to meet with you and your client tomorrow morning. Would you both be receptive to that?"

Larkyn didn't need to check with Madison before replying. She knew Madison Cavanaugh would make herself available no matter what.

Larkyn assured Linda. "I can arrange for my client to be available. Where would you like to meet?"

Linda was not sure how Larkyn would react to the meeting including both attorneys and detectives, but she needed to be up front. "Attorney Jackson requests that you come to our offices. We will meet in our large conference room. I will tell you that there will be some other professional individuals in attendance. I don't want you or your client to be surprised by them."

Larkyn was surprised at Linda's last remark and asked, "What kind of professionals? Will Attorney Jackson's client be there?"

Linda was truthful in answering. "Attorney Jackson has the DA's office and some officers of the law involved in the case. She feels it best not to have her client in attendance tomorrow. The attorney would like to hear from your client first. I hope that is not a problem."

Larkyn got a bit defensive when Linda mentioned the DA and officers of the law. She wanted to protect Madison.

"I hope that my client is not walking into a meeting that could result in her having criminal charges filed against her."

Linda was quick to respond. "No, it's nothing like that. I see no reason why charges would be brought against her."

Elaine LaForge

Larkyn was very curious as to what Madison's fate held, "Linda, could you give me some kind of hint as to who wrote that note, or who 'Baby M' might be?"

Linda wanted very much to reveal 'Baby M's' identity, but knew it was too soon. "Larkyn, I truly wish I could tell you more, but I can't at this time. You and your client will learn everything you need to know tomorrow. May I schedule the meeting for ten o'clock?"

Larkyn was disappointed, but had not expected more. "Ten o'clock will be fine with us. We will be there."

Linda could not totally contain her excitement when she ended the conversation. "Larkyn, let me just say one thing. This could be a very big case for both of us. I can't wait to see you and meet your client tomorrow morning."

Larkyn Belanger sat at her desk with Linda's last words repeating over and over in her head. "This could be a very big case."

What had Madison stumbled onto? Better yet, who might Madison Cavanaugh turn out to be?

Chapter 89

Madison had just left the hotel with Ray and Megan for lunch when her cell phone rang. She looked at the call ID and announced, "This is Larkyn. Maybe she has more news for me."

Ray and Megan exchanged a hopeful smile in the front seat of Ray's SUV.

Madison quickly answered the call. "Hello Larkyn. Do you have something more? Did that woman call back?"

Larkyn could hear Madison's excitement. "Calm down Madison. I need you to listen carefully."

Madison tried to become calmer. "What do you need to tell me?"

Larkyn recounted her call with Linda Butler and ended with the news of the next morning's meeting,

"Attorney Jackson would like us at her firm's office by ten in the morning."

Madison was astounded that the call Larkyn received the previous day had been from a law firm. That was a good sign, right? Madison just wasn't sure whether the police presence was a bad sign.

She agreed to the meeting. "Of course we should meet. Do you want us to meet you at your office?"

Larkyn felt that she and her client should attend this meeting alone. "Madison, I was thinking that I should pick you up at your hotel. I did not mention Ray and Megan when I set the meeting up. I think you and I should field this one alone. Are you okay with that?"

Madison became defensive. "Larkyn, Uncle Ray is the one who first saw me with my mother, Rosemary. He might be able to answer some questions that I would have been far too young to know about."

On the other end of the line, Larkyn Belanger thought about Ray's involvement in the case and agreed. "I see your point, Madison. We should take Ray and Megan with us. I will explain to Linda when we arrive tomorrow."

Madison smiled and said, "That's great. We will all be ready for you tomorrow morning. See you then."

Ray looked over at Megan from the driver's seat and could see her relief. He knew Megan did not want Madison to deal with any news, good or bad, alone. He felt better too. They had agreed from the beginning that they were in this together.

Chapter 90

The tall, thin, older businessman had just left a meeting when his cell phone vibrated in the pocket of his very expensive black suit jacket. He answered the call using one word, "Yes?"

The businessman listened to the voice on the other end of the call describe a situation. He had heard the same type of distress call from this caller in the past. He knew what had to be done.

"I will take care of it. I always do. Don't I?" the businessman said gruffly into the phone.

The caller continued on but the businessman was no longer giving his full attention. He was short when he ended the call.

"I'll be there. Don't worry so much. Everything will be fine. Our plan is working. It's almost over now."

By the time the call ended, he was back in his private office.

"So much for a relaxing holiday weekend," he mumbled to himself.

Chapter 91

Julie Collins awoke Friday morning feeling somewhat better. She was still glad that she had told Mrs. Meriweather that she needed the day off so as to not expose Mr. Meriweather to her cold. Tomorrow was the fourth of July so she would have an extra long holiday weekend now. Suddenly, Julie had an idea pop into her head. She grabbed her cell phone and dialed her sister Katelyn's number.

Sounding as if she had been awakened, her sister answered groggily, "Hello."

Julie felt bad at calling so early. "Katie, I'm sorry if I woke you. I just had an idea for the holiday weekend. Would you like your big sister to come for a visit?"

Katie Collins was two years younger than Julie, a fact that Julie never seemed to resist rubbing in.

"I don't have any big plans. It would be great to see you. We could go to the fireworks display together tomorrow night. When will you be here?"

Julie's car had not been running the best lately. She was hesitant to set out on a three-hour drive. She thought for a moment before answering.

"I think I will take the bus to Fort Worth. I can get around this morning and take the afternoon bus. I should be to your place by dinner time."

Katie was more awake by this point. "That sounds great. I work from eleven till four today. Text me what time the bus gets in and I can pick you up at the station."

Julie was already mentally packing her bag. "That sounds great. I could really use some time off to relax and have fun. I'll see you later today. Bye."

Julie hurried around her downstairs apartment. She needed a cup of coffee, then a shower, and then she had to pack a bag. She calculated she could catch the city bus a block from her apartment and that would take her downtown to the main bus station. She could leave her car parked in her driveway and save parking fees.

Julie lived on Baker Street in a residential neighborhood. Her one-bedroom downstairs apartment was quite small. She had one neighbor, Mrs. King, who lived in the other lower half and there was a larger apartment in the upstairs portion of the house. The larger apartment was currently vacant, which made the house seem quiet. Mrs. King was an older woman, who was hard of hearing. Other than when she fell asleep with her television still on and the volume set loud, she was a perfect neighbor.

Julie did not take the time to pick up after herself that morning. She dumped her clean clothes from a clothesbasket onto her bed and pulled out what she needed for the weekend. As if to disguise the mess, she pulled her bedding up and over the remaining pile of clothes. Julie was anxious to get out of town and see her sister.

Chapter 92

Madison, Megan and Ray were standing outside the main entrance to their hotel at eight o'clock waiting for Larkyn to pick them up. Everyone was nervous but trying not to show it.

Ray spotted Larkyn's vehicle pulling up and said, "Here's our ride, Ladies."

Ray opened the front passenger door and motioned for Madison to get in. "You should sit up front with Larkyn. Megan and I will hop in the back. You two might need to go over things on the way."

Madison climbed into the vehicle with her tote bag. She had brought along the photos of herself as a baby, her monogrammed baby blanket, the lone pink bootie, and of course, the notes she had been given by Father Gomez. Madison felt quite prepared for the meeting.

Larkyn took some of their travel time to advise Madison on how she wanted the meeting to go. Larkyn believed that the group Linda Butler described would basically be interviewing Madison to determine whether her story of how she came to possess the notes was true.

When they arrived in Las Cruces, Larkyn parked in the garage nearest the law firm. Larkyn and Madison led the group as they walked to the front entrance of Jillian Jackson's office building. They rode the elevator up and checked in with the receptionist. Linda Butler soon appeared. Larkyn took Linda aside and explained the relationship of Ray Davis and his niece Megan. Linda nodded and walked over to shake hands with everyone. She then escorted them to her firm's large conference room.

Most of the people sitting at the long rectangular table were sitting in the same seats they had the day before. Manuel Escobar, Brian McGregor, Tim McGregor, Sami Harper, Brock Richards and Evan Gibson were seated. Jillian Jackson stood at the head of the table and Melanie Duncan was positioned at the side to take the day's notes.

Linda introduced the four new attendees to Jillian Jackson and in turn to the group sitting at the table. Jillian gave introductions of the individuals at the table. Though she introduced each by name, she simply identified them as Attorney, Investigator or Detective. Jillian Jackson did not want to tip her hat just yet that the case covered a multi-state region. Just as Jillian was asking Madison to take the seat at the head of the table, Carol Storms slipped quietly into the room and sat in a corner chair.

Chapter 93

Jillian began the meeting by addressing Madison. "I would like you to start at the beginning and tell us what events led you to place the personal ad in the newspaper."

Madison nodded and began the same as she had to numerous people over the past few weeks.

"About a month ago my mother, Rosemary Cavanaugh, was in a tragic car accident. She was seriously injured and brought into the hospital where I am a nurse in the ER."

The story made her sad no matter how many times she repeated it. "Before going into emergency surgery, my mother kept saying that she was sorry she had never told me something. She did not mention what that something was, but she was quite agitated at the time. Just before she fell unconscious she told me to come to Deming, New Mexico and find a Father Francis Gomez at Saint Gabriel's Church. She said that the priest held information that I would need. She kept saying that I needed to start at the beginning."

Madison took a sip of water from the glass that sat in front of her before she continued. "My mother died during surgery. She was never able to tell me more. The loss of my mother was very hard on me. She was a single mother who had raised me, her only child. We had an extremely close relationship. I felt as if her death was the worst thing that could happen to me. But I was yet to learn a very shocking truth."

Madison's audience was drawn into her story and she continued. "A few days later the surgeon who had operated on my mother came to visit me. He had noticed something strange while operating on her. He had medical evidence that my mother had never given birth. After DNA testing, it was proven that Rosemary Cavanaugh and I are of no blood relation."

Madison then explained how Ray Davis had met Rosemary and herself, as an infant, in Deming, and had given them a ride to North Carolina where they lived as mother and daughter for twenty-seven years.

Brian McGregor was now quite intrigued by the young woman sitting at the head of the table.

Madison went on to tell how she had found Father Gomez. She explained that he had given her the envelope and notes from Rosemary he had been holding for many years. She gave a summary of what the notes said.

Madison went on to describe the meeting with Ned Tuttle and Jackie Potter from the *Deming Daily* newspaper office. Madison acknowledged that Jackie had introduced her to Larkyn Belanger. She explained how together they had devised a plan and had written the personal ad which appeared in the paper.

Madison concluded by saying, "Apparently I was abandoned by someone that December night so long ago. Rosemary Cavanaugh found me and raised me as her own daughter. I never had a clue that she was not my birth mother. I placed that ad to try and locate the person who left me in that manger. I would like to know if I have a family that is still looking for me."

Madison then pulled items from her tote and explained. "Ray Davis said I was wrapped in this blanket the night he met my mother and me. I also found an unmatched bootie tucked inside this blanket in my mother's cedar chest."

Brian McGregor sat up and took a closer look at the pink bootie. It was a match to the bloodied bootie in an evidence bag inside Olivia Meriweather's case file. "Is it possible that this young woman is Olivia?" he thought to himself.

Madison continued to bring items from her tote. She laid photos of herself as a young child on the table and finally placed the note Rosemary had written to Father Gomez and the note to

Madison for all to see. Her last item was the note that had been scribbled on a torn piece of paper and left in the manger with her.

Tim McGregor was the first to closely examine that last piece of paper. He remarked, "This note seems to have been written on the back of some kind of receipt. Maybe the crime lab can pull information from it."

Sami Harper had the same idea when she said to Tim, "I can get it to our lab right away."

Jillian Jackson took the lead again. "I think it's time for a short break. I want to thank you, Madison, for telling us what you have been through the past few weeks. You have certainly been on a journey and I speak for all of us in the room when I say how sorry we are that you lost your mother."

Madison nodded and Jillian continued. "If you wouldn't mind, I believe we need to confer without your presence after the break. I will have my secretary Carol Storms take you to a smaller room. We will come for you in a few minutes."

Madison replied, "That's fine. I understand."

Chapter 94

When Jillian Jackson resumed the meeting after their short break, she started with a question. "I want you to think about the two interviews we have done with Nina Perez and Madison Cavanaugh. Does everyone in the room feel we have enough evidence to proceed with the assumption that our case is related to the Olivia Meriweather kidnapping?"

Brian McGregor was the first to respond positively. "Both Nina Perez and Madison Cavanaugh have pieces of information from the Meriweather kidnapping that were never released to the public. Since we have both of their statements now, I can enlighten the rest of you.

"While searching the apartment of Mia Sanchez during the initial investigation, a bloody pink baby bootie was found. While DNA testing was not available at that time, the blood type was consistent with Olivia Meriweather's. The pink bootie that Madison Cavanaugh produced today is a match to the one found in that apartment.

"Also, both women mentioned the monogrammed baby blanket. Today, Madison Cavanaugh also produced that item. I believe that this case is not just related to the Meriweather kidnapping case. I believe it is highly likely we just reopened the original case. I feel we may have just been speaking with the now adult Olivia Meriweather."

Sami Harper agreed with Brian. "I believe both women's stories. Are we able to get a DNA sample from Mr. Graham Meriweather to compare to Madison Cavanaugh?"

Brian started shaking his head before Sami had finished her question. "Asking to get a DNA sample from Mr. Meriweather would be blocked by lawyers, doctors and a lot of red tape. I have another idea."

Jillian was interested in what Brian had to say. "I'm listening."

Brian continued, "Over the years I have developed a relationship with Catherine Wallace. Mrs. Wallace was Lydia Meriweather's mother. Catherine Wallace calls me once a year; on what would be Olivia's birthday. She likes to make sure her granddaughter's case is not forgotten. I believe if I called her, she would consent to a DNA test. That would prove whether or not Madison Cavanaugh was Lydia Meriweather's daughter. If that proves negative, the case is closed again. However, if that proves positive, it could give us more leverage to obtain a DNA sample from Graham Meriweather himself."

Jillian was smiling at the suggestion. "I like your idea. Would you be able to ask Mrs. Wallace in a way that keeps her from going to the public?"

Brian was sure that would not be a problem. "The last thing Mrs. Wallace wants is publicity. She always felt that the fame of the Meriweather family contributed to her granddaughter's kidnapping."

Jillian asked the group, "Do you all agree?"

When she noted all heads shaking affirmatively, she turned back to Brian. "Let's make the call."

Chapter 95

In San Angelo, Texas, Catherine Wallace was about to prepare lunch when the telephone rang. She walked over to the remote set on her granite kitchen counter, picked up the receiver and said, "Hello."

Brian McGregor was on the other end of the line. "Hello, Mrs. Wallace. This is Chief of Detectives McGregor from Abilene. Would you have a moment to speak with me?"

Catherine Wallace steadied herself by grabbing onto the counter's edge. She slowly made her way to a chair at her kitchen table.

It took Catherine a moment to reply to Brian. "Yes, Chief, I certainly do. You have information about Olivia, don't you?"

Brian had planned to ease his way into the conversation, but Mrs. Wallace was making that difficult.

"What would make you say that?"

Catherine Wallace replied, "Chief McGregor, I have called you twenty-seven times, once every year, on Olivia's birthday. It has been over twenty-six years since you have called me. I don't have to be a detective to know that you must have something to tell me."

Brian McGregor smiled to himself as he replied, "Well, Mrs. Wallace, you would make a fine detective. Some new evidence has just been presented to me. I feel this evidence is quite compelling, as well as factual. I need to ask you a favor."

"You know I would do anything to help you find out what happened to my little Olivia. What is it that you need?"

Brian took a deep breath before he spoke. "I would like you to agree to a DNA test."

That had not been Catherine's first guess at what his favor would be. "You want me to take a DNA test? Of course I would do that. May I ask whether you have requested the same from Graham Meriweather?"

"Mrs. Wallace, to be perfectly honest, I am coming to you first. I foresee more red tape in my way with Mr. Meriweather than with you. I hope you don't mind."

Catherine smiled. "Not in the least. I would like to know one thing first though."

"What would that be, Mrs. Wallace?"

"Will my DNA be matched against someone living, or against the remains of a deceased child?"

Brian McGregor wanted to reassure her, but did not want to give out false hope. "Mrs. Wallace, I can say that we have found no remains at this time. We need to prove or disprove a theory based on this new evidence. Does that satisfy your question?"

Catherine Wallace was relieved. "That is just fine. Please tell me where and when you need me. I will be there."

Brian explained that an exact time and place would be determined and he would call her back with that information. Before he ended the call, he made one more request of Catherine Wallace.

"Mrs. Wallace, I would ask that you not share this information with others. We are not at the point of making any public statement."

Catherine reassured him. "I don't plan on sharing your call with anyone, not even my husband. I also want to have the facts verified before I make any announcement. You can count on my discretion."

After the call ended, Catherine sat at her table and sobbed. For the first time in years, tears of hope ran down her face.

Chapter 96

After Chief Brian McGregor spoke with Mrs. Wallace, he made some calls to arrange for the lab at San Angelo Mercy Hospital to perform the tests. His medical liaison would arrange for confidentiality of the names of the participants. Brian then met with Jillian to finalize the arrangements. Together they called the larger group back into the conference room, including Madison, Ray and Megan.

Jillian introduced Brian more formally. "Madison, Chief Brian McGregor is from Texas. He would like you to submit to a DNA test. Would you agree to that?"

Madison smiled as she answered. "I actually brought my DNA profile with me. It is the one that was compared to my mother, Rosemary."

Brian McGregor shook his head and said, "I'm sure your profile sheet is fine. However, for this to be an impartial investigation, we will require that you submit to another test. I hope that will not be a problem."

"It is not at all. I am anxious to find my family. Do you have a suspicion about who my parents might be? Will you be comparing my DNA with them?"

Brian tried to stay vague. "We have a working theory at this time. All I can say is that we will be comparing your DNA with someone we feel you are related to."

Madison nodded. "That's fine. When and where do I need to be?"

"We have actually arranged for the test to be performed on Monday, in San Angelo, Texas."

Larkyn Belanger was the first to jump at the mention of the location. "Texas? Are you telling us that Madison is originally from Texas?"

Brian had expected this reaction and was prepared. "I am not telling you anything about where Madison is from. As I said, we are working on a theory. The relative that we want to perform the DNA compare with lives in San Angelo, so I have made the arrangements in that city. Will it be a problem for you to be in San Angelo by Monday?"

Madison looked in Ray's direction, who immediately spoke up. "I can have Madison wherever she needs to be."

Brian continued, "We would like you to be at San Angelo Mercy Hospital at one-thirty Monday afternoon. You can go directly to the lab. I will make sure that the paperwork is there. I will write down the address and the technician's name for you."

Chapter 97

The next day, Saturday, was the fourth of July. Madison, Megan and Ray were packing and making plans to travel to Texas. Madison felt fortunate to have made so many new friends during her two weeks in New Mexico. She was finding it sad to say goodbye to them.

It was determined that Larkyn Belanger would also travel to Texas. She wanted to follow through on her investigation of Madison's case. Larkyn was quite anxious to learn Madison's true identity. She hoped there would have a happy ending.

Megan was the one least happy about leaving Deming, New Mexico. She and Ned Tuttle had become close friends. Megan thought that if she and Ned lived closer, their relationship might actually turn into something serious. Ned asked Megan to attend the fireworks display with him that evening. She had happily accepted.

Ray spent Saturday preparing his vehicle for the trip. He made sure the gas tank was full and had the oil changed at a local shop. Ray also notified the hotel clerk of their departure early Sunday morning.

By Sunday night the group expected to be checked into a hotel in San Angelo that was recommended by Detective Timothy McGregor. Everyone had mixed emotions over Madison's DNA test on Monday. It was a combination of excitement and nervousness. Hopefully there would be an answer soon as to who Madison Cavanaugh truly was.

Chapter 98

While the fireworks were booming and bursting in the air over the city of Abilene, Texas, a burglar was sizing up Julie Collins' apartment. He noted a car in the driveway next to the front door, but there were no lights on inside the apartment. The burglar assumed the tenant was in bed. The tall man dressed in dark clothing with the hood of his sweatshirt pulled over his head was hidden in the tall bushes outside Julie's living room windows. The man attempted to open them, but found they were locked.

The burglar then crouched and snuck around to the rear of the house to a back door. The door also was locked, but he found he could unlock it from the inside by breaking one small pane of glass.

The burglar could hear the television from the neighbor's apartment. He was nervous that someone would see him. As he peered into the window of the other apartment, he realized he had nothing to worry about. An elderly woman was sound asleep in her recliner as her television continued to entertain her on a high volume setting.

"Between the fireworks and that old lady's television, no one will hear this glass break," he thought to himself.

He used a rock and shattered the small pane of glass. Though he was wearing gloves, the burglar used the cuff of his sweatshirt for added protection over his hand. He was able to reach and turn the lock. The burglar was quickly inside.

The burglar looked at the contents of the apartment and became familiar with the layout. He crossed a small living area that included a table for two, a love seat and a small desk holding a laptop computer. From the love seat the man took a decorative throw pillow. He noticed that in one corner of the living area stood a stand with a small flat screen television. A doorway was open to the right of the television that appeared to lead to the bedroom.

As the burglar stepped into the bedroom doorway, the light shining in the window from the streetlight allowed him to see what he was looking for. On the twin size bed, he noticed a rounded shape covered with a floral quilt. From his pocket he drew a handgun and placed the throw pillow over the end of the gun as a silencer. The burglar aimed and fired two shots into the mound on the bed. As the cotton stuffing fell to the floor, the man tossed the now destroyed pillow across the bedroom where it fell into a corner.

As the burglar turned to retrace his steps and leave the apartment, he yanked on the cords attached to the flat screen TV and laptop. He placed both items under his arm and fled out the back door.

Chapter 99

Monday morning Judy Rockwell was up early and eager to get back to her office. She had spent the long weekend with her daughter, Danielle. Judy enjoyed the time with Danielle and was pleased they had been able to accomplish many tasks in preparation for Judy's first grandchild. However, she had to admit she was a bit tired and ready to get back into her own routine.

As Judy gathered her belongings together to leave for work, she rechecked her cell phone for messages. She seldom found any, and today was no different. She once again noticed the missed calls from the previous Thursday identified by the unfamiliar name of Julie Collins. She would delete them later.

Thinking about her schedule for the day, Judy remembered the card addressed to her boss, Graham Meriweather, from Catherine Wallace that had arrived just as she was leaving for the long weekend.

Judy thought to herself, "I might try to deliver that today on my lunch hour."

When Judy arrived at the office building of Meriweather Associates, she was greeted once again by Charlie Armstrong in his security uniform. As usual, Charlie was smiling behind the circular desk near the building's entrance.

Judy beat Charlie to the morning greeting. "Good Morning, Charlie. I had a marvelous weekend, how about you?"

Charlie replied, "I sure did Ms. Rockwell. Thank you for asking. Summer is officially here now that the Fourth of July is over."

Judy nodded and headed for the elevators. When she arrived on the twentieth floor she found the main doors to the Meriweather office suite unlocked. As she entered and walked to her office, she noticed that Harrison Meriweather was in his office and already on a call. Judy performed her usual morning tasks; she turned on her computer, made sure the copy machine was on, made a fresh pot of coffee and returned to her desk to check her electronic and voice mail accounts.

Judy was multi-tasking as she scrolled through numerous emails while punching her access code into the voice mail system. From habit, she pressed the appropriate number to listen to her first voice message. Her face paled as she heard a weak voice say, "Judy, help me."

Judy quickly pressed to replay the message and noted the date and time. She realized that the message was received just as she had left the office on Thursday. As Judy concentrated on the caller's voice, she became convinced it belonged to Graham Meriweather.

Judy saved the message and was about to stand up when Harrison Meriweather appeared at the front of her desk.

"Good Morning, Judy. I hope you and your daughter had a nice time together this weekend."

Judy was shaking as she tried to explain the message. "Mr. Meriweather, I believe Graham left me a message last Thursday. Here, I will play it for you. He sounds in trouble."

As the message was played over the speaker on Judy's phone, Harrison Meriweather became concerned for his cousin.

Judy looked Harrison in the eye and said, "Have you actually spoken with Graham in the past few weeks?"

Harrison Meriweather looked ashamed as he answered her question. "As I said awhile ago, I received an email from Graham stating he was taking some time off and requested I respect his privacy. To tell you the truth, I have been so busy trying to manage all of our client accounts alone, that I haven't taken the time to check in with Graham since that email. I just assumed he would be back in the office soon."

Judy was not about to wait any longer. As she reached into the pile of mail on her desk, she told Harrison, "Graham received this card last week. I was going to deliver it to his home on my lunch hour. I suggest you and I go over there right now."

Harrison was nodding his head as he spoke. "I think that's a good idea. Let me get my car keys and I will drive us."

Chapter 100

Julie Collins wanted to spend as much time as possible with her sister Katie. That was why she took the overnight bus from Fort Worth back to Abilene. She arrived back at her apartment a few minutes after seven o'clock Monday morning. She would have to hurry to be to work on time.

When Julie unlocked her front door and entered the main living area of her apartment, she quickly realized that her flat screen television and laptop were missing. Julie dropped her duffel bag of clothes by the door and looked around the room. Someone had stolen her electronics.

Having found the front door locked, Julie walked through her apartment to the back entrance. There she found the broken glass at what must have been the burglar's entry point. Julie grabbed her cell phone from her pocket and dialed 9-1-1 to report the break in. She was told not to touch anything and that a patrol car was being dispatched to her address.

Julie was not comfortable staying in her apartment so she knocked on her neighbor's back door. She knew that Mrs. King would be up and halfway through her first pot of coffee.

Clarissa King was an eighty-year-old woman who used a cane to help herself get around. She would not admit to being hard of hearing, so it was Julie's third round of knocking that finally got Clarissa's attention.

When the small framed, gray haired woman opened her back door she found her younger neighbor in a state of hysterics.

"Someone broke into my apartment while I was gone," Julie yelled as she entered Clarissa's kitchen. The smell of fresh brewed coffee and bacon cooking on the stove seemed to temporarily calm Julie.

Clarissa was confused by Julie's statement. "What do you mean? I was right here all weekend. I'm sure I would have heard if someone broke in your place."

Julie knew that certainly wasn't true, but did not want to offend her elderly neighbor.

"They probably broke in during the night, when you would have been asleep. Do you mind if I wait here until the police arrive?"

Clarissa liked Julie and was happy to oblige. "Would you like a cup of coffee, dear? You are welcome to join me for breakfast as well. I can put a couple more slices of bacon in the pan."

Julie smiled at the woman's gesture of kindness. "I would love a cup of coffee, Mrs. King. I'm afraid I don't feel much like eating right now, but thank you."

As the two women sipped their coffee they heard a car come to a stop outside their home. The patrol car had arrived.

Julie stepped out onto the small front porch of Clarissa King's side of the house. She watched as a young patrolman got out from the passenger's side of the vehicle. He was six feet tall with a thin frame. His blondish hair was cut short beneath his hat. An older officer who appeared to be a couple inches taller with much broader shoulders exited from the driver's door.

Julie greeted the patrolmen from the porch. "Thank you for coming so quickly. My apartment is the other side. I haven't touched anything, just like I was told. I came over to my neighbors until you arrived."

Officer Dylan Quigley introduced himself, and then took out his notepad and pen. He asked Julie for her general information, her name, when she noticed the break-in and where she had been.

Julie explained her weekend visit to her sister and that she had just returned home to find her items missing.

"I'm Sergeant Leroy Decker. May we go in your apartment, Miss Collins?" the older patrolman asked when he joined Officer Quigley on the sidewalk.

Julie gestured to her front door, "Of course. Do you want me to come in with you?"

The Sergeant nodded. "Yes. That would be fine. If you could stand near the doorway and point out where your stolen items were for us that would be good. We need to examine the scene and look for any evidence the burglar may have left behind."

Julie did as the Sergeant asked. She motioned to her empty television stand and the open area on her small desk where her laptop had been. From where she stood, she did not notice any other missing items. The two policemen wandered throughout her apartment, making notes and whispering to each other.

Officer Quigley wandered into Julie's bedroom and soon called out. "Sergeant, you need to see this."

Sergeant Decker made his way quickly from the kitchen area into the bedroom where he found Officer Quigley pointing to the bedding on Julie Collins' twin bed.

Officer Quigley commented to his Sergeant, "Do those look like bullet holes to you?"

He was pointing at two round marks in the floral quilt Julie had thrown over her pile of laundry before leaving for Katie's. Sergeant Decker was nodding in agreement as he bent to inspect closer. It was then he noticed the throw pillow in the corner of the room.

The sergeant pointed and said to Officer Quigley, "That would be the reason no one reported hearing a gunshot."

Chapter 101

In San Angelo, Chief Brian McGregor and Detective Timothy McGregor were sitting in their unmarked vehicle in the parking lot of the San Angelo Mercy Hospital. The father and son were assigned to watch over the arrivals of Catherine Wallace and Madison Cavanaugh. Catherine Wallace was scheduled to be at the hospital's lab at eight-thirty on this Monday morning. Madison Cavanaugh was not scheduled until one-thirty in the afternoon. The times were specifically set five hours apart to insure the women did not encounter each other. The lab was prepared to take blood and saliva samples to determine whether they shared common DNA.

The same lab technician was selected to collect the samples from each woman. Giselle Dubois was informed that two individuals were being sampled to determine whether a family relationship existed. The women would identify themselves only with a coded identification number. The officials involved did not want any public awareness of the testing until the results were known.

In addition to the testing of Catherine Wallace and Madison Cavanaugh, Brian had recovered the bloody pink bootie from the Meriweather kidnapping evidence box. It was also being profiled for DNA to compare with both women. The advancement in testing could tell whether the blood on the bootie belonged to Olivia Meriweather.

As Brian and Tim sat in their unmarked vehicle, they discussed both Meriweather case files. Brian had obtained the homicide file of Lydia Meriweather's death from Luis Fuentes over the weekend. Brian wanted to review the file for any common links to the kidnapping.

Tim was reading the file aloud to his father. "The report states that Lydia Meriweather was taking her daily walk when she was struck down. The driver of the car never stopped. Witnesses reported the car was dark in color, mid-sized and that it possibly had out of state license plates. Not much for the police to go on."

Brian had seen many cases like Lydia's in his career. "Hit and run accidents are always the toughest. Luis said they canvassed the neighborhood and local body shops for damaged cars, but came up empty. The police theorized it was a tourist or an out of state businessman who didn't stay in the area. Somebody got away with murder that day."

Tim read on. "Several witnesses told the officers of a man who ran over to help Lydia after she was hit. They said the man sat on the pavement beside her and lifted her head. He held her head in his lap for a couple minutes. He ran off when he heard sirens approaching. Some witnesses felt Lydia may have spoken to the man."

Brian wondered aloud. "I gather that man was never located. Makes you wonder what, if anything, Lydia said as she lay dying in a stranger's arms."

Brian then looked out across the parking lot and pointed. "Here comes Catherine Wallace. She's right on schedule."

Catherine Wallace was escorted to the hospital's main entrance by a male police officer dressed in plain clothes. The officer would take her to the lab and present the coded paperwork to Giselle Dubois.

Brian's mind went back to Lydia Meriweather's case file and he asked, "Tim, were the witnesses able to describe this stranger who went to Lydia's side?"

Tim scanned the reports before answering. "They all agreed he was tall, wore a baseball cap and walked with a limp. They remembered the limp as being quite discernible when the man hurried away from the scene."

Brian rolled his eyes. "Well, that narrows it down, doesn't it? We are looking for a tall man, wearing a baseball cap and walking with a limp. There must be hundreds of men with those characteristics."

Tim started to chuckle at his father's remark. As he glanced out the side window of the car, he gestured to his father. "Look, there goes a man fitting that exact description right now."

Chapter 102

Milton Donovan arrived at the San Angelo Mercy Hospital just before eight-thirty Monday morning. He was not sleeping well since his mother's fall. Milton's mother was scheduled to be released from the hospital the following morning, and that would be none too soon. Milton was having trouble keeping his medications straight. He was becoming more confused each day.

As Milton walked from his car's parking spot toward the main entrance, he noticed Catherine Wallace headed toward the doors from a different direction. He became confused and started pulling at his hair through his favorite baseball cap.

"What is she doing here? I can't let her see me. What if she recognizes me? What if she remembers seeing me in the cemetery?" Milton's mind was full of paranoid questions.

Milton decided to return to his car until after Catherine Wallace entered the building. He would then feel safe to go in the building and visit his mother in her room.

Milton waited beside his car for five minutes after Catherine walked through the doors. He was giving himself plenty of time to ensure he would not run into her in the lobby.

When Milton finally felt safe, he walked cautiously toward the entrance. Milton was looking over his shoulder and from side to side as he limped along.

Milton's limp and his nervous movements were what caught Tim McGregor's attention as he walked across the parking lot and along the side of Chief McGregor's parked car.

Chapter 103

Harrison Meriweather was kicking himself mentally while he drove with Judy Rockwell to Graham's residence. "I should have checked on Graham more this past month," he thought.

Judy Rockwell was also worried about her employer. "Why wouldn't Graham call you?" she asked Harrison.

Harrison shook his head. "I don't know. He sounded fine in the last email he sent. It just stated he wanted some time and privacy. You know how often he used to act like this. Years ago he spent weeks at a time searching for Olivia. Lately it seemed as if he has become fixated again with finding her. I just assumed that was what this recent time away was about."

Judy nodded. "For some reason he has seemed more depressed lately. He went through so much, but that was almost thirty years ago now. I never felt it was healthy for him not to move on."

Harrison knew one fact that Judy did not. "Judy, there could be another reason for Graham's renewed search for Olivia. The original trust fund from Graham's father, Oliver, naturally included Olivia, his granddaughter. After Olivia's kidnapping, the trust was changed to exclude Olivia if she was not found by her twenty-fifth birthday."

Judy was confused. "But that date has already passed."

Harrison continued. "Yes, but shortly before that date, Graham petitioned the court to extend the date. The judge ordered that Olivia would not be excluded until what would be her thirtieth birthday. But in that ruling he stated no further extensions would be allowed."

"That would give Graham only two more years to find his daughter."

"That's correct. At the time, five years seemed like quite a long time, but now three years have passed and what would be Olivia's twenty-eighth birthday is just around the corner. Graham may feel he is running out of time. He is obviously stressed and might not be thinking as clearly as he should be."

Judy agreed. "It's quite doubtful, that after all these years, Graham will ever find Olivia."

Harrison felt the same way. "Nothing short of a miracle will bring Olivia Meriweather home."

Chapter 104

Harrison and Judy pulled into Graham's long, circular driveway and parked in front of the large golden double doors. They were quick to exit the car and Harrison pressed the bell to the right of the doors. After the third time, Patricia Meriweather opened the doors.

Harrison had never been fond of Patricia. Though she was married for several years to his Uncle Oliver, he had never referred to her as his aunt.

Harrison was somewhat curt when he addressed Patricia. "Hello, Patricia. I didn't expect you to answer the door. Where are the servants?"

Patricia responded. "If you must know, I have let many of them go. There isn't a need for a large staff for just Graham and myself. We have a woman to tend to the laundry and cooking on a daily basis and a weekly cleaning service. How may I help you today?"

Judy was already tired of the chitchat. She wanted to know about her employer. "Where is Graham? Is he alright?"

Patricia was formal in her reply. "Graham has taken to staying in his room. He has not been well of health lately. We have hired a nurse to assist him. He does not wish to be disturbed."

"We have reason to believe he may be in trouble. I insist on seeing him. I know the way," Harrison said firmly as he walked past Patricia. Judy was right at his side.

Harrison started up the long, winding open staircase that led to the second floor of Graham's home. He assumed Graham still occupied the same master suite he had shared with Lydia. When he came to that room, he opened the door quickly and rushed inside. Harrison was shocked to find the room empty.

"Where is he?" he demanded of Patricia.

"He has moved into the other suite", she replied.

"You mean the suite where my uncle died?"

Patricia nodded as Harrison continued down the hallway to the next set of double doors. Again, he didn't pause to knock. He pushed the doors opened and entered to find Graham Meriweather in a large bed in an otherwise empty room.

Harrison's entrance roused Graham from his sleep. He looked at Harrison and Judy with pleading eyes. Graham's skin color was quite gray and his face was thin and drawn. With one glance Harrison could tell that Graham Meriweather was indeed in poor health.

Harrison searched the room for a phone. "We need to call for an ambulance. Isn't there a phone in this room?"

"Graham did not want to be disturbed. He asked that there be no telephone, television or computer."

Judy wasted no time in pulling out her cell phone and dialing 9-1-1. She gave the address to the dispatcher.

Patricia was stumbling over her words. "I have been away for a few days. I didn't know he had gotten this bad. The nurse should have alerted me of his condition. In fact, she is late for work. Julie hasn't even called with an excuse. She said she was ill last week. Maybe someone should check on her."

Judy's ears perked up. "Julie? His nurse's name is Julie?"

Patricia nodded and said, "Yes, Julie Collins. Obviously she isn't much of a nurse to let her patient get this ill. I will be ending her employment immediately. That is, if she shows up for work."

Judy did not comment, but excused herself for a few minutes. She ran back down the staircase and went out to the driveway. She intended to give directions to the ambulance crew, but she also had a second motive.

Chapter 105

Judy Rockwell rechecked her cell phone for the missed calls logged from the prior week. As she read the caller id again, she exclaimed. "Julie Collins. Why was Graham's nurse trying to call me?"

Judy quickly pressed to return a call to Julie Collins' number.

Julie answered the call on the fourth ring. "Hello."

Judy introduced herself as Graham's administrative assistant and then asked the young woman, "Did you try to reach me last week?"

Julie was stunned. "No. I didn't call you. Until this minute, I didn't even know your name or your association with Mr. Meriweather. What is this about?"

Based on the condition she had just found Graham in, Judy was quite angry when she answered. "We have just found Mr. Meriweather quite ill in his home. It does not appear as though you have been taking very good care of your patient. Patricia Meriweather states she has been away and was not informed of the decline in his condition. Then today, you did not show up for work"

Julie Collins became defensive to Judy's remarks. "For your information, I have spoken on several occasions with Mrs. Meriweather regarding Graham Meriweather's condition. Just last week she had Dr. Haskins examine him and the doctor told me that it was Mr. Meriweather's choice to remain in his home for what time remains of his life. He was to be given pain medication to keep him comfortable."

"Are you sure it was Dr. Haskins? He was here last week?"

"That's who he said he was. He was an older gentleman, short and balding."

Judy had never actually met Dr. Haskins. However, she did remember seeing an announcement in Graham's mail stating the doctor was not seeing patients for a few weeks and giving a colleague's contact information.

Julie continued, "For another thing, Mrs. Meriweather has not been away. And for the last thing, my apartment was broken into this weekend while I was visiting my sister. I just arrived home this morning and had to call the police. But that's not the worst part. The police discovered that the burglar shot at a mound of laundry I had left under my bedding. Someone tried to kill me."

Judy's mind was in turmoil. Who should she believe? Patricia Meriweather had no reason to lie? Or did she? Julie Collins was just a young nurse who might be trying to cover up her medical inexperience.

At that moment Judy heard the ambulance's siren as it reached the end of the drive. Once Graham was in the hospital all of this could be straightened out. She only hoped it wouldn't be too late.

Chapter 106

In San Angelo, Brian and Tim McGregor were back in the parking lot of San Angelo Mercy Hospital. After seeing Catherine Wallace leave the hospital with her police escort, the men took a break and had lunch at a local deli. It was one o'clock now and Madison Cavanaugh was expected to arrive shortly for her one-thirty appointment with the lab. Local authorities would also be escorting her.

Tim had been thinking of their case at hand. "This must be terribly difficult on Madison. One day she is a happy young woman with what appears to be the perfect life, and the next day she has no idea who she is or where she came from. I can't imagine what she must be going through."

Brian sensed that the mysterious young woman intrigued his son. "It certainly appears as though she has had a rough time these last few weeks. But you and I can't get soft on her. We have to stick with the facts. She could be a young woman trying to scam everyone. She may have discovered that her lost mother was not her birth mother, but that alone doesn't prove she is Olivia Meriweather. Let's wait until all these DNA tests are complete before we assume anything."

Tim was less of a skeptic than his father. "I'm not assuming anything either. I just wonder whether Madison has any idea what these tests could mean for her."

"Everyone has made it a point not to divulge the identity of the person we are trying to determine Madison Cavanaugh is or is not. Unless she has discovered the Olivia Meriweather kidnapping case on her own, I doubt she realizes she might be an heiress."

Tim pointed out, "If Nina Perez had not seen Madison's personal ad no one would have tied this all to the Meriweather case either."

Brian nodded. "That is one point I keep going over. There is a small chance that Nina Perez and Madison Cavanaugh are conspiring together. But, as I said before, these tests will tell us the truth."

Tim was the first to spot Madison walking with a female officer toward the entrance. Forty minutes later, Madison emerged from the hospital doors with her escort. A driver pulled a car up to the front entrance, parked and was attempting to unload a woman from the backseat into a wheel chair. Another gentleman stopped to assist the driver. Madison and the officer stopped while the woman was wheeled toward the lobby. As they waited, other people exited the hospital and a pedestrian traffic jam was created on the sidewalk.

Brian McGregor became a bit concerned over the congestion that was being created. He was relieved to see the crowd start to break up and Madison head up the sidewalk with her escort at her side. It was then he noticed a familiar figure from earlier in the day.

"Isn't that the same guy with the baseball cap and limp you pointed out this morning?" he asked his son.

"I think it is. I remember how disheveled the man had looked."

Brian and Tim watched as the man started toward the parking lot and then, as if something caught his attention, abruptly limped down the sidewalk in the same direction Madison had just walked.

Tim became worried. "I thought he was parked a few rows behind us. That was the direction he came from this morning. Why is he suddenly going in the other direction?"

Brian was watching the man closely. "I think he's following Madison. He appears to be speaking aloud. Let's go check him out."

Brian and Tim were out of the car and caught up to the limping man in a matter of seconds. It was as they drew closer that they heard what the man was saying.

"Lydia," they heard him shout.

Brian and Tim looked at each other in astonishment, and said in unison, "Lydia?"

Madison's female escort had become aware of the commotion behind them and was hurrying Madison to the safety of the unmarked police vehicle. After Madison was placed in the front seat, Detective Karen Simpson turned to head off the man in the baseball cap. The man was boxed in with Brian and Tim just behind him.

Brian McGregor put his hand on the man's shoulder. "Were you following that young woman?"

The man was shaking and noticeably confused. "Was that Lydia? Has she been in the hospital all this time?"

Brian took the man's wallet out of his jacket pocket and announced his name, Milton Donovan.

Brian then turned to the man and asked, "Mr. Donovan, who do you think that woman is?"

Milton Donovan replied. "She's my Lydia. Her name is Lydia Wallace Meriweather."

Brian could not believe his ears. Had this man known Lydia Meriweather? Could this man be the stranger who held Lydia Meriweather as she lay dying in the street?

Brian was handcuffing Milton as he spoke to Karen Simpson. "I believe we need to ask this man some questions. Could we use one of your interrogation rooms?"

Karen Simpson had not been fully briefed on her assignment. She knew it was considered quite secretive. However, she did recognize the name Lydia Wallace Meriweather. Karen immediately knew why this case was not being publicized.

Karen replied to Brian. "I will call the station and arrange for a room. But, if you don't mind, I would like to watch and listen. This is my jurisdiction, after all."

Brian smiled. "No problem. It seems the proverbial cat was just let out of the bag. We'll meet you downtown in twenty."

Karen joined Madison in the vehicle as Brian and Tim walked Milton Donovan back to their vehicle and ducked his head into the backseat. While Tim drove, Brian thumbed through Lydia Meriweather's case file again. Thumbing past the accident photos, Brian finally came across a photo of a very beautiful Lydia taken prior to the accident.

Holding the photo up so that Tim could see, Brian asked the younger detective, "Do you see any resemblance?"

Tim was amazed at the similarity between the photograph his father was holding and the young woman they knew as Madison Cavanaugh.

Chapter 107

Downtown San Angelo in the police headquarters building, Brian and Tim McGregor ushered Milton Donovan into the interrogation room that had been reserved for them by Detective Karen Simpson. Milton was seated on the side of the table with one chair. His handcuffs were removed and a glass of water was set in front of him. Brian and Tim sat on the other side of the table. Karen was observing from behind the fake mirror.

Brian started the questioning. "Mr. Donovan. May I call you Milton?"

An intimidated Milton Donovan answered, "Yea, that's fine."

Brian continued, "Milton. You seem to think the young lady you encountered at the hospital today was one Lydia Wallace Meriweather. Is that right?"

"Yes, she looked just like Lydia."

"Milton. I would like to know how you know Lydia Meriweather. Can you tell me that?"

"She was my nurse. A long time ago I was in an accident, at my work. I was in the hospital for many weeks. Lydia took care of me. She helped me with my therapy."

Brian dug deeper. "So, Lydia was your nurse. Did you and she become closer than the normal nurse-patient relationship?"

Milton blushed. "She told me she would always be there for me. She promised. Then she left the hospital for a different job. After I got released I looked her up. She was working for some rich family in Abilene. In a few months I heard she married the rich man's son. She lied to me. She didn't stay with me."

"Did you contact her after she moved to Abilene?"

"No, I went by their house a couple times, but I never got the nerve up to talk to her."

Tim jumped in. "In other words, you were stalking her."

Milton started rubbing his hands together in a nervous manner. "No, it was nothing like that. I loved her. I would have protected her. Lydia would still be alive if she had stayed with me like she promised."

Brian and Tim both knew Milton Donovan was obsessing over emotional feelings that had not been reciprocated from Lydia Meriweather.

On the other side of the mirror, Karen Simpson made notes to herself to check with the hospital. Maybe Milton Donovan had approached the then Nurse Lydia Wallace inappropriately while he was a patient. That could have been part of the reason she changed jobs.

Brian was anxious to get to the day of Lydia's death. "Milton, were you there, on the street, the day Lydia was killed?"

Milton's voice became sad. "Yes. That was one of the days I had gone to see her. She left her house alone that day, without her baby. I thought maybe I could talk to her while she was alone."

"Were you able to speak with her?"

Milton shook his head. "Not before the accident. I was parked about a half a block away from the intersection. I watched her start to cross the street. Then, out of nowhere, a little dark car sped by me and headed straight toward Lydia in the intersection. I knew the car would not be able to stop in time. I screamed as I watched the car strike her and she fell down."

"Milton, did you see the driver of the car?"

Again, he shook his head. "No, but I believe it was a man. He was wearing sunglasses and had a beard. It all happened too fast."

Brian asked, "Did you go over to Lydia after she was on the ground?"

"Yes. I wanted to hold her. I didn't know what else to do. I knelt down and lifted her head and held it in my lap. She told me to press on her hand, which I did. She died in my arms."

Brian was somewhat cynical. "You want us to believe Lydia Meriweather asked you, her stalker, to hold her hand as she was dying?"

Milton got upset with Brian. "That's not what I said."

"Yes it was. You just said Lydia asked you to hold her hand and then she died."

Milton banged one fist on the table. "No, she didn't say to hold her hand. She said 'Press on my hand'. She kept saying it over and over."

Tim didn't see much difference in the wording. "Milton, tell us exactly what Lydia Meriweather said to you. Tell us every word."

Milton tried to calm himself before he began. "She said 'Press on hand. Press on hand, Milton.' She called me by name. That's how I knew she recognized me. She said it several times before she passed out. I pressed as hard as I could, but I don't think it helped."

After the interview, the three had no reason to hold or charge Milton Donovan. They arranged to have him driven back to the hospital parking lot. They could see that Milton was a somewhat delusional man.

Brian and Tim were both surprised with the specific details Milton had been able to relate to them about the day Lydia Meriweather was killed. One fact in particular stood out.

Tim was the first to state it aloud. "Dad, did you catch the fact that the driver wore sunglasses and had a beard?"

Brian knew where his son's detective mind was going. "Yes, I did. We've heard that description before in this case. Do you suppose Olivia's kidnapper killed her mommy first?"

Tim nodded in agreement. "That was the scenario I was putting together. We might be looking for one criminal involved in both of these cases."

Chapter 108

Tuesday, July 7th was a bright and sunny day in San Angelo, Texas. Brian McGregor and his son Tim had enjoyed a good night's rest in their room at a well known chain hotel. They had discussed the two Meriweather cases over burgers and beers the night before. Brian and Tim agreed that the hit and run death of Lydia Meriweather could well be connected to the kidnapping of her daughter just a few months later.

Late Monday afternoon, Brian had called the District Attorney's office in Abilene and explained their new theory to Betsy Littleton. She said she would contact Graham Meriweather's attorney the following morning, today. Hopefully they would be able to speak with Graham Meriweather regarding his wife and daughter. If Catherine and Madison's DNA proved to be a match, they would ask for a sample from Graham to positively confirm or disprove Madison Cavanaugh as Olivia Meriweather.

As the two men ate breakfast in the hotel's small café, Tim asked his father, "What's on our agenda today? When do you think we will hear any results from the lab?"

Brian finished swallowing his latest bite of eggs before replying. "It seems as if today we wait for the phone to ring. I'm expecting to hear back from the DA's office this morning. The lab should have the testing complete by early afternoon. The calls we receive today could make or break our case."

Tim was not so secret in his hopes that Madison Cavanaugh would turn out to be the long lost Meriweather child. "I feel good about this one. I think we are about to make a family quite happy. It seems to me Olivia's family is long overdue for some good news."

Brian couldn't agree more. He, of all people, knew how Catherine Wallace had never given up hope that her granddaughter might still be alive. He hoped he would soon be able to tell her that she had been right to hold on to that hope.

The first call came in just after the two men had finished breakfast. The caller was Betsy Littleton from the Abilene DA's office.

"McGregor," Brian answered his cell phone.

"This is Betsy Littleton. I was able to contact Graham Meriweather's attorney. His name is Thomas Abbott. There's a bit of bad news. It appears Mr. Meriweather has taken a bad turn on the health front. He was admitted to the hospital Monday and is in serious condition. His lawyer refuses to let us near his client. Abbott says his client is not up to an interview and might not be very coherent even if we did meet with him. I'm sorry, Brian."

Brian was disappointed. "I'm sorry to hear about Mr. Meriweather. We might be close to something big here. He's waited so long for an answer. I hope he hangs on long enough to get it. Thanks for trying, Betsy. I'll keep you up to date with any new developments."

Brian updated Tim on Graham's condition and his attorney's stand. Before they could discuss it, Brian's cell phone rang again.

"McGregor," he said again.

The newly familiar voice on the other end said, "This is Sami Harper in Las Cruces, New Mexico. How are you today, Chief McGregor?"

Brian was curious what Detective Harper had for him. "I'm doing just fine on this sunny morning. Do you have something for me?"

"I do in fact. Our crime lab ran that piece of paper found with the baby in the nativity manger. They were able to determine it was a car rental form. The name was quite faded, but they were able to enhance it. One Dennis Holmes signed for the rental. We are running the name now in both New Mexico and Texas. It could take awhile, but it's a top priority."

Brian was smiling with satisfaction as he said aloud, "Gottcha!"

Sami wasn't sure she heard correctly. "Excuse me?"

Brian stammered. "I'm sorry. I was imagining talking to our perp. You just might have discovered his identity. This is great news. Thank you for rushing it through. If you come up with a suspect, we will want to check if the same guy rented a car about the time Lydia Meriweather was killed. We now suspect the same person may have been involved in both cases."

Sami was not surprised to hear this revelation and answered, "Will do. I wondered whether the two would ever be tied together. Two crimes committed against the same family seem like too much of a coincidence. I'll stay in touch," she said as she hung up.

Again Brian had to update his son on the latest evidence.

Tim commented on the information. "I wonder who this Dennis Holmes is and what he had, or possibly still has, against the Meriweather family."

The best call of all arrived at about two o'clock. Brian and Tim had the case files laid out across the small table in their hotel room. They were continuing to review the statements and evidence.

"McGregor," Brian said in his usual deep voice.

"This is Giselle Dubois from the San Angelo Mercy Hospital's lab. I was assigned to your recent subjects' tests."

"Yes, Ms. Dubois. It's good to hear from you. Have you completed the comparison on the two women?"

"Yes, I have. Feel free to call me Giselle. Based on the DNA profile results, the two women you tested are indeed related. The tests confirm a maternal relationship based on the mitochondria. They are two generations apart, so that would make them grandmother and granddaughter. I hope that was what you were looking for."

Brian McGregor could not be more thrilled. "Yes, Giselle, that was exactly the result we were hoping for. I cannot thank you enough. May I pick up the official report from you?"

Giselle had the paperwork ready. "Yes, but I have a second report for you."

"You do?"

"Yes, you had given me a baby's bootie from the original crime scene. The blood on the bootie is an exact match to the younger of the two individuals tested. I have both reports in an envelope waiting for you. Should I expect you this afternoon?"

"I will see you shortly. I just have one call to make before I head to the hospital. Thank you again."

Brian McGregor could not have been happier with the results.

Tim did not need to be told in words to know what news the latest caller had delivered. The look on his father's face confirmed the test results. He too was smiling as his father dialed Catherine Wallace's phone number.

Chapter 109

Catherine Wallace was sitting in her living room trying to read a book. She was much too nervous to be able to concentrate on the words written on the pages she held. Catherine knew the phone could ring at any moment with the test results. She still had not mentioned her trip to the hospital to her husband, Nathan.

As if hearing her mind the phone rang. "I'll get it," she called out.

"Hello."

"Mrs. Wallace, this is Brian McGregor. I have the test results. Do you want to hear them over the phone?"

Catherine knew she couldn't wait for him to drive to her home. "Yes, please tell me now."

Brian took a deep breath before he said, "Mrs. Wallace, I am thrilled to tell you that the tests do confirm a relationship between you and the young woman who has come forward. The lab results prove that you are grandmother and grand-daughter."

There was silence on Catherine's end of the connection.

"Are you still there? Are you okay Mrs. Wallace?"

Catherine had tears of joy running down her cheek. "Yes, Chief, I'm still here. This is what I have been waiting twenty-seven years for. It is what I've been praying for since you called to arrange the test. So why is it that I am still shocked?"

Brian was smiling. "The realization has not sunk in yet. You may have been hoping for a long time, but the actual truth has just been realized. Congratulations, Mrs. Wallace."

"Thank you so much. When do I get to see her?"

Brian had previously arranged for a meeting location. He replied, "I actually reserved a small conference room here at my hotel. It's nothing fancy, but I can almost guarantee we will not be recognized."

Catherine was glad of that fact. "I don't want any press involved in this. I need to meet my granddaughter privately. The press will eventually have their heyday with all of this, but I want to keep our first meeting quiet."

"I couldn't agree more. Could you be here around ten o'clock tomorrow morning?"

"Nothing could keep me away. Nathan and I will both be there."

"I'm glad to hear that," Brian said before giving Catherine the hotel's name, address and room location.

As she hung up the phone, Nathan walked into the room. "Who was that on the phone?" he asked.

Catherine looked at him and asked a question. "Did you say we have an extra bedroom in the rental house for next month's family vacation?"

Nathan nodded as he replied. "Yes, there are five bedrooms in total. Did that call come from one of the grandkids wanting to bring a friend?"

Catherine stood up and took her husband's hands in hers. She quietly said, "No, dear. We need the extra bedroom for our other granddaughter. Chief McGregor has found Olivia. We have her back."

Nathan's knees started to buckle beneath him. "I need to sit down. I'm not sure I heard you correctly."

Catherine helped her husband to the sofa and sat down beside him. "You heard me right. Olivia is alive and well. We are going to meet her tomorrow morning."

"How can McGregor be sure? I don't want you to get your heart broken."

Catherine had to reveal her secret. "Nathan, I didn't tell you sooner because I didn't want your heart broken. Chief McGregor arranged for a DNA test. I went to the hospital lab Monday morning. The test results are in and the young woman is truly our granddaughter."

Nathan Wallace embraced his wife and his tears of joy ran onto the back of her blouse.

Chapter 110

Madison was trying to relax in her hotel room with Megan on Tuesday afternoon. Trying was the key word. She was very anxious over the testing that was being performed in the hospital's laboratory. She was playing out the two outcome scenarios in her mind.

If it turned out that she was a match to the person Brian McGregor had found, it meant she had a new family. If it turned out she was not a match to this person, she would be right back at the beginning of her quest. She would still not know who she truly was or where she came from.

She was startled back to reality by the ringing of her cell phone. Megan looked across the room at her and said, "Are you going to answer that?"

Madison opened her phone and pressed the key to answer. "Hello."

Detective Tim McGregor was the caller. He had persuaded his father to let him contact Madison. "Miss Cavanaugh, this is Detective Tim McGregor. We have received your test results."

Madison's hands were shaking as she asked, "Was I a match to the other person?"

Tim's cheerful voice delivered the results. "Yes, you were a match. We would like to arrange a meeting in person for tomorrow morning. Would that be good for you?"

"Yes, the sooner the better. I can't wait to meet this person. May I ask what relationship this person is? Is it one of my birth parents?"

Tim did not want to tell Madison over the phone that her birth mother was deceased. He calmly said, "The other person tested is your grandmother. She is your mother's mother and she is quite anxious to meet you."

Tim gave Madison the location and time of the meeting. He purposely told her to arrive at ten-fifteen. The two men planned to have Catherine in the room before Madison arrived.

After Madison said goodbye to Tim, she closed her phone, beamed a big smile at Megan and proclaimed, "I have a grandmother."

Chapter 111

On Wednesday morning, Nathan and Catherine Wallace arrived at the hotel before ten o'clock. They couldn't wait to meet the granddaughter they had not seen since she was five months old. Neither of them knew quite what to expect.

Brian and Tim had been waiting in the hotel lobby. After introductions were made to Tim, Brian walked Nathan and Catherine to the conference room at the end of a long hallway. The room was quite secluded. The hotel staff had delivered coffee, tea, water and a tray of assorted fruit and mini muffins. Catherine was too nervous to eat, but poured herself a cup of coffee to hopefully steady herself. Catherine had dressed in navy slacks with a brightly flowered blouse. She wanted her attire to reflect the joy she was feeling.

Madison, with Ray and Megan at her side, arrived at the hotel entrance just after ten o'clock. Tim saw them walking from the parking lot and held the door for them to enter. He could tell Madison was nervous as well.

Tim tried to calm her. "There is nothing to be nervous about, Miss Cavanaugh. These people are going to be quite happy to see you."

Madison caught Tim's words, stopped short and said, "THESE people? I thought I was meeting my grandmother. Who else is here?"

"Your grandfather is in the room as well. I should have said that on the call yesterday. I apologize for that, Miss Cavanaugh."

Madison's heart was beating fast. "Please call me Madison. At least that's my name for now. If I am meeting two relatives, I am now twice as excited."

When the group arrived at the meeting room door, Tim asked Madison, "Are you ready?"

Madison nodded and Tim turned the knob on the door.

Brian was standing just inside the door of the room. He held out his arm in a gesture for Madison to stand beside him. She studied the kind-looking elderly couple sitting at the table.

Catherine watched as the young woman wearing white jeans and a blue, green and white striped shirt walked across the front of the room. She saw Madison's shiny brown hair bounce as she walked. Catherine noticed the shape of her face, her big brown eyes and her skin tone, which was even more tanned thanks to the southwest summer sun. She did not need a DNA test to know that the young woman walking into the room was her granddaughter.

Catherine gasped and grabbed her husband's arm. "Nathan, look. She looks just like Lydia."

Nathan Wallace could not find any words. He sat in his chair with his eyes fixed on Madison.

Madison was searching the faces of the elderly couple seated at the table. She was trying to find a likeness to herself in their faces. After all, these people were her grandparents. Madison thought her face was shaped similarly to the woman and she suspected her slightly above average height might have come from the man sitting before her.

Brian broke the silence. "Nathan and Catherine Wallace, I would like to introduce you to Madison Cavanaugh. This young woman has been through a great deal during the past few weeks. She has traveled a long way to find you, her family. I am happy to present her to you as your granddaughter, Olivia."

Madison heard her birth name for the first time. "Olivia? That's my real name?"

Catherine was on her feet and walking slowly toward Madison. "Yes, my dear, your birth name is Olivia Catherine Meriweather. But I can see that the name Madison fits you just fine. It's a lovely name. May I hug you?"

Madison so needed a hug at that moment that her arms reached out to Catherine without answering the question. As the two hugged, Nathan stood and walked over to the women and embraced them both in his long, willowy arms. All three had tears in their eyes.

Closer to the doorway, Ray Davis listened as the elder woman declared Madison's true identity. The name sounded vaguely familiar. He wondered how that could be when he lived hundreds of miles away in North Carolina. By the end of the meeting, Ray would remember that the kidnapping of Olivia Meriweather had made headline news across the entire country.

When the hug was broken Madison introduced Ray and Megan to her newly found grandparents. She briefly explained how she and her mother, Rosemary, had been extended members of Ray's family.

Nathan walked over, shook Ray's hand and said, "Then I want to thank you for making our granddaughter a part of your family. She seems to have grown into a lovely young woman."

Ray nodded in agreement.

Chapter 112

After everyone had been seated in the room, Brian McGregor explained the circumstances of Olivia Meriweather's kidnapping that occurred over twenty-seven years ago. Even with their granddaughter sitting safely at the table with them, Nathan and Catherine still felt pain as they listened yet again to the horrible events they had lived through.

Tim McGregor was watching Madison's face for her reaction. He wondered how she would feel learning how infamous her kidnapping had been and how famous she would now become. He hoped Madison would be able to hold up to the pressure that would fall upon her soon.

Madison's mind was going in an entirely different direction than Tim's. She could grasp the fact that she was kidnapped as an infant. But why would a kidnapper simply abandon her?

Madison could not contain her questions any longer. "If I was kidnapped, how was it that I was found at the church?"

This was the first time Nathan and Catherine Wallace learned where their granddaughter had been found. They were even more curious about the person who had found her.

"You were found at a church?" Catherine asked Madison. "We have always assumed that if you were alive, the nanny must have had kept you."

Tim McGregor took control of the conversation and explained the recent revelations from Nina Perez. Tim then asked Madison to explain the events that led her to Father Gomez in New Mexico. When the full story had been laid out, Catherine and Nathan seemed as astonished as Madison had been not many days earlier.

"Chief McGregor, are you saying that the nanny was not the actual kidnapper?" Catherine asked.

"It appears that Mia Sanchez, who we now know as Nina Perez, was also a victim in the case. The man who actually kidnapped your granddaughter also held Nina hostage. We believe he used Nina to care for the infant until he received the ransom money."

Nathan was trying to make sense of all the information. "So while everyone was looking here in Texas and south of the border in Mexico for Olivia, she was actually on her way to North Carolina."

Ray spoke up. "That appears to be correct. I met Madison's mother, Rosemary, and agreed to give them a ride to California. As you heard from Madison, her mother decided not to stay there, but rather traveled back east with me. She raised your Olivia there as her own daughter, Madison."

Catherine looked deeply into Madison's eyes. "My dear, you never suspected that this woman was not your true mother? Did you resemble her enough to not question?"

"My mother, Rosemary, and I were very close. I always felt lucky to have such a wonderful mother. There was no inclination that this big secret existed, until she revealed it on her deathbed. And, yes, I shared some features with my mother. Any others, I simply assumed came from my father's genes."

"How did she explain who your father was?"

"She told me she did not know who my father was. I see now that she was telling the truth. I led myself to think that my mother might have been attacked by an unknown assailant."

There was one question Madison felt was being avoided. "Where are my parents?"

Catherine was the one to tell Madison that her daughter, Lydia, who was Olivia's mother, had been killed. Catherine explained that her father, Graham, lived in Abilene.

Madison was quite sad when she said, "So both of my mothers were killed in accidents."

The questions and answers continued amongst the group. The Wallace's were glad to learn Madison had a happy childhood. They were very proud to learn that their granddaughter had become a nurse like Lydia. Madison was amazed to learn that not only had her mother been a nurse, but also that her grandfather was a surgeon. Madison learned of her mother's brother, Luke, his wife Emma and their children, her cousins. Nathan proudly told her of the upcoming family vacation and made sure she knew she was included.

After about an hour Brian McGregor took back the lead.

"Mr. and Mrs. Wallace, I am quite happy that we have been able to reunite you with your granddaughter. However, a couple pieces remain to this puzzle.

"First, I need to gain access to Graham Meriweather. His lawyer tells me that Graham has been hospitalized in serious condition. I have been denied visitation."

Catherine responded immediately. "I'm sorry to hear about Graham's health. However, if he knew his daughter has been found, he would demand to see her."

"The Meriweather lawyer has me in a catch-twenty-two situation. He refuses to believe Madison is Graham's daughter, but he is refusing to allow a DNA test that would prove or disprove it. Just because Madison has been proven to be your granddaughter, does not make her a Meriweather in the lawyer's mind."

Catherine had an idea. "Though Graham and I have not remained as close as when Lydia was alive I know for a fact he would want to know the facts. Let me contact his assistant, Judy Rockwell, and see if she can help circumvent the lawyer. Judy works in the same office as Graham's partner, his cousin Harrison."

Brian nodded and said, "Thank you. That might help us. Now, let me explain the second problem. There is still a kidnapper out there who has not been caught. If we make any of this public, Madison and Nina Perez might be in real danger."

Brian hesitated before continuing. "There is one more thing. We have come to believe in the possibility that the same person who kidnapped Olivia may also have been your daughter's killer."

After all the details Nathan and Catherine had learned over the past two hours, Brian McGregor's last statement did not shock them.

"Do you have any leads as to who that might be?"

Brian shook his head as he replied, "None at this time. We interviewed a man who witnessed the accident."

Nathan thought before he spoke. "There were many witnesses, but the police were never able to find the car."

"That is correct. But many of the witnesses mentioned a man in a baseball cap who seemed to have tried to help Lydia."

"Yes, I remember that now. It sounded like a Good Samaritan who left the scene before the ambulance arrived."

"We have found that man."

Brian explained to the group how he and Tim had noticed Milton Donovan at the hospital and later questioned him. Catherine was able to remember her daughter mentioning a patient who had developed a crush on her, though she could not remember the patient's name. Brian felt confident Milton Donovan was that patient.

Chapter 113

While the group took a greatly needed break, Catherine used her cell phone to call Graham Meriweather's office. Judy Rockwell answered the call.

"Good Morning. This is Graham Meriweather's office. How many I help you?"

"Hello, Judy, this is Catherine Wallace. I hope you remember me."

"Yes, of course, Mrs. Wallace. If you are calling about the recent correspondence you sent Mr. Meriweather, I have not been able to deliver it. I'm not sure if you are aware that Mr. Meriweather is in the hospital."

"Yes, I have just learned that fact. Please don't worry about the card. I have a much larger concern."

Judy was intrigued. "I hope it's not anything serious."

Catherine had to determine whether she could trust Judy to secrecy. "Judy, I have something to tell you, but you cannot breathe a word of it to anyone, with the exception of Harrison Meriweather. Can I trust you?"

"Yes, of course, Mrs. Wallace. I am quite capable of holding things in confidence. That's a large part of my job. What is it?"

Catherine took a deep breath. "The detectives have found Olivia. She is alive. I just spent the last few hours with her."

It was a good thing Judy Rockwell was sitting at her desk, because she would have fallen over with Catherine's announcement. She was speechless for a few seconds. "That is wonderful news. Are you sure?"

Catherine explained the DNA test match that proved Madison to be her granddaughter. She went on to explain how Graham's lawyer was refusing a similar test to prove Madison as Graham's daughter.

"This is where I was wondering if Harrison Meriweather would be able to influence the lawyer. Judy, we both know Graham would want to know Olivia is alive. He would want to see her. Do you think you can help?"

Judy said with certainty, "Harrison knows how Graham has held out hope for Olivia's return. When I tell him this, he will probably get you the sample himself. Can I call you back on this number?"

Catherine and Judy made arrangements to speak later. When the group returned to the room Catherine explained her call. Brian then took it upon himself to make a decision.

"I think we should plan to travel to Abilene later today. I spoke with Sami Harper in Las Cruces and she is prepared to meet us there with Nina Perez and her attorney Jillian Jackson. I believe Larkyn Belanger also plans to travel to Abilene. I will set up a meeting location for tomorrow afternoon."

Everyone around the table nodded in agreement. The sooner they arrived in Abilene, the better. If they were able to obtain a DNA sample from Graham Meriweather, the results could be known by the end of the week.

Chapter 114

At the Meriweather Corporation in Abilene, Texas, Judy Rockwell was anxious for Harrison Meriweather to return from his meeting. She needed to discuss Catherine Wallace's call with him immediately. When Judy heard the door open and Harrison walk through, she was on her feet.

"Sir, I need to speak with you."

"Sure Judy. Did the hospital call about Graham?"

"No, but I just had a call from Catherine Wallace."

Judy went on to tell Harrison that a young woman had been located whose DNA profile proved her to be Catherine's granddaughter. She also explained how Graham's lawyer was denying access to Graham's DNA for the final proof that this young woman was Olivia.

Harrison was stunned. "I can't believe Olivia could be alive after all this time. How can I help?"

"The police need a sample from Graham. It could be his saliva, his toothbrush or comb. They need something that they can get his DNA from."

Harrison wanted to find the truth for his cousin. "I won't let Graham lie in a hospital, possibly dying, and not realize his daughter is alive. I'll get that sample, if I have to take it myself."

Judy had never seen Harrison Meriweather so adamant. "Thank you. There is one more thing I wasn't sure whether I should mention."

"Is it about Graham?"

Judy hesitated before she answered. "Yes, but it concerns his nurse Julie Collins. Someone tried to call me from her cell phone last week. When I realized whose phone it was, I returned the call Monday morning while we were waiting for the ambulance. This nurse said she had not called me. Julie also mentioned having met Dr. Haskins in Graham's home a week or so ago. She described him as an older, short bald man. Something about that statement didn't seem right to me. When I got in the office this morning I went back through Graham's stack of mail. I found a letter from Dr. Haskins' practice stating he was on a leave of some kind for a few weeks."

"Yes, I believe I heard he needed some surgery," Harrison added.

"Anyway, I looked him up in the medical database and found a photo of him. He is older, and of course I can't tell if he is short, but he certainly is not bald. Do you think this nurse is covering something up by saying Dr. Haskins made a recent house call?"

Harrison became very concerned. "Judy, I have another bit of information from the hospital. It seems Graham has not been getting his proper medication. That alone could be what put him in the serious condition he is now in. It is starting to sound like Julie Collins isn't much of a nurse."

Judy was more puzzled as she said, "Maybe, maybe not. There is one more thing Nurse Julie told me. It seems her apartment was burglarized over the weekend. That alone is no big deal, but the police found a startling discovery."

"What was that?"

"It seems the burglar fired two shots into what was a pile of laundry under her bedding. Julie believes someone tried to kill her."

Harrison Meriweather and Judy Rockwell both knew there was a lot more going on than they could figure out at the moment.

Harrison returned to the most current need. "I'm going right over to the hospital and see about getting Graham's DNA sample."

Chapter 115

On Thursday afternoon, a meeting room was used in a hotel in Abilene, Texas to hold the larger group that had arrived. Brian McGregor made the introductions. For the time being, Madison continued to be referred to by the name Rosemary had given her. Ray and Megan were with Madison, Nathan and Catherine Wallace had arrived, and Tim McGregor was standing next to his father.

In attendance from New Mexico was Attorney Jillian Jackson, who had brought Nina Perez and her husband Hector. Sami Harper had offered a ride to Larkyn Belanger, bringing the total to five.

Nina Perez could not believe her eyes. It was as if Lydia Meriweather were back from the dead. Madison looked so much like her birth mother it was uncanny.

Madison was the one who approached Nina and said, "I understand you were the one who placed me in the manger. From what I understand you risked your life to save mine. I owe you much gratitude."

Nina smiled and reached out to hug her former ward. "I am very happy that you were found by someone who loved you and kept you safe. I only wish I had come forward long ago so that you could have found your real family sooner."

"I had a real family. A family is made up of people who do those things you just mentioned. They love you and keep you safe. I don't feel badly about my life in the least. I had amazing people who supported me and cared for me. We can't look back and wonder 'What if?' What is past is past; the future is what we have to look forward to."

Nina wiped a tear from her eye as she said, "You even sound like your mother. She was a very wise and caring woman. She would be very proud of you."

Madison added, "I like to think that both my mothers are proud of me."

As Nina nodded in agreement, Catherine Wallace approached. Catherine placed her hand on Nina's shoulder as she asked, "Do you remember me?"

"Yes, of course, Mrs. Wallace. You and Lydia spent much time together. I hope you can forgive me."

"It is you who will have to forgive me. For all these years I thought you had taken Olivia from us. Now I learn that you, too, were a victim of some horrible man."

Nina still grimaced at the thought of him. "He was worse than horrible. I was so afraid he was going to kill us both, that I had to do something. I took the only opportunity I had and ran away from the car with Olivia in my arms, wrapped in her blanket. When I saw the nativity display I knew she would be safe there."

Madison added, "My mother, Rosemary, kept that blanket all these years. I found it in her cedar chest. From the notes she left with Father Gomez, she believed the monogrammed 'M' was the initial of my first name. That is part of why she named me Madison. I realize now that it was the monogram for my family name of Meriweather."

Catherine smiled as she remembered and said, "I gave that blanket to your mother before you were born. We had every intention of having your first and middle initials added after you were born. It was just one of those things we never got around to."

Turning to face Nina, Catherine said sincerely, "You saved our granddaughter's life. I don't know how we can repay you."

Nina knew how and explained, "All I have ever wanted was to see that Olivia was alive and well. Now she can be reunited with her family. This is all I need."

As they continued to get to know one another, the time flew by. Brian announced that he had received a call from Harrison Meriweather. A saliva sample was taken from Graham at the hospital. Brian had provided Giselle Dubois' name and fax number. Once the DNA profile was completed in Abilene, a copy of the report would be faxed to Giselle in the lab in San Angelo. She would compare Graham's profile to the profile from Madison. Giselle Dubois was one of the people on Brian McGregor's short list of people he trusted in this investigation. The results would be available by midday on Friday.

Not wanting to leak information to the press, Brian reminded everyone of the importance of not discussing Madison's identity outside of the immediate group. It was decided to have the group meet at the hospital late the next morning. With any luck, the test results would be known and Graham Meriweather could be reunited with his daughter. It was one family reunion no one wanted to miss.

As the group was disbanding, Madison asked to speak with Larkyn off to the side of the group.

"I haven't had the chance to thank you for all you did to help me find my family. I could not have done this without you."

Larkyn was truly amazed how Madison's story had turned out. "You don't have to thank me. I am so happy that things turned out the way they did. I had no idea the great mystery we would be able to solve. I believe this is about the most prominent outcome to a case I have ever had. I should be thanking you."

Madison was not done with Larkyn's services. "There is another case I would like you to work on."

Chapter 116

Friday, July 10th was another day filled with bright sunshine. According to plan, Madison, Ray and Megan arrived at Abilene Memorial Hospital at eleven o'clock. Brian and Tim McGregor met them at the main entrance. Tim greeted Madison first. His father was quite confident that his inclination of his son being deeply infatuated with this young woman was correct.

Just as Brian was about to shake Ray's hand, his cell phone rang. Brian looked at the call ID, quickly greeted Ray and excused himself to take the call in private.

"Good Morning, this is McGregor," he said in a less formal tone than usual.

Giselle Dubois was calling from San Angelo. "Chief, I think you will find this to be a very good morning. I have compared the DNA profiles from your male subject and the younger of the two females tested here on Monday."

Brian was anxious to get what he hoped was a positive match. "What is your expert opinion, Giselle?"

"The two profiles show a relationship of father and daughter. I hope these test results bring about a very happy family reunion. Will I be reading about this one in the newspaper?"

Brian smiled as he answered. "Yes, Giselle, you will. In fact, this particular family reunion should make the front page headlines."

"Glad I was able to help you, Chief. Where should I send the full report?"

"I left my business card with you. You can send it to my station's address on the card. I really want to thank you for your quick attention to my case. Many people are appreciative of your hard work."

The call ended and Brian rejoined the group, smiling.

Madison noticed the elder McGregor's expression and asked, "Was that good news, Sir?"

"Let's just say that you should be meeting your father today."

Ray reached out and hugged Madison. "Congratulations. I am so happy for you."

Brian was instructing Tim on what the next steps should be while Madison was celebrating with the people who had shared the quest with her.

When the celebratory hugs were over, Tim motioned for the three to follow him.

"We have arranged for a private waiting room for your use while my father advises the Meriweather family and legal representatives. The room is on the fourth floor, right this way," he said as he led them to the bank of elevators. What Madison was not aware of was that the waiting room was near the very room in which her father lay in serious condition.

Tim ushered the three into the room and turned to leave. "I am meeting Nathan and Catherine Wallace downstairs. I expect that Nina Perez will be arriving about the same time with her husband and Attorney Jackson. Detective Sami Harper and your personal investigator, Larkyn Belanger were given the same meeting time as well. I should be right back with everyone."

Tim closed the door as he left. Fifteen minutes later he was back with everyone he had been expecting. He made sure all were comfortable and left the room again to join his father in a smaller room down the hall.

Chapter 117

Brian McGregor was meeting with Harrison Meriweather in the smaller private waiting area while Tim was gathering the others.

After introductions, Brian explained the entire complex chain of events that had just recently been uncovered. Harrison was astonished to say the least.

"I just can't believe that Olivia has been found. All these years, Graham never gave up hope, while I tried and tried to get him to move on. This is unbelievable."

"Mr. Meriweather, I would like to introduce Madison to Graham as Olivia as soon as possible. I have been running into legal roadblocks from Attorney Abbott. Can you help facilitate the meeting?"

Harrison nodded in agreement. "There is nothing I would like to do more. I believe finding out that Olivia is alive and well will only accelerate Graham's recovery."

At that very moment, Attorney Thomas Abbott appeared at the door. "Good Morning, Harrison. You must be Chief McGregor, nice to meet you. I am Thomas Abbott. I represent Graham Meriweather."

Harrison was determined to step up on behalf of Graham. "Good Morning, Tom. The DNA test results are in. Chief McGregor has indeed located Olivia. We have to tell Graham immediately. This is what he has been living for all these years."

Tom Abbott was still somewhat skeptical. "Now, hold on, Harrison. We need to be absolutely sure before we present this young woman to my client. Have you met her yet? She could be a fraud."

Harrison shook his head. "No, I have not met her. However, I don't believe she can fake a DNA test."

Brian was not about to waste any more time. "I can have her in this room in less than one minute."

Tom said in a surprised tone, "You mean she's here, in the hospital, now?"

"Yes, I have a host of people waiting just a few rooms away," Brian said as he gestured to Tim, who had just entered the room.

True to his father's word, in less than a minute, Tim escorted Madison into the room.

Harrison took one look and knew what everyone else already believed. The young woman who stood in front of him was certainly Graham and Lydia's daughter. The resemblance to her mother was undeniable.

Harrison looked at Tom and said, "I think it's time to prepare Graham to meet his daughter."

Chapter 118

While Harrison Meriweather and Tom Abbott were being introduced to Graham's long-lost daughter, another gentleman was making his way toward Graham Meriweather's hospital room. This gentleman's mood was definitely not good.

Preston Hamilton stormed into his stepbrother's hospital room and found his mother sitting in a padded chair by the window. Patricia Meriweather had gotten wind of the situation from her own attorney, who had shared a round of golf with Tom Abbott.

Preston was not being quiet when he spoke to his mother. "I got your message. What do you mean they think they found Olivia? That just can't be."

Patricia tried to quiet her son. "Calm down. We both know this must be some woman trying to pose as Olivia to gain access to our money."

Just then Harrison Meriweather entered Graham's room with Tom Abbott. Harrison was quite surprised, and displeased, to find Patricia at Graham's bedside. He was even more displeased with Preston Hamilton's presence.

Harrison turned to Tom. "I don't believe they should be here at this time."

Tom seemed to be defending Patricia when he responded. "Patricia has a shared interest in the Meriweather Trust Fund. If a situation has arisen that affects the trust, she has every right to know about it."

Patricia could hold her own defense. "Harrison, you can't believe this nonsense about Olivia being alive. That is simply preposterous."

312

"Patricia, I only wish to present the truth. The facts prove that the young woman who has just surfaced is biologically Graham's daughter. I feel Graham should be aware that his daughter is not only alive, but very anxious to meet him."

Preston could not contain his anger any longer. He began to speak, his voice loud again, "It just can't be true. Olivia is dead. That nanny, Mia, kidnapped her and killed her. We all know that. Mia killed Olivia! This woman is a fraud."

Harrison would not tolerate another moment with this man in Graham's room. He turned and shouted on his way out of the room, "I'll be back with security. You will be leaving this room."

Chapter 119

Madison had just returned to the larger group of people when she heard a disturbance in a nearby room. Before she could close the waiting room door, one of the voices had become very loud. As she started to finish closing the door, she looked at a seemingly shocked Nina Perez.

"Nina, are you alright?"

The hairs on the back of Nina's neck were standing on edge. Her body was trembling with fear. Nina recognized a voice from her past.

Jillian Jackson saw her client's face go pale. "Nina, please tell us what is wrong. Are you ill? Do you need a glass of water?"

Nina could not speak. She simple made her way to the open door and walked past Madison. Her ears were searching for the source of the voice. She became focused on a nearby room and, as if in a trance, walked toward it.

Madison was the first to follow Nina into the hallway and toward the room. Nina seemed to be mumbling something.

"What is it Nina?"

Nina Perez whispered, "It's him. I remember his voice. He's here. I can hear the Bad Man who hurt us. I have to find him."

Nina continued to walk toward an open doorway.

Madison could not believe her ears. She called back for someone to help her. Hector and Jillian were soon outside the waiting room. Before Madison knew it, everyone was behind her following Nina toward an open door to a patient's room.

Nina stepped into the room and saw the man's profile as he stood with his back to the door.

She said in a forceful voice, "Turn around. Look at me."

The tall man turned to face a petite, middle-aged Mexican woman standing just inside the door.

Preston Hamilton responded sarcastically. "Who the hell are you? Don't you have a floor to mop, or a bedpan to empty? Get out of here."

Nina stood her ground. "Take a good look at me. Look me in the eye."

"Look, lady, just who do you think you are?"

Nina Perez said in her firmest tone. "I am Mia to you. I'm the woman you tried to kill."

Chapter 120

Brian and Tim McGregor were discussing what would happen next when they too heard a disturbance coming from down the hall. As they started out of the smaller waiting room, they saw Harrison Meriweather approaching them.

"Can you help me call security?" Harrison said in a frustrated tone.

Brian was immediately concerned and asked, "Why? What's happening? We heard loud voices."

Harrison explained. "My late uncle's widow is in Graham's room and I don't believe she has a right to be involved in this matter. To make matters worse, her son from an earlier marriage is here. He has become quite agitated. I would like to have security remove them."

Brian nodded, but asked further, "Who exactly is this man?"

"His name is Preston Hamilton. He especially has no right to have a say in how Graham is treated."

A light went on in Brian's head. "What is his name again?"

Harrison repeated, "Hamilton, Preston Hamilton."

Brian was digging deep into his memory banks. "Tim. Why does that name sound familiar? Was he listed in the case files at all?"

Tim remembered. "I think he was in Olivia's case file. He arranged to get the cash."

"Yes, that's right, I remember now. He also dropped the moneybag off to the kidnappers. But I think his name came up again recently. Do you have the notes from our interview with Milton Donovan?"

Tim dug into the breast pocket of his suit jacket. He pulled out his note pad. "Sure do. What are you looking for?"

Brian was confident he was on to something. "What did Donovan say that Lydia's last words to him were?"

Tim scanned his notes and replied, "Press on hand, Milton."

"That's it!"

Both Tim and Harrison asked at the same time, "What's it?"

Brian shook his index finger at Tim. "I'm going to say a few words slowly and you look at Lydia's last words."

Tim nodded. "Okay, but I'm not sure where you're going with this."

"Just hear me out. Here's the first word, 'Preston.'"

Tim looked at the words. "Press on."

Brian said the next word. "Hamilton."

Tim's eyes showed that he caught his father's train of thought as he read aloud the next two words, "Hand. Milton."

Tim gasped, "Oh, my God. Lydia Meriweather didn't say 'Press on hand, Milton.' She was trying to say 'Preston Hamilton.' Lydia saw her killer."

At the same instant, Brian, Tim and Harrison all turned and started running toward Graham Meriweather's room.

Chapter 121

Preston Hamilton stared with disbelief at the woman who just identified herself as Olivia's former nanny, Mia. He looked at the woman's face, saw some of her physical scars and looked deep into her eyes. Preston saw how much this woman despised him.

Patricia Meriweather overcame her shock and yelled at her son. "You said she was dead. It appears this is something else you didn't get right."

At that moment Preston used one hand to reach for Nina and pulled her in front of him, facing her outward. He used his other hand to retrieve a revolver from his suit coat pocket. He held the barrel of the gun to Nina's temple.

Brian, Tim and Harrison arrived just in time to hear Patricia's proclamation to her son and see Preston pull a gun on Nina. Brian and Tim drew their weapons and pointed them at Preston. Harrison tried to get Madison and the rest of the group away from the open doorway.

Brian didn't want any weapons fired in this crowded hospital room. He tried to calm things down as he addressed the man holding the gun, "Preston Hamilton. Put your gun down. You have nowhere to run. There is no way for you to get out of this room."

Preston started waiving his gun in the air and around the room. "No. I have to finish what I failed to do before."

Tim tried to assist his father. "Preston, you don't want to kill anyone today. You see that Mia is still alive. You didn't kill her before. That's a good thing. Let her go now and we can talk things out."

Preston felt as if the walls were closing in on him. His hands were shaking and sweat was running down his forehead. He glanced over at Patricia as if begging for her support. That was when he saw his mother grabbing at the center of her chest.

Seeing that, Preston dropped the gun and screamed, "Mother!"

Preston pushed Nina away from him and ran to his mother's side just as she suffered a heart attack. Brian was instantly behind Preston pulling his arms around to where he could handcuff him.

Tim yelled out to the nurses' station. "We need a crash cart in here."

Chapter 122

Patricia Meriweather was taken out of the room on a gurney headed for ICU. Preston Hamilton was handcuffed, read his rights and escorted out of the hospital by Brian McGregor. He was being taken to the Abilene Police Headquarters.

Graham Meriweather was heavily medicated and had not been aware of the great commotion that occurred in his room. After things were cleared away, Catherine Wallace walked to the far side of Graham's bed and looked down at the man her daughter had fallen in love with. She wished that Lydia were still alive today to stand beside her husband.

Graham sensed a presence at his side. When he opened his eyes, it took him a few seconds to focus on his former mother-in-law's face.

Graham was taken aback. "Catherine. I didn't expect you here. What a pleasant surprise. I just had the loveliest dream."

Catherine took his hand and smiled. "You did?"

"Yes, I dreamed someone told me that Olivia was still alive and with us. It made me feel so peaceful, even though I never actually saw her. Catherine, I know it was just a dream, but it gives me peace to know that someday I will see my daughter again. I know my life is coming to an end. I've come to terms with that."

Catherine's eyes were watering. "Graham, it wasn't a dream. You don't have to wait any longer to see your daughter."

Graham felt as if Catherine must be a continuation of his dream. He stared into her eyes and then followed her gaze to the other side of his bed.

There he noticed a lovely young woman who looked amazingly like Lydia. Her brown hair was tucked behind her ears in a manner that reminded him of his late wife. She was standing next to Nathan Wallace.

Catherine squeezed Graham's hand and said, "Graham, we would like to introduce you to this young woman. She is your daughter, Olivia."

Madison stood looking at the man lying seriously ill. Though his face was thin and drawn, she could see this was from whom she inherited her slightly pointed chin and the shape of her nose. Madison looked into her father's eyes with tears streaming from her own.

She had no idea what to say, so she said the first thing that came into her mind, "Hi, Dad. I'm home."

Graham reached out his hand to his daughter. Madison took it and held it between both her hands.

That was when Catherine made another startling announcement to Madison. "I would like to wish a Happy Birthday to my dear granddaughter. Today, July tenth, is your twenty-eighth birthday. I can't think of a better way to celebrate."

Madison was stunned. "I kept forgetting to ask that one little detail. I have always celebrated my birthday on the fourteenth of July. This is surely the best present. I have found so many wonderful additions to my family tree."

Megan smiled as she lightened her friend's mood. "All this detective work and you find out you're four days older."

Everyone laughed.

The group turned to leave Madison alone with her father and grandparents. They felt this particular family reunion should be a private affair.

Chapter 123

On Tuesday, four days later, Brian and Tim McGregor arranged for one more meeting in a room at their precinct's headquarters. They wanted to make several announcements involving the case.

In attendance were Madison, Ray, Megan, Nathan and Catherine Wallace, Hector and Nina Perez, Jillian Jackson, Sami Harper and Larkyn Belanger. Added to the group were Harrison Meriweather and Judy Rockwell.

Brian began the conversation. "I'm glad to report that Graham seems to be doing some better. I'm sure the presence of his long-lost daughter has given him a renewed purpose for his life."

Everyone looked at Madison and smiled.

She added to Brian's comments. "He is still a very ill man, but it looks like with the proper medications and dialysis treatments, he will be able to function with his disease."

Brian continued. "Preston Hamilton was arrested for the murder of Lydia Meriweather. Additionally he was charged with the attempted murder of Nina Perez, kidnapping of both Nina and Olivia Meriweather, and many other assorted charges. We are still searching his property, so more charges are likely. It is likely Preston Hamilton will die an old man in prison."

Tim took the nod from his father and presented the next bit of information. "While searching Preston Hamilton's home, fake identification papers were found in the name of Dennis Holmes. As some of you know, this was the name discovered on the rental lease Nina wrote her note on and left with the baby Olivia in the manger.

"We have also located a safe deposit box in New Mexico under this fictitious name. Yesterday, upon receiving the proper search warrant, the box was opened. Inside we found the majority of what we believe was the ransom money used to pay Olivia's supposed kidnappers. We also found several pieces of jewelry belonging to Lydia Meriweather. Those items will be returned to Graham and Madison as soon as they have been processed."

Brian smiled at Nina. "Included were the pieces you were accused of stealing. It appears Patricia Meriweather was the insider who was setting you up for dismissal due to stealing."

Nina shook her head. "Why would she do that?"

"It was greed, pure and simple. As you witnessed, Patricia had a heart attack Friday while we were at the hospital. She recovered enough to be able to give us a statement over the weekend. Apparently Patricia Meriweather must believe that confession is good for the soul. She explained that many years ago she married Oliver Meriweather simply for his money. Patricia knew he was a terminally ill, older man. However, Oliver surprised everyone and lived several years longer than he was expected to. By the time he actually passed away, his son had a family that would be sharing what Patricia thought of as her private trust fund."

Catherine gasped and said, "So, Preston Hamilton killed my daughter to get more money for his mother?"

"It would appear that Patricia and Preston were trying to get everyone who shared the trust fund out of the way so that Patricia would inherit the entire fund. That would eventually put all the money into Preston's hands.

"We believe that the original plan was to have both Lydia and Olivia killed in the hit and run accident. But, as we have learned from Nina, Olivia had a cold that day and only Lydia went on their usual walk."

Harrison questioned Brian. "So they waited a few weeks after Lydia's death and kidnapped Olivia? If they never intended to return her, why ask for ransom?"

Tim fielded that question. "By asking for ransom, the attention was drawn off the family. Graham figured the kidnappers were just using Olivia as a means to obtain a large amount of cash. He fully expected his daughter to be returned after he paid the money. Graham had no way of knowing that the man he sent out to deliver the money that night was the actual kidnapper. After Olivia was not returned and Graham called in the police, it was too late. By then Preston had returned to New Mexico, with his two victims."

Judy Rockwell was still curious about Graham's recent illness. "Was Graham's in-home nurse working with Patricia? It appeared she was not taking good care of him."

Brian shook his head when he responded. "We do not believe she was aware of their plan. It seems as if Patricia hired Julie Collins as the nurse's aide specifically because she was not a Registered Nurse. Patricia didn't want someone questioning Graham's care. Without Julie's knowledge, Preston was substituting Graham's pills with sugar placebos and empty capsules. That was why Graham's health was failing so quickly. We also believe Preston was the man who burglarized Julie's apartment. He and Patricia may have thought they needed to get rid of her as a witness. Had Julie been home, Preston would likely have killed her."

Tim added a comment. "It appears both Patricia and Preston have been scheming for several years to get control of the Meriweather fortune. By spreading the crimes out over so many years, they almost got away with it. The timing of Madison's arrival and Nina's testimony most surely saved Graham Meriweather's life."

Catherine looked across the table at Nina. "Not only did you assist in saving Graham, but I give you full credit for saving Olivia's life. If you had not gotten her out of Preston's car, I'm confident he would have killed you both."

Madison was sure of that as well. "Yes, Nina, I will be eternally grateful to you for what you did that night. It took a great amount of courage on your part. I only wish you had not suffered such pain from that man."

Hector placed his arm around his wife's shoulder and said, "My wife is the strongest person I know. She endured great harm then and has lived with the scars since that time. I'm glad she can finally see justice served to Preston Hamilton."

Brian nodded. "Amen to that. Between his mother's statement and the mound of evidence we have accumulated against him, Preston Hamilton should be locked away for the rest of his life."

Chapter 124

Three months later, Madison was in the passenger seat of a car being driven by Tim McGregor in California. They were traveling west of Sacramento to the small town bearing the name of Madison.

"I find it amazing that my Mom named me after this little town in northern California. Her mother, Ellie, had talked about this place as being her hometown. In her note, Mom said the name Madison had come to mean family to her. I think she was looking for a family that night she met Ray in Deming. She may not have stayed in California, but Mom certainly found a great family that night. The Davis family took us in and we quickly became part of their lives."

Madison had made two trips back to North Carolina to wrap up loose ends there. She turned in her resignation at the hospital and gave up the lease on her apartment. Madison spent several days cleaning and sorting through her mother's and her own belongings at the home they shared while she was growing up. With both return trips to Texas, she drove a car full of her possessions. Madison found no problem fitting her property into the many rooms at the Meriweather estate. She could not believe how beautiful her new home was.

After Madison's father was released from the hospital, she arranged round-the-clock care for him at their home. She made sure to hire only Registered Nurses and arranged for a newer home dialysis machine. Graham had a long road ahead of him, but Madison was confident he was making progress.

Madison turned to Tim and said, "I want to thank you again for all the help you have given me these past few weeks. I had so many things to work through, both legal and personal, and you never tired of my many questions."

Tim smiled at the woman he was slowly losing his heart to. "It has been my pleasure. I wanted to make the transition to your new life as easy as possible. You always seem to take things in stride, but I'm sure some of this must have overwhelmed you."

Madison rolled her eyes. "Overwhelmed is probably understating it. When I think of everything that has changed just since June, I almost can't believe it. First, I lost my Mom and discovered I wasn't her daughter. Then I traveled across the country to solve an almost three decade old mystery. From that experience I found my father and an expanded family. I have a new address, new friends and even a new birthday. Oh, let's not forget a new name."

Tim chuckled at Madison's light-hearted summary. "Have you made a final decision on that last one?"

Madison nodded as she answered. "I wanted you to be the first to know. I felt wrong simply taking back my birth name. Doing that erased too much of whom I have always been and how my Mom saw me. So, I am petitioning the court to become Madison Olivia Meriweather. My father and grandparents have given me their blessings."

"That name suits you well."

"There's one thing I didn't realize right off. My new initials will be M O M, Mom. I think that is a fitting tribute to both women who held that title in my life."

"I think they would both be proud of you. I'm curious though how you distinguish them in your everyday life."

Madison paused a moment, then said, "I have decided to refer to Rosemary as Mom. That's what I always called her and she did raise me for over twenty-seven years. Lydia is my birth mother, so I refer to her as Mother."

Tim pointed to a road sign stating they had five miles to go until they reached their destination.

He asked, "Are you ready for this?"

Madison was nervous, but anxious to arrive. "I'm not sure how to explain it all, but this is something I have to do for my Mom."

"Larkyn did a great job in finding this woman. I hope she turns out to be who you suspect she is."

"When I asked Larkyn to look into finding Rosemary's mother's family, I didn't hold out much hope. Ellie had stated her family was dead, but I needed to know if that was true. With all that I have been through, I couldn't let another family go without closure."

Tim reassured her. "You're trying to doing a good thing. We should know in just a few minutes if Larkyn's discovery is the right one."

Chapter 125

Tim and Madison pulled up in front of a large two-story home on a quiet tree lined street. The yellow house with white trim had a wrap-around porch that extended the full width of the front and halfway back on the left hand side. White wicker furniture lined the porch and flower boxes hung from the rail with fall mums blooming in harvest colors.

Tim asked once more, "Are you sure you want me to come with you? I'd understand if you want to do this alone."

Madison smiled at the man she was becoming quite fond of. "I would appreciate you being at my side. You might be able to help me with specifics if I forget or get sidetracked. We aren't even sure we have the right family yet."

Together they walked up the sidewalk, climbed the porch steps and rang the bell. When the door opened, a woman who appeared to be in her middle sixties greeted them. She was wearing a red and white checkered apron over blue jeans and a red, long sleeved shirt.

The woman smiled at her guests and said, "Hello, may I help you?"

Madison started with the opening she had been practicing in her mind. "Good Morning. We are looking for the former Elizabeth Brewster. By chance would that be you?"

The woman's face became quizzical as she answered. "Yes, that's my maiden name. Most people call me Beth. My married name is Parker."

"My name is Madison. You may have read about me in the news. My last name is Meriweather. This is Detective Tim McGregor. We have traveled from Abilene, Texas."

Beth Parker's eyes opened wide with surprise. "Of course, I know who you are. I've followed your heartwarming story in the newspapers. Oh, my goodness. I can't imagine why in the world you would be knocking at my door."

"Mrs. Parker, I wanted to talk to you about your sister."

Beth was shaking as she asked, "My sister? I haven't heard from her in more than fifty years. Do you know something about her?"

Madison did not want to continue the conversation on the front porch, so she asked, "May we come in, Mrs. Parker?"

Beth stepped back and motioned for them to enter her home. The smell of freshly baked cookies filled their nostrils. Madison smiled and nodded a thank you to their hostess.

Beth led them into her living room, which looked as if it had probably been used as a parlor a few decades ago. Tall windows lined two walls of the room letting a great deal of the morning sun into the room. Situated between two windows on the far side of the room was a fireplace with a large mantel. A comfortable looking floral print sofa with a matching loveseat was situated at right angles to each other. Two solid colored padded chairs accented the room and faced the sofa.

"Please have a seat. May I get you a cup of coffee or tea? I just made some molasses cookies. I will bring us a plate."

Tim and Madison were receptive to her offer and Beth left the room. That gave time for Tim and Madison to look around the room. On the mantel were several framed photographs that told Beth Parker's family history.

Beth returned while Madison was still admiring the photos. She turned to Beth and said, "You have a lovely family."

"Thank you. My husband and I had four great children. Unfortunately my husband passed away a few years ago. Since then I have been blessed with five grandchildren. Two of them are coming over later today. That's why I was baking their favorite cookies."

Madison sat next to Tim and took a sip of her tea before she got to the reason for her visit.

"Mrs. Parker, if you have followed me in the news, you realize that I was raised by a woman named Rosemary Cavanaugh, in North Carolina."

Beth nodded, and sipped from her cup. "Yes, I know that. I believe I read that she found you abandoned in New Mexico and then you somehow ended up in North Carolina."

"Yes, those are the basic facts. I am trying to locate any living relatives that Rosemary may have. That is why I wanted to speak with you about your sister."

Beth was confused. "This Rosemary would be too young to be my sister and, as you know, our family name is not Cavanaugh. I'm not sure how you think information concerning my sister, who ran away from home as a teenager, is going to help you."

"Rosemary's mother was named Ellie Cavanaugh and she told people, including her young daughter, that she was from Madison, California."

Something Madison said rattled Beth. She set her cup down.

"Wait a minute. Did you say her name was Ellie?"

Madison nodded. "An investigator I hired found your sister Shellie Brewster listed as a runaway a couple years prior to when Ellie Cavanaugh gave birth to Rosemary. I realize it seems farfetched, but I was wondering whether you might recognize the name Ellie Cavanaugh."

Chapter 126

Madison could tell from Beth Parker's facial reaction, that something she said triggered a memory.

Trying not to pry, she asked gently, "Mrs. Parker, does that name sound familiar?"

"First, please call me Beth. I don't know an Ellie Cavanaugh, but you should know that I used to call my sister 'Ellie.'"

Madison and Tim said at the same time. "That's interesting."

Beth continued, "Yes. I was four years younger than Shellie. When I started to talk, apparently I could not pronounce the 'sh' sound very well. So, I would call my older sister, Ellie. Before long, it was a nickname that stuck and even my parents called her that."

Madison smiled as she said, "That sounds like a nice memory. I actually have a photograph of the woman I am inquiring about. It was taken when her daughter, Rosemary, was just a baby. Would you like to see it?"

Beth reached out her hand. "Yes, of course."

Madison pulled the old black and white photo she had been given from Christine Morgan out of her bag. She handed it to Beth and waited for a response.

Beth studied the photo carefully before she spoke. "This could certainly be my sister. I was only twelve when she ran away, so my memories are somewhat cloudy after all these years."

Madison then retrieved a second photo from her bag. It was the family photo labeled 'Mom, Dad, Beth and me'. She held it out.

"Beth, this picture was also found with Ellie Cavanaugh. Is this your family?"

This time Beth Parker gasped and started to cry. "This was one of the last pictures taken before they died."

Tim was curious and asked, "Before who died?"

A tearful Beth explained, "My parents, Bill and Martha Brewster. They were killed in a car accident. Ellie was in the car with them but she survived. After the accident, my sister and I went to live with our father's sister, Aunt Ruth, in Oakland. Ellie was quite upset by the loss of our parents. She did not adjust well to living with our aunt. After a few months, she ran away. No one was ever able to find her."

Tim proceeded with the facts. "Ellie told people in New Mexico that her entire family was dead. She never mentioned a sister, or your aunt."

"Ellie felt responsible for the accident."

Madison was stunned. "How could she? She was just a child."

Beth wiped her eyes with a tissue and explained, "To say my sister was a handful might be an understatement. She was a rebellious teenager at the time. The night of the accident, Ellie had snuck out of the house and gone to a party my parents had prohibited her from. My parents found her missing from her room and took the car to bring her home. When they found her they pulled her away from the party in front of all her friends. On the car ride home, apparently Ellie and my parents were arguing. Ellie felt that our father was distracted by the argument and that was why he lost control of the car on a sharp curve in the road. She blamed herself for their deaths."

Madison could understand the pressure that must have created for a teenage girl. "I'm sure no one else blamed her."

"No. Everyone knew it was a devastating accident. But that didn't ease the pain for Ellie. Instead of the tragedy shocking some sense into her, it seemed to cause her to rebel more. It was as if she were punishing herself by getting into even more trouble. As I said, Ellie ran away from our aunt's home a few months later."

Tim asked, "You must have eventually adjusted."

"Yes, I did okay with my aunt and her family. This house is actually my parents' old home. My aunt sold it soon after their death. However, about the time my husband, Henry, and I had our second child, this house came on the market and we were able to buy it. Maybe subconsciously I came back to this little town and bought this particular house just in case Ellie ever found her way home. Do you know where Ellie is now?"

Madison had prepared the answer for that question. "I'm sorry to say that Ellie passed away many years ago. She died when her daughter was only six years old."

Beth nodded quietly. "I see. May I ask what caused her death?"

"I'm afraid she became addicted to drugs. They ultimately caused her death. I am so sorry."

"I was always afraid something like that happened. At least now I know for sure."

Madison wanted Beth to know the good Ellie had brought into the world.

"Beth, Ellie's daughter, Rosemary, was a wonderful person. She was kind and gentle. She was the best mom I could have had. I want you to know that. Ellie also gave Rosemary the middle name of Elizabeth. I believe Ellie loved and missed you very much."

Beth smiled as she said, "I just realized why Ellie might have picked the first name of Rosemary for her daughter. Our grandmother's name was Mary and our mother had a lovely rose garden. Mother was quite proud of her roses."

Everyone smiled and Tim said, "It sounds like Ellie created a lovely tribute to her entire family when she named her daughter."

They sipped their respective tea and coffee and ate Beth's delicious cookies as Madison showed yet more photos depicting Rosemary's life. Beth was grateful to see the photos and learn about the woman she had never met, but who had been her niece.

Before they left, Madison had one more item to discuss with Beth Parker. She wasn't sure how to approach the subject.

"Beth, you might find this a strange question, but I was wondering where your parents are buried?"

Beth wasn't sure why Madison had asked the question, but she replied. "Our family has a plot in a local cemetery. I'm not sure why you're asking."

Madison had been struck with an idea a few days ago that she explained to Beth now.

"It seemed that your sister, Ellie, always thought of this town as her home, where her family was. If you would allow me, I could arrange for Ellie to be brought back home and reburied near your parents."

Beth Parker started to cry as she ran the idea through her mind. "Have you located where Ellie was buried in New Mexico?"

"Yes, between the investigator I hired and a wonderful, caring social worker, they were able to identify her current grave site."

"I would like that very much. I don't know how I can ever thank you. Not only have you brought me closure as to what happened to my sister, but now you are bringing her home. This is where she belongs, resting eternally with her family."

Madison gave Beth a hug and said, "Just knowing you have closure is all I need. I have come to realize how precious it is to learn the truth about one's family."

Beth was thinking aloud. "Madison, you know there is plenty of room in our family plot. If you wanted Rosemary to rest beside her mother, I would be honored to have her here."

Madison was now the one on the verge of tears. "Let me think about that. Now that I have moved to Texas, that might be a nice idea. It would be like reuniting three generations. I will start making the arrangements when I get home."

Beth initiated another hug. "I would like to stay in touch with you after all this. You were raised as my niece's child. That makes us family too."

Madison smiled and nodded as she and Tim prepared to leave. "I agree. One can never have enough family."

Chapter 127

It was on September 27th of the following year that Madison Olivia Meriweather stood in front of the Three Angels Day Care and Clinic ready to cut the ribbon for the grand opening. She had worked hard for countless hours over the past year preparing for this moment. A portion of the Meriweather trust fund had enabled her to renovate an older building into a well equipped, functioning business in a neighborhood with a desperate need for such a facility.

As Madison reflected over the past months of her life, she realized that she had found peace and put closure on many issues of her life. She was completely relocated to Texas. Madison was making new friends and with the opening of the clinic, would be starting a new job as the administrator.

Patricia Meriweather had suffered a second heart attack at the end of January, which had proven fatal. With the loss of his mother, Preston Hamilton pleaded guilty to the charges filed against him and had been sentenced to life in prison.

Graham was able to identify the jewelry found in the safe deposit box Preston had maintained under the alias name of Dennis Holmes to be Lydia's. After Preston's sentencing, the jewels were returned to Graham, who presented them to his only daughter. On this special day Madison was proudly wearing the ruby and diamond necklace Graham had given Lydia upon her own birth.

Madison acquired a renter for her mother's home in North Carolina. She was not overly surprised when her friend Megan announced that Ned Tuttle was relocating from New Mexico to

North Carolina. Madison had seen the attraction building in the couple of weeks they spent together researching her identity. Ned secured a job with a local newspaper and was looking for a place to rent. Madison was confident that one day Megan would be joining Ned in the home Rosemary raised her in. She hoped they would be very happy there.

As she discussed with Beth Parker, Madison arranged for both Ellie's and Rosemary's remains to be exhumed, transported to California and reburied in Beth's family's plot.

As Madison looked out over the crowd of people attending the grand opening, her heart was swelled with all the love she felt for her friends and family. Debbie and Doctor Steve were married earlier in the summer and were happily settling into wedded bliss with the blessings of all their children. Megan and Ned were standing near Debbie. Ray and Susan were also in the crowd. Madison knew she would never have found her birth family without the Davis family's help.

Madison spotted her grandparents, Nathan and Catherine Wallace. She had come to love them so much over the past months. Madison accompanied her grandparents, along with her Uncle Luke's family on two vacations since she returned to Texas. She was certainly lucky to have such loving families to share her life with.

Hector and Nina Perez were also in the crowd. Hector told Madison recently that Nina has never been so relaxed in her life. He feels that keeping such a huge burden all those years was causing stress on his wife that no one had seen.

Father Gomez and Sister Mary Louise Lopez sent Madison a lovely bouquet of flowers as congratulations for her work.

Madison looked down to see Tim McGregor standing in the front row. Madison and Tim began dating soon after their trip to California. Their romance was growing stronger by the day. Tim's eyes met hers and she saw his love and admiration. Tim's parents, Brian and Kiera were at his side. Madison had been welcomed into their home on many occasions.

Sitting on Tim's other side was Beth Parker, who had flown in from California to attend the dedication in honor of the niece she never got to meet in life.

A couple rows behind Tim was seated Larkyn Belanger. Because Larkyn was so instrumental in discovering Madison's true identity as the long ago kidnapped Olivia Meriweather, her Personal Investigation business gained much publicity. Madison smiled when she spotted Larkyn who had become one of her newest friends.

As Madison looked to the left side of the platform, she saw her father. Graham was in a wheelchair attended to by his assistant, Judy Rockwell. Madison had grown very fond of Judy over the past year. She knew her father relied on Judy greatly as his administrative assistant dealing with his business affairs. Madison thought happily of her private notion that Judy was also becoming Graham's personal assistant, with the greater emphasis on personal. Her father's health was improving and Madison felt he should learn to enjoy life more.

Madison also made a business deal with Graham's former nurse's aide, Julie Collins. Madison agreed to fund Julie's continued education to become a Registered Nurse. In exchange, Julie agreed to three years of employment at the clinic being opened today.

The mayor motioned that it was time for Madison to take her place near the podium. She reached for her notes to the speech she had written as she was handed the microphone.

"I would like to thank each of you for being here for this special moment in my life. I am here today to dedicate this childcare, elder care and health clinic to the three mother figures I was blessed and honored to have in my life. These three women are my angels. I feel they have watched over me my entire life from both near and far.

"My first honoree is Lydia Jayne Wallace Meriweather, my birth mother. She gave me life. Though we had only a few months together, I understand she loved me very much.

"Next, I would like to honor Nina Perez, also known as my Nanny Mia, for saving my life when I was but an infant. Without Nina's quick actions, I would probably not be standing before you today.

"Lastly, my dedication goes to Rosemary Elizabeth Cavanaugh, the woman who created a wonderful, loving life for me for more than a quarter of a century. Rosemary was the only Mom I knew. She may have left a staggering mystery for me to solve, but I am a better person because of her upbringing. I am honored to celebrate the grand opening of this facility on what would have been Rosemary's fifty-first birthday.

"I am proud to officially open and dedicate this facility as Three Angels' Day Care and Clinic."

Madison cut the bright red ribbon with the oversized scissors and the crowd cheered. While she was returning the scissors to the mayor, she did not see Tim climb the steps to the platform.

When she turned to face her audience, Tim was reaching for the microphone.

"Ladies and Gentleman, I would like to take this opportunity to ask this distinguished businesswoman a very personal question."

Madison started to cry as he saw Tim bend down on one knee and reach for her hands.

"Madison Olivia Meriweather, I would like to proclaim my love for you in front of our family and friends. Would you do me the honor of becoming my wife?"

Tim produced a black velvet box and opened its top to reveal the most gorgeous solitary diamond she had ever seen. Madison could find only one word to say, "Yes."

The audience cheered and clapped as Tim and Madison shared a long kiss that would start them on their next journey in life.

CPSIA information can be obtained at www.ICGtesting.com
Printed in the USA
LVOW13s1041200813

348774LV00001B/27/P